The BLACK FURY

The BLACK FURY

ZEETA SHERIN

PARTRIDGE
A Penguin Random House Company

ISBN: Hardcover   978-1-4828-2197-0
             Softcover   978-1-4828-2198-7
             eBook   978-1-4828-2196-3

To order additional copies of this book, contact
Partridge India
000 800 10062 62
orders.india@partridgepublishing.com

www.partridgepublishing.com/india

To my four granddads . . . . One, whom I was not fortunate enough to meet . . . the other who I knew only for a while but cherish every little memory we had. And the other two who are established writers. Thank you for your inspiration and for the motivation.

Contents

Sara Jane Salvatore

Introduction

Every step I took towards the ball made my heart thump harder against my chest. Tonight was my last night as a player on this field . . . . I can't lose, not tonight.

Extra time was getting over in nine more seconds, we had to avoid penalty round because our opponent had an excellent player readied for it as though they knew that the game would come to a penalty. It was 2-2 draw and if I scored this goal, we were winning. I looked at the face of the goal keeper, I sensed nostalgia in her eyes and it said that she was afraid but was simultaneously excited about how the game was still suspense. My teammates were keeping our opponents from getting to me. 'C'mon SJ! It's open . . . it's now or never!' I heard a voice in my head. I took the ball to the right and the goalie followed my every step but I kicked the ball to the left of the net and the keeper, as she was quick, leapt to her left like she was expecting it. My heart was pounding faster. I could feel the beats in my temples. It felt like time had paused. It was the most nerve-wrecking pause in my life! The ball flew past the goal keeper's glove, just a few millimeters away. I breathed out after a long time of holding air in. I shut my eyes in relief, we won! A male voice boomed from the speakers 'Salvatore goals! Home team wins!' The referee blew his whistle, indicating extra time was over. I looked around the cheering crowd, I saw dad, Suzie and Ashley in the front row. Wonder where Sammy is? He never missed one game of mine. My team mates jumped on me, all at once, I fell on the moist grass. We straightened up after our coach came. She put one hand on my shoulder and the other on our team captain's, Jamie Watson. She looked into each of our eyes and smiled. She actually smiled! She hadn't smiled in a very long time, after we lost last year's inter-school league. 'Girls, you did an excellent job today. If you guys keep playing like this, I guarantee that each one of you will make it into the national team. Every drop of sweat, blood and tear that you guys sacrificed, here's your result. Look at that trophy girls . . . it's yours!' She patted Jamie on her shoulder. 'It's ours!' She said. 'But girls, remember not to be over-confident and proud. One victory never makes history.'

We dispersed into a gleeful locker room. Our school principal took the trophy and handed it to Jamie. 'St. Edison's Middle School wins inter-school soccer league!' The same voice that I heard earlier spoke again from the speaker. Jamie handed the trophy to me and said 'We're going to miss you. It's a loss that you're leaving.'

After long hours of celebration, I said a final goodbye to my old classroom, locker, and soccer field and hopped into Ashley's blue tuck.

I jumped out with my gym bag and medal, Ashley too followed. She was a twenty five year old sports coach. She trained archers, horse riders and sword fencers. I have been training with her from when I was five. She was the only person I would miss. I didn't have a lot of friends, after I lost a close one, I didn't dare to create such a strong bond with anyone else. Ashley wiped away a tear that tumbled down her rosy cheek. She ran her fingers through her honey coloured hair and said 'I'm going to miss you.' Her hazel eyes watered again. I hugged her. She said 'Keep in touch, alright.' After that, her blue truck rumbled along with her down the road. I turned back to see Mr. Jacobs, our chauffer, loading our hummer. All the other cars had already left to our new home. We were packed tight and heading to THE BLACK FURY.

Chapter 1

The Salvatore Mansion

$\mathfrak{I}$ had never known I was from this little town with a mysterious name. I always thought I was a city girl.

I'm Sara Jane Salvatore, soon going to be fourteen years of age, you can call me SJ. I lived in New York all my life, now I'm moving into this town named Black Fury. It's a very strange name, isn't it?

My dad is the owner of the Salvatore suites and the mall Mack Splash, which is located all around the world so you might already be familiar with those names. My mother is the editor of the magazine 'Scarlet' which is more like the 'writer's digest', and a well-known writer, and buys a lot of art but it's only a hobby.

Now my brother, Samuel Salvatore, is a smart sixteen year old hunk. He's the kind of guy who would even give his life for his sports, has great dedication for . . . . um all the games that you can think of.

My twelve year old sister, Suzie Salvatore, is well . . . . a very girly girl in general. There's not much to say about Su, you see, she's the total opposite of me. Her tastes very rarely match mine. But we get along fine. It's mostly me and Sam. Sam is an expert at annoying me but he's also a very caring brother. He's very sarcastic, so don't blame me for anything I say, I got it from my brother.

I got down from the car and stared at the huge palace which my dad said was a "house" in which we were going to live in. My jaw dropped open, I was in utter shock. It was much huger than the previous house. There was a large silver and golden gate with a fancy-looking security booth at one side. To the right there was a gleaming golden plate that said 'THE SALVATORE MANSION'.

The gate opened automatically and inside stood a piece of architecture which I thought was like Paradise. There was a fountain in the centre, right in front of the house, which gushed with sparkling water.

The air smelled of fresh flowers, I took a deep breath, inhaling the scent of nature. There were lots of marigolds around as they were mum's favourite.

The place looked like a maze of trimmed bushes with beautiful flowers growing out of them. And in the middle lay the Salvatore mansion, each engraving so original and artistic. The outer house was painted white, brown and cream. 'What do you say?' Dad asked 'I wanted it to be a bit royally old fashioned.' I, Sam and Su looked at each other and then back at dad. 'Expected reaction' Dad said. 'Guess who designed it?' I shrugged.

'Tomas Martin' dad answered himself. 'You mean the guy you were talking to a week back, who designed the president's beach house.' Sam said. 'He's my best friend; you don't call him 'the guy'. Now c'mon, your mom will be waiting for us.' Dad said.

A long bricked path led to the front porch from the fountain; on either side grew rows of flowers (probably mom's choice). They were of different kinds, roses, jasmine, marigolds and plenty of others I couldn't name. The porch had a white swing on one side with red cushions and a comfy looking two-seater sofa that was also red and white. I could smell the teak wood as I climbed up the porch.

The polished brown door had a big handle on it to knock but I rang the door-bell and mom opened the door. She smiled and said 'Hey, honey! How are you?' as she gave me a warm and soothing hug. I hugged her back and said 'I'm fine. We won the inter-school soccer league! What about you?'

- 'Oh, such a pity I missed the big match. Nothing much going on, I was just visiting all my friends. All of them are longing to meet the three of you, especially Julie; because of the pro-'she stopped. Her expression changed.
- 'Because of what, mom?' I asked suspiciously.
- 'Well, why am I killing your time. Go a trip around the house first, and then I'll introduce

you to my friends. Mrs McClellan is up in your room, arranging your belongings. Make sure she's placed everything in the correct place.'

- 'Oh mum, Mrs McClellan knows where my stuff belongs more than I do.' I rolled my eyes, put my bag pack on a table near and ran upstairs.

I went up and down the house and long corridors. All the corridors had many pictures of the five of us, my grandparents who I have never been fortunate enough to meet and many people I didn't know but I guess they were my parents' friends.

Finally I came to the first floor where my room was. On the right was a hallway, with doors on both the sides. Okay, maybe I'll be able to find my way to my room. Even if I would never agree to this, I have to say I seek to excel in everything I do but I suck at finding my way. My weak point is routes. I'm the worst at remembering my way.

I yelled 'Mom! Where's my room?' After a moment mom's voice floated up the stairs saying 'The second room on the right side!'

The ground floor was divided into a huge living room, a dining, a parlour, kitchen and my mom's study. The first floor was partitioned into my room, Sam and Su's room, a room where we preserve trophies and a sound proof music room where Sam and Suzie can play all the noisy tunes they like to play. That was something common with those two. The second floor was separated into my parent's room, my dad's den, the library, an art room and a huge room where my parents can have meetings. The third floor was just split into four guest rooms and a store room and gym.

I walked into the long corridor and found my room. I flung the door open. Inside I saw plump Mrs McClellan shutting a drawer. She said 'Sara!' 'Mrs McClellan! I prefer being called SJ, just SJ.' I said

- 'I know dear, take some rest, alright.' I nodded. She left the room thinking I'd be very tired.

Come on, why would I sleep when there is a big house to explore? There was much more exploration left to do, especially in the library.

On the left side there were dim yellow lights and a door had already been open. Inside were three long tables. One table had the letters S-A-M engraved on it. The other had S-J, the next had S-U carved. On the table were all the trophies, medals, certificates, photographs, of all our victories. For once I had realized I really have had a whole lot of victories. I looked over at my brother's table and my sister's. My medal from last night stood right in front on a tiny pedestal which said 'Inter-school soccer league'. On the centre of the wall stood a huge portrait of mom, dad, Sam, I and Su. It looked so life—like. We were all so young in the picture. It took me back to the old days. The beautiful and juiciest of memories, maybe there were more exciting ones lying ahead!

Chapter 2

The discovery

I had tried all the passwords that dad would possibly think of. But yet I couldn't open the door. The room with the portrait had an automatic lock system which needs a password for opening. I hadn't even noticed that I had shut the door. I gave up! I was stuck there for about an hour. I slumped down on the floor and put my head down.

Suddenly I heard a voice say 'Don't you know this door has an automatic lock system?' I looked up to see Sam. I said 'How did you get in?' 'Well . . .' He hesitated. I knew he never was in the room and my back was against the door; there was no way he could've got into the room that way. 'Sam, what's going on with you?' I asked. He'd been acting weird lately like he was trying his best to keep himself from telling me something. He's been ignoring me a lot. I and Sam are not the kind of siblings who are poles apart, we are very good friends. He quietly walked past me and typed the password, the door opened with a loud beep. He opened it and said 'The pass is 12937. And dad specially printed out a map of the whole house just for you.' He mocked. 'It's on the dresser in your room.' I punched his shoulder. I complained 'I want to talk with you.'

- 'That's what we're doing now. About what, anyway?'
- 'Well . . .' what was I going to talk to him about? Why was he ignoring me? I'm sure I would get a "I never ignored you"
- 'Fine, today we'll go around town alright. We could talk about whatever you wanna talk about then.' He said as he left. He kept fixing his hair as he walked away. He had dark chocolate brown hair which was always spiked. My brother was tall for an eleventh grader. And he had a great physique. I must mention he goes to martial arts classes or whatever. And he works out more than anyone I know, it was his favourite hobby.

He turned back and looked at me. He bit his lip and deep dimples fell on his lightly tanned cheeks. His light hazel eyes like freshly baked cookies widened. I knew he was hiding something from me. He always tells me everything. 'You know where you're room is right?' He asked. 'Like you care!' I snapped as I headed towards my room. He raced behind me and said 'Hey, what's wrong?' catching my arm. I brushed his hand off. He was getting on my nerves. He wasn't there at my soccer game nor was he the Sam I liked. He had changed, and I didn't like the new Sam.

I heard mom's voice say 'Kids, come down for breakfast!' I took one last glance at Sam. He gave me his usual pleading for apology look which was pretty satisfying. But I wasn't going to fall for it; I'd already fallen for it too many times.

He said as he followed me down the stairwell, 'I'm really; really sorry for whatever I did, alright. Why are you mad at me?'

I looked at him and said 'Sammy, I have so much to tell you. Remember after Nancy died, we'd play this game every evening, after school about whatever happened that day? You know I wouldn't tell anybody else, what I'd tell you.'

- 'Now is a perfect bro-sis moment? Let's play, what is it that's disturbing you?'
- 'I'm hungry.' I snapped.
- 'Okay, if that's disturbing you, let's hog down some food.'

After breakfast I, Sam and Suzie went around town. The three of us sat at Simon's Smoothies, which looked like a pretty popular place as it was packed with teens. 'Hmm . . . There's nothing fancy about this place except its name. You know what; I think I'll go home for a swim.' Su said as she got up to leave. Sam asked 'Are you sure you can find your way home?' She smiled and said 'I'm not SJ.' I frowned. I have one bad quality and everybody takes advantage of it. I mean, why do they always have to see what I can't do? I have a lot of other extraordinary things that I can do. Only later did I learn that my 'extraordinary' abilities were not that ordinary.

There was long moment of silence. There were a bunch of kids sitting next to our table playing with cards. Suddenly a chill ran up my spine. I shivered, my brother touched my hand, it was so cold, and my head felt so heavy. 'Nerdo,' he began. But at that state of time I realized I could literally see through things. I could see through the cards, through the doors, through the walls . . . . I gasped when Sam shook me. 'Are you alright, Nerdo?' He asked. 'I . . . . I . . .' I gasped for air. I told him what had happened. And he wasn't surprised at all. He said 'That's what I've not been telling you all this while. I'm sorry okay; I mean you would've thought I was crazy if I told you this before you experienced it yourself.'

- 'I don't understand.' I muttered.
- 'It's evolution. Everyone in our family has . . . what do I say . . . a supernatural ability, like an out of the ordinary power. I can see and move through solid substances, I mean literally walk through things.'
- 'What?!' I exclaimed. I didn't understand a word he said. He literally pushed his hands through the table to prove himself honest.

- 'Yes, Su, you know why she always was a good swimmer and so fond of water? And why she's so good at sprinting? Because she has super speed and she doesn't need oxygen. Well mom's is the coolest. She flies and when she does she turns into fire like real, blazing, hot fire. She's radioactive. And dad has telekinesis; he can move things with his mind.'
- 'No wonder mom always does something with all the new clothes she buys.'
- 'Yes, because she wears fire proof clothes.'
- 'Oh my gosh, this is all too much to–'
- 'I know the information is too hard to digest. But that's the truth. That's what I've been hiding from you since the past two weeks. And I saw through the door that you were stuck in the room earlier today morning.'
- 'Okay so why didn't you show up at the game?'
- 'I . . . I forgot.' He gave me that apologetic look again. 'Sam, you know that that look won't work on me like other girls. I'm your sister not your girlfriend.' He smiled and said 'It works really well with mom.' I sat uncomfortably on the chair; I had an odd feeling of being out of place. I felt really dizzy; maybe I'll even pass out. And I sure did.

I kind of had a very weird dream but I guess it was just a supressed memory that I suddenly remembered. Is my brain allowed to play tricks on me like that?

I was just two years and there were three other kids around me of the same age. One guy had black hair and eyes; they were of the same color. Looking into his eyes was like falling into a black abyss. His eyes were staring right at me, he looked so familiar. It was one of those moments—where you know the face and you know the name but you can't put it together. He was chewing on a batman toy's head.

The other guy, who had a toy truck in his hands, had blonde hair and calm sky blue eyes like a sunny and gleeful morning; he gave me a warm smile. The girl who stood next to me had brown hair like melting chocolate and sea green eyes; she seemed to be busy playing with a doll. I guess the location was a play school or a baby sitter's place, because there were plenty of other kids around. A woman in a skirt and shirt sat at a table in front of the room. She wore thick reading glasses, too big for her face. She was young and pretty. The whole place smelled like milk and baby lotion.

My mother accompanied with three other women entered the room. My mom was very young; I really mean it, very, very young. The other three women were probably of her age. My mom lifted me and asked 'How are you doing SJ? Missed mommy?' Was I supposed to reply?

The lady next to me was holding the hand of the boy with black eyes. He was too involved at the sight he looked out of the window. He hugged his mom; she knelt down to him and asked 'Hello Jake! Honey, guess what? Daddy will take you to the park today, you want to go?' He said 'Yes' in a cute voice. My mom asked the lady 'Julie, will you be leaving Jake here tomorrow?' So this lady was Julie, my mom's best friend. 'Well, I guess I have to. I mean, I can't look after both Jake and Alex at the same time at home. And also have to help Alley with her spelling bee after work. I don't have an option.' Julie replied.

'Then can you pick SJ up tomorrow?' My mother questioned. 'I have to go to the doctor.' Then I realized my mother was pregnant with Suzie, very pregenant that I was surprised I didn't notice before. I searched the room for a calendar. It had to be somewhere. Then I spotted it, it was October 29, which meant Suzie would be born after 20 days.

I woke up to find myself on the big brown and cream coloured sofa near the fire place. I sat up, rubbing my forehead. My father was talking to this man. He realized that I had woken. 'Hello, there SJ! This is my good friend, Dr Jack Robinson. He's an old neighbour of ours'.' My hot-shot of a dad said with a smile showing off all his pearly whites. I said 'Good morning Dr Robinson.'

- 'Hello Sara Jane!' He replied. I gave my dad a stare and he said 'Remember she hated it when we called her Sara Jane, Jack. She's still the same kid. SJ, please.'
- 'Well you have grown, child.' He said 'I saw you as a little kid.'

- 'Wait a second, was I born here?' I turned to my dad. He gave me a nod which made his brown hair bounce. Mr Robinson said 'I have to go now. Lunch at my place would be nice, you and your family' as he got up to leave. My father nodded a yes with a hair-bounce again.

Chapter 3

Meeting strangers and strangeness

I headed upstairs, changed and sat down at my dresser, observing the map. The house was really huge; in fact my room was like a mini apartment. Outside the mansion we had a servant quarters, a small dining and a parlour. My dad even gave us a small portion to play soccer. Everyone in my family loved soccer, and baseball . . . and tennis . . . and football . . . . and cricket, oh the list will just keep going on forever!!!

My dad has been forcing me and Sam to go to this charity ball. I understand him; I mean it is a *charity* ball. But dad doesn't get me, it is a charity *ball*. And it doesn't matter if I don't have a date, what matters is what I have to wear. I don't get why you can't come to a charity ball with comfortable jeans and T-shirts.

I pulled my short hair into a tiny ponytail. My hair was feathered, black, spiky and short. My grey eyes were usually stormy and fresh but today they were dull, I was tired. I crept on my bed and pulled my sheets up. There were a few more minutes through which I could sleep till we had to leave to the Robinsons to have lunch. I thought of what Sam had told me. It was really true, all the strange things, I asked both mom and dad. I really had a supernatural ability, life is growing awkward.

Some odd power ran in the blood of few families in the town, and slowly generation after generation, it transformed into a unique talent within us, like another sense. We usually had symptoms of it when we are young, like about seven or eight, but it was delayed for Su, I and Sam because of the long term separation from the town.

The same strange feeling was felt; I looked out the window at Suzie getting out of the swimming pool. An insane thought struck me. I raced downstairs; was fast, super-fast, and maybe too fast for a normal human. In a blink of an eye I found myself in front of the pool. Without even taking off my shoes I jumped in. I heard Su yell 'At least take off your shoes, SJ! Mom, SJ has completely lost it!' I stayed underwater for about a few seconds. I pulled my head out of the water to see mom standing there with a towel, looking at her wrist watch. She looked at me and said 'Twelve minutes under water. Wow, that is interesting. You can play Sam and Suzie, the prophecy surely has passed over to you.' My mother sighed. Whatever the prophecy was, I guess it wasn't a good thing. So, was I supposed to be worried? I got out of the water and grabbed the towel out of mom's hand.

I asked 'What is this prophecy?' A part of me didn't even want to know but my curiosity level is very high, it always wins.

My mom looked at me with her dove coloured, grey eyes. They were like the silver moon. She said 'It was about 1943 when all of it started. Way before even I was born. A man walked into the town, no one knew anything about him. He was an immortal, a bad man. From when he came to town, a lot of murders had started; the town was full of fear and chaos. The truth was that, that man went searching for people with a supernatural power and drained it out of them. But there was no legal proof for this.

Unlike other mortals, our life depends on one strand of DNA. It is through which our powers are inherited. It is what keeps us alive. Once that strand is lost, we will grow weak and die.

Like I said this man is immortal. That is when we knew that there was a way to get rid of this man. Not for long, but for a while. Any person with ability like yours would be accompanied by a guardian, a soul mate who has a very unique ability like yours and who will protect the chosen one that is you. And there will be four people, brother, sisters or close companions who will be able to control the four elements of life: Earth, sky, water and fire. And together—the chosen one, her protector and the four holders of life as we call them, they will be able to defeat the man but if you fail, it may even decide the end of the world for our kind. And if we don't live mortals can never be in peace. This man's name is Lucifer Cyrus. As he is immortal, the adults, the more experienced of our kind have decided, whoever this prophecy falls on, has to tear the man apart and throw him outer space, and he won't find his way back to earth for a century or so. A person with a power like yours will come only once in a hundred and thirty five years. You have a lot of responsibility, SJ.'

I was astounded, all I could do was blink. I finally asked 'Well, what is the power that I possess? I mean, nothing makes sense.'

- 'You my dear, have the ability to absorb others powers.'
- 'Well, that means I'm nothing. I'm not a specialist in any particular supernatural talent. I only can copy others' power. That is dumb.'
- 'Oh SJ, it means you are the most powerful, silly. It means you are a specialist in all kinds of supernatural talent, if that's what you call it.'
- 'Okay, that . . . . that is not good for me at all.'
- 'Don't worry; you love mysteries and adventures, don't you? Then you have just got the biggest adventure of your life coming. Enjoy!'
- 'Enjoy? This whole prophecy thing is giving me the creeps! Can't I just quit?'
- 'No, of course you can't quit! The best blood is always chosen for this. Don't worry, fate never

does anything wrong. Okay come on, let's get you into dry clothes and hit the Robinsons. Well you have to meet many of my friends. Julie and Tom are the closest. The eight of us were very close; we went to school together . . . .'She said as she walked to the door. But I couldn't hear what she was saying because I was still aw-struck. Just before sliding open the gigantic mahogany door to enter the house, she said 'Our abilities do not work on new moon and full moon days.' Before I could ask her more questions she left saying 'Get dressed, we got to leave in five minutes.'

As I changed I just kept thinking. All this information was way too much to take. Firstly, I couldn't believe all this was true, it feels like a dream. Secondly, there's this totally insane prophecy which is driving me nuts. Thirdly, the whole planet earth is depending on me and some other guy who I have no idea about. Oh my God! All of this is not real, I said looking at my reflection in the mirror. Everything's going to be fine. You'll wake up from your dream and you'll see that none of this was real. Suddenly Sam barged into my room, flying right out of my wall. He said 'C'mon, we got to go.' I took a deep breath and followed Sam downstairs.

Dr Robinson opened the door with a big bright smile. I stepped into the house after all the others. The house was pretty huge I say, just a little smaller than ours. They're house was just opposite ours. I stuck with my mom going around everywhere she went. She entered into the kitchen, inside stood a tall lady with pale blond hair which was twisted into a pony tail and oddly familiar emerald eyes. She said 'Hello Kelly!' They hugged. She observed me for a moment as those olive eyes widened 'Oh look at SJ, you're all grown up. The last time I saw you, you were four years old. You don't remember me do you?' I nodded a yes. She resembled the women from my dream. But this lady in front of me was older. 'Well then this is our first meet. I'm Annie Robinson and I'm a dentist. I have five children—Alexis, Jonah, Katarina, Karen and Mathew.' I shook hands with her.

A girl walked into the kitchen. She wore a pink tank top beneath her purple sweater. Her hair was so long it went all the way to her waist. It highly resembled melting chocolates which formed ringlets as it passed down. It was like chocolate might drip right out of her hair. Her hair seemed a bit . . . yummy. And her eyes were the colour of the leaf. The same set of sea green eyes I'd seen in my dream perfectly going along with her tanned complexion. Her skin was just a little bit lighter than espresso. She said 'Table's set.' She looked at me and said 'Sara Jane Salvatore, hello!'

- 'Please call me SJ. And you?'
- 'Katy.' She replied. 'I don't like to be called Katarina.'
- 'Katy, it is.'

- 'Seems like the new trendsetters in town.' She said narrowing her eyes at her mom.
- 'Me? Trendsetter? Please.' I dragged the syllables of 'please'. So it sounded more like Pll-eee-ssss.
- 'Of course you are. I mean everybody in school has been talking about you for the past two weeks. Every girl and guy in the whole school knows your name. Especially our coach is looking forward to meeting you.'
- 'Coach? You mean soccer right? And anyway, I can't be a trendsetter, I mean . . . . I wear sneakers, I'm a total . . .'
- 'Tomboy, I see that. Well, you are lucky to have such a great coach as your aunt.' It hit me. I just had one aunt. My mother's sister, Sylvia Ryan. 'Okay, let's go have lunch alright.' Dr\Mrs Robinson said. 'Katy, get Jonah to shut his text book and come down stairs for lunch.' She sighed and started out the door. My mother signalled me to accompany Katy. I said 'I'm coming with you.'

I followed her upstairs into a long corridor. 'Hey wait a second, this resembles my house.' Katy stopped and turned to me, laughing. 'Both the houses are designed by the same architect and interior designer, so it has a little similarity.'

- 'Same architect and interior designer?' I echoed.
- 'Mr and Mrs Martin. Mr Martin is an architect, he's a busy man, and you see he's preferred by

a lot of people for his amazing designs. And Mrs Martin, gosh, no words to say about her, whatever she puts in a room are just amazingly perfect!'

She knocked the door. A tall and pale guy with dark hair just like my brother's and soft eyes just like Katy's opened the door. 'What do you want? I got another few chapters to finish.' Then he looked at me and smiled. 'Are you SJ or little Su?' He asked with an eyebrow raised. 'Yeah, that's me . . . SJ' I said.

- 'I cannot believe this, you were so tiny the last time I saw you!' He said.
- 'Well, I've grown up. I couldn't stop it.' I said.
- 'I'm sorry, you won't remember me. I am Jonah, soon Dr Jonah Robinson.'

'Will you quit your whole 'I'm going to be a doctor in a few months' act for now? I'm fed up.' Katy said. 'You don't know how hard it is to study medicine, and how much hard work I do day and night to accomplish my dreams. And the fact that I study in Harvard has to be stressed.' This Jonah brother was a nerd, a good-looking nerd. Before Katy could reply I said 'Seems like you're very ambitious. That's a very good thing. You know, it's good to have a target in life, and when you finally achieve it, the pleasure is indescribable.' Jonah's expression softened. 'See, she understands me better than you.' He snapped at Katy. 'Okay, both of you. Stop it.' A voice said from behind me.

I turned to see this little boy with green eyes and flushed face. He said 'Mom's calling you guys downstairs.' He gave an angry expression and signalled both of them to follow him. He turned and marched the other way. I looked at Katy 'That's Mathew.' She said. I nodded with a smile.

All of us sat at the table and had our lunch. Sweet-sour soup as a starter, main course was roasted beef with baked potatoes and dessert was blue berry pie.

It was very awkward but my mom and dad seemed to be very happy. When I sat there at the table, it was so real, everyone was so gleeful and the atmosphere was filled with joy and excitement. These stranger that I just met, made me fit in just right. I sat next to Katy and on my left sat Karen, Mathew's twin. She hardly spoke; she looked more like her mom. And I don't think she likes me.

Chapter 4

I burnt it down

After lunch Jonah, Mathew and Sam were playing video games. Suzie and Karen were upstairs in Karen's room. Our parents sat in the living room. I and Katy decided to sit on the front porch. She said 'It's pretty boring at my place. I mostly hang out at Luke's or Jake's.'

-   'Who?' I asked. Jake, familiar name.
-   'Luke's my boyfriend. Well, I, Jake and Luke have been together since we were little kids. Even you were pretty close when we were young, at least that's what mom says. Then fate brought me and Luke together.'
-   'Well, why do you feel so bored? I mean, you have a big and nice family.'
-   'Only now. Jonah will soon leave to collage, he's here for his study hols and he has his big exams coming up. Alexis is hardly in town. She's a professor at Harvard, so Jonah gets to see her

every day at school. It's mostly Mathew, Karen and I. Both of them are kids and Mathew is bossy, very bossy. Karen, she's very sacrificing. I guess that's why she gets along with Mathew. I'm mostly with Luke and Jake. Jake is very fun to hang out with, he's like my brother. What about you, how is it in your place?'

- 'Well I do not have many friends. It's mostly I, Sam and Suzie. My siblings are fun-enough for me. And I didn't have any time for friends. You see, my life was really tight.'

- 'No hanging out with friends, partying, sleep over's?' She exclaimed.

- 'No, not one. My schedule doesn't spare time for that. That's why I decided to drop it. My dad said that it was time for me to get to know people, have some friends, to have an adventurous life. And when you have your life scheduled, I mean it's kinda robotic. You don't have any adventures.' I sighed. 'Are you coming to school tomorrow?' Katy asked.

- 'I have to. I don't have an option!' She told me more about the school and she said the principal rocks, which was a fantastic thing, because my ex-principal, Ms. Parker, there were rumours spread about her that she didn't get married because of her mean behaviour and she decided to become a nun, but you need patience, glory, honesty, kindness to be one, which she didn't possess.

The name of the school was Mid-Springs Academy; it had all grades from nursery to high school. It has a big soccer field and lot more sports. I couldn't believe it, but there's just one school in the whole town.

We were sitting in the living room and my mom asked 'So, how did you spend your time at the Robinson's?' 'I had fun!' Su said. 'It was nice. I caught up with a lot of things.' said Sammy. 'It was fun.' I said. 'I got to know a lot about school.' 'Hon, when's the charity ball?' My dad asked mom. 'It's on the day after tomorrow.' Mum said. Dad turned to us 'Sam and SJ, you have to go to the ball. I'm sorry, if the age limit included me and your mother, I would've gone but it's not for us. It's for both of you, and its charity, how could I not contribute?' I and Sam sighed. Going to a ball means we have to go shopping, which was not good, and both of us didn't have a date. And if we didn't find one, we might have to go with each other.

That evening my mom dragged me and Sam to go shopping. Oh no! Going shopping was even worse than doing math homework with Ms. Parker.

My mother said 'I think this will look good on you.' I looked at the red dress in her hand. I said 'I don't care, just get whatever you think will look good on me.' Suzie said 'Oh come on, this dress looks awesome! I wish it was there in my size.' 'Alright, I'll go try it out.' I went into the trial room and changed. I let myself out, and when mom saw me she exclaimed 'You look wonderful!' That means I look like a witch from an evil and extremely odd fairy tale, I thought.

While my mom paid for the dozens of bags Su and her bought for themselves and for the one dress I bought, I and Sam went into a cafe. I felt an ache in my head. I was shivering even if it was just early October. I pulled my jacket closer around me. I sipped from the cup. I felt like I was going to throw up so I went into the washroom. I took deep breaths and tried to relax. But suddenly I felt this burning sensation, it was within my body, the burning crawled into my throat and when I coughed, ashes came out. Oh Lord! What's happening to me?! Suddenly my hands went up on flames, my skull felt hot. I dashed open the door to my stall and looked at myself in the mirror. I was on fire, but yet the fire didn't burn me, it was under my control; at least I guess it was. But then I realized, oh no I wasn't in control of it. All I remember was that I coughed and breathed fire. My whole body was up on flames and I was floating in the air. Then suddenly I felt a pull in my gut, the sprinklers began to spray water but yet I wasn't put off. The fire alarm began to ring, when I breathed out a big wave of fire spread out. After a state of time the wave grew so big I had caused a huge explosion.

I was lying down on my bed. I saw a glass of water on my dresser. The flat screen TV in front of me was switched on. A news channel was going on which said, ' . . . . The mall had been set on fire, no one got injured and no harm was caused to the people, but the police have still not found the source of the explosion.' 'That was me, wasn't it?' I asked to Sam who had just walked through my door. 'Yeah' he said switching the TV off and he handed over the glass of water to me. I gulped it down, my throat was warm. It felt better.

I had just burnt down a whole building, thankfully no one got hurt. 'Don't worry; it was a small mistake . . .' Sam said 'Actually a huge colossal mistake but still it was not your fault.'

That evening at dinner all of us sat at the long dining table. There was complete silence, I had a feeling I was getting grounded the first day in Black Fury. Yeah, I walk into a town and burn my father's mall, that's a cool hobby; everyone does it, all the time, don't they?

The only noise that came was from the forks and spoons. My dad cleared his throat and began 'The three of you should go to bed right away. Sleep well and get ready for school early in the morning.' Suzie rolled her eyes and sighed. 'I'm sorry about what I did to the mall this evening. I know it will cost a lot to fix the damage. You could sell my pass to the charity ball and fix it.' I insisted. 'Well then let's see, you have to get punished for this sin, so you . . .' I interrupted dad saying 'Getting grounded for two weeks.' 'No, you have to go to the charity ball. That is my final word and I am not going to change my statement, I guess that's a deal.'

I nodded. My mother caught my hand and said 'I know it wasn't your fault, honey. You do not know how much power you possess. You are the most powerful living creature on earth. Do you understand what I'm saying?' I nodded. 'I know at this state of time you feel uncomfortable, insecure maybe even a little bit sick, right?' My mother questioned. Well, I was definitely feeling something like that. I nodded again.

I came into the kitchen to put my plate into the sink but Mrs McClellan insisted that I left the plate on the table but I said that it was okay, and when I stood at the corridor connecting the dining room and kitchen I heard mom say 'We got to keep an eye on SJ. She's still not mature enough to handle all the power within herself. We should take good care of her now.' When I passed through the room, everyone remained silent. When I went up the stairs, they continued their conversation.

I sat on my bed, leaving my room door open. I held out my hand towards the door and concentrated. Nothing happened, I tried harder. Then I felt the same chills run down my back and the pull in my gut, the door began to shake. With all my energy, sitting on my bed, I slammed the door shut. Wow, that was so cool! I snapped my fingers and the lights went off. I pulled up my sheets and slept through a long night.

Chapter 5

First day of school!

I sat on the dining table with my father, brother and Suzie, dipping our spoons into our favourite family cereal. My mom sat down on her chair, she had the month's edition of her magazine in her hand. Dad was reading the morning newspaper, Suzie was rattling with her new science text book. I think she was trying to catch up as the kid's in MSA were two chapters ahead of us. Sam had his laptop computer in front of him and he was watching this guy with blue hair skate board. I guess I was the only one actually concentrating on my food.

After breakfast Mr Jacobs pulled out the hummer-limousine from the drive way. The three of us drove in the ride. It was a peaceful and lengthy drive. When we got out of the ride at the school parking lot, all human eyes were set on us . . . . or the ride. I signalled Mr Jacobs to leave immediately, and he did so.

As the three of us went into the school, even more people stared at us. From high schoolers to the elementary, everyone knew who we were. Before I entered the principal's office a girl with pink hair and a pierced eyebrow came running and said 'Cody Ryan's your uncle, right?' I nodded and stepped inside the office. Damn Uncle Cody! I thought. My uncle was an actor and model, but he didn't have to mention the names of the three of us to the whole universe, did he?

The principal said 'The Salvatores. Am I right?' The three of us didn't utter a word, and she knew who we were. 'How did you find out?' Suzie asked. 'Madam . . .' She added. 'I heard all the muttering from the students. My name is Edina Griffin. And I am your principal.' She said with a smile. She handed our schedules and said 'Welcome to mid—Springs academy!' She mentioned our locker numbers and gave us the combination. The three of us got our stuff and went our way. Here comes my first day of eighth grade in Black Fury.

I opened my locker and stuffed my books in. I was in Ms. Green's class; she was our home room teacher and taught English. I pulled out my English text book and other things needed and started searching for room 252. I finally found the class. When I was on my way to enter my room, I ran into someone. We knocked our heads and fell on the ground. The guy got up and held out a hand and said 'Sorry.' I ignored his help, and picked up my things. He said 'It wasn't my fault, he kept the bet.' He said pointing to a guy in the crowd. I leaned to see a guy with blonde hair, sapphire eyes and a flushed face. He looked totally innocent. I then looked at the guy who had pushed me again. For some reason the atmosphere tightened around me. He was impressive—tall, in good shape, muscular and lean, deep mesmerising black eyes like utter darkness and silky, partially spiked black hair. He wore a shirt that hugged his frame perfectly under his black leather jacket. And he probably had a pretty good tan in the summer. It just made him look extra-good. You could clearly see his high cheek bones and his square-jaw tightened. But I wasn't interested anyway. I was mad at him. It was so embarrassing because everyone was looking. After all I was the new gossip in town. I frowned and walked to the class. His features relaxed as he looked at me.

I sat on the second last desk. Few minutes before the bell rang the class was getting full. I spotted Katy, two seats away. I waved at her and she waved back. She switched seats and sat next to me. There was just one empty seat in front of Katy. The blonde guy I had seen earlier sat on Katy's desk and they spoke. Katy turned to me and said 'This is Lucas McQueen, Luke this is Sara . . . . sorry SJ Salvatore.' He smiled and said 'It's been a long time since we met. I don't remember you at all.' I smiled and said 'Neither do I.' someone banged their books on my desk which startled me. I looked up to see the guy who knocked me down. He said 'I'm sorry, but this is my desk. See I got my name on it.' I looked down to see the name 'Jake Martin' carved on the table. 'You're Tomas and Julie Martin's son!?' I exclaimed. 'Yeah, and your Benjamin and Kelly Salvatore's daughter!' He replied, sarcastically. I frowned and said 'Why can't you sit anywhere else?' 'Why should I?' He questioned with an eye brow raised. Before I could say anything, Katy said 'Oh come on Jake, let it go for a day. She's not like other girls, she's definitely different.'

'Yeah I can see that. If it was any other girl she would've just let me sit in my place.' He replied, his eyes glaring right at me with irritation. I couldn't look at him directly, his eyes were just so . . . disturbing. 'And would've said some extremely flirty lines and would follow you around everywhere you go which would annoy you.' Katy helped him finish. 'She didn't do that. So let her off the hook. It's her first day. Cut the kid some slack.' He gave an expression like a little kid who was told not to play in the rain by his mother and strutted to the seat in front of Katy's.

The bell rang and the teacher entered the class. Unlike other teachers, Ms. Jessica Green wore jeans and T-shirt. She looked 20's and wore florescent green spectacles. She said 'I heard there's someone new to class?' I slowly stood up. 'Sara Jane Salvatore. Well there is no need to introduce you. Everyone knows Salvatore here, right?' Some half-shook their head, some only noticed my presence then, most were just staring right at me. Jake just took out his phone and began listening to music. 'Martin?' She asked. He rolled his eyes and said 'Does it even matter?' Katy tapped his back telling him to shut up. Ms. Green walked up to him and whispered loudly 'Jake, I will not consider you as my sister's child if you have this attitude, I'll just break your arm and shove it up your, you know what. You've been annoying me since school started.' 'I'm sorry Aunt Jess; some idiot ruined my mood in the morning. And anyway, I am stronger than you. And you will need me to go fishing' Jake said. 'Ms. Green, Martin.' She corrected.

After half the day went by, I realized that this Jake guy's locker was right next to mine and he happened to be in all my classes. Could there be anything more annoying than that? At recess, I took my tray of food and walked down the hallway to Katy's table. Suddenly some guy walked into me and unfortunately both our shirts got covered with food. I looked up knowing that this time, it was definitely Jake. He said 'I swear to God I didn't mean to do that.' I looked at him with disgust. A girl saw this scene and walked up to Jake. 'Do want me to help you change?' She asked. He looked at her, horrified. He started moving away as she came closer and closer. He looked at me as though he was pleading me to save him. Maybe I hated this guy, but I imagined myself in his shoes. He needed help and I was the only person around. She was harassing him and he was really uncomfortable. I said 'Hey girl, I'll give you two new shoes if you let him go.' She turned towards me and asked 'And an autograph from Cody Ryan?' I nodded 'I'll try Uncle Cody to sign an autograph.' She said 'Bye Jake, I'll be waiting for those shoes.' She reminded as she left. When she reached her gang of friends she yelled 'I'm going to get two pairs of shoes from Sara Jane Salvatore! And Cody Ryan's autograph!' 'Thanks.' Jake said. 'How'd you do that?'

'The only thing a *normal* girl is crazier about than boys are shoes.' I said. 'What do you mean by *normal* girls? Like you're not one?' He questioned. 'Well, I guess I don't fall under that category. And you owe me one.' He nodded. I went to the table Katy and Luke were sitting. Katy looked at the mess and said 'I'll give you my spare T-shirt.'

It was Phys Ed, and I was sitting in the crowd of kids who were here for the try outs. I was the only eighth grader among them. The rest of them were from high school. My Aunt walked into the huge soccer field and said 'we got try outs after school. If you are interested in joining the team, you may try out as long as you are a student of this school and are from eighth grade to seniors in high school.' She zoomed through the crowd and spotted me. Her hard expression softened and she smiled at me. She had the same shade of grey in her eyes, just like mine, the colour of salt and pepper. Other girls were standing in another big area; I guess they were trying out cheer leading. Katy came up to me and said 'You'll get into the team, don't worry. By the way, I'm a mid-fielder, Luke's a goal keeper and Jake's a striker.'

- 'Back in New York I was a striker too.'
- 'O yeah I heard of you getting that trophy in your hand. I saw you strike the final goal too, in YouTube. I guess we'll be winning this year. We got the star player of the league now.'

- 'No you haven't got me yet. I've got try outs afternoon.' She chuckled and ran into the field. Each player got two members to train. Aunt Sylvia came up to me and said 'That last strike you did at the inter-school soccer league, that is what I want a team captain to do. Your dad took a video and sent it to me. That's my female Maradona; she does it clean and tidy.' I smiled as she patted my back, I felt a weird clink.
- 'How are my sis and your daddy? They never came by to meet me.' 'Well Aunt Sylvia, you see we just moved in yesterday and we got a lot of things going on, a lot about me.' I said. 'You burnt down the mall didn't you?' She questioned.
- 'Who told you?
- 'Your mom tells me everything.' I gulped down water and when I started running back into the field, she said 'Hey SJ! You don't have to come for the try outs. You're too good for that.'

'But officially you can't do that, I mean it'll be like you're showing partiality amongst us just because I'm your niece and I don't want people to take it that way about you.' I said. She smiled and said 'Don't worry; I received a recommendation letter from St. Edison's middle school to get you into the team. They said you were an excellent player and things like try outs aren't what you have to go through. So did your brother, what was his school's name, Brain whatever high school.'

'Brian Marcus Carleton high school' I said to myself as though I was trying to get myself back to New York.

After Phys Ed, the creep's locker was next to mine so I had to see his face; I went to my locker and dropped my stuff inside. Jake said 'You got nice moves, and a lot of speed. Your speed amazes me.'

It hit me why people were staring at me. I hadn't taken control over my speed. Oh darn! I hope I wasn't too fast. 'Don't worry, it wasn't all that fast. No one's faster than me.' Jake said as though he had read my mind. 'Oh yeah, let's race then.' I said. 'You want to race me?' He questioned, his face showed a lot of attitude. 'Duh, didn't you hear me' I raised an eyebrow.

- 'Are you sure? Because I know I'm going to win!'
- 'You can't be so sure about that dude. No one can beat me.'
- 'Okay right now.' He asked. He gave me an evil smile which created dimples in his macho cheeks.
- 'Under one condition.'
- 'What?'
- 'Somewhere where there are no public around.'
- 'I know why, because you'll be embarrassed if you lose in front of all those people.'
- 'No, because *you'll* be embarrassed in front of a lot of people.'

- 'Fine, let's go right now. I got the perfect spot.' Katy came along and asked 'Perfect spot for what?' 'To race.' I answered. 'Look, I know both of you aren't so smooth with each other but SJ under any circumstances I would never dare to race Jake Martin . . .' 'I'll win, just watch. I've never lost and I will never lose.' I said interrupting Katy. I heard Sam press the horn on his car real hard for me to come. I ran over to the car and said 'I'll come home myself. I got someone to beat.' I ran back before Sam could say anything. There was an advantage of Katy being my neighbour; I could reach home without knowing the way.

Katy, Luke, I and Jake went off to some deserted place where there was absolutely nothing. And when I mean nothing, I mean literally nothing: just sand, everywhere.

We decided the length of our track and Luke would see who would come first. Katy had to begin the game. And the moment she shouted 'go', I got on my feet and shot forward. I felt that pull in my gut and a cold feeling down my spine. The world around me slowed down and I moved like wind. Before I could blink I was at the finish line and Jake was far behind me. I stood at the finish line when Luke, Katy and Jake were shocked, astonished actually.

Chapter 6

I fight the strongest guy in the world

Jake was glaring at me and was profoundly thinking like he'd just got to know how to launch a rocket. Katy asked 'How come you never told me you were one among us? And you run like the wind. And you just walked through that wall and the bottle just floated to your hand and you can fly!' I nodded as I sucked milkshake from the straw. We were sitting at Fury Cafe and Jake was still too stunned to utter a word and take his eyes off me. He probably thought I wasn't human. 'So you guys got this supernatural power thing too. I thought only my family had it?' I said. 'Yes, the three of us do. And a lot of people around town do. We even have our school for this.' Katy replied.

- 'You guys go to school for this?'
- 'Yeah, weekend school. Right now we're on hols but we'll have school starting again soon. I am a healer.'

'What about you guys?' I asked to Luke and Jake. Jake snapped out of his fantasy. Luke said 'I'm a shape-shifter.' I turned to Jake who sucked in chocolate milkshake and said 'Mine's complicated.' 'Try me; I'll try to keep up.' He took a deep breath and started 'I have two powers actually, one even you can't absorb: super strength. And as for the other, just like how you can absorb people's ability even I can, but you absorb abilities for life time. You will have the power with you till you die. I'll give you an example of mine: When I touch Katy, I absorb her power so I can heal and then if I touch Luke I can shape shift but I can't heal anymore because the previously absorbed power is eliminated. You understood?'

- 'Um . . . I guess.' I said. There was no noise from the four of us till I said 'I got to go home.' When I stood up the door flung open and I found my mom with another lady. I think it was Jake's mom because when Jake saw her he crouched behind the table. My mom came up to me and I knew that second, I was busted. Jake's mom stared at him and he got up pursing his lips which created deep craters in his cheeks. She said 'Jake Martin, you were grounded weren't you?' He nodded. 'Get into the car.' She ordered. Jake ran out the cafe. Then she turned to me and said 'Hello Jane. You don't mind me calling you Jane do you?' I nodded a no. As long as she didn't call me with my first name, which was also my biggest enemy's first name, it was fine with me. But 'Jane' did bring back a sad memory. 'I'm Julie Martin, interior designer. Jake's mom and your mom's best friend. 'My mom rolled her eyes and said 'Julie I came here to yell at her.' 'Come on, the kid just got here, she's probably just hanging around and checking things out. You know Kelly, she's so . . . .' Mrs Martin stopped. My mom said 'so much like me when I was young.' She smiled and said 'Alright, alright, goodbye kids. And Lucas, tell your mom to call me.' He nodded. With the look my mom gave I knew that if I didn't hop into the car, I'll get yelled at in public. When I got out of the cafe, Jake was not getting busted, and Mrs Martin was not yelling at him. And I was hoping to witness Jake's mom scolding him.

Instead both of them were sharing a laugh. I got into the ride and we drove with complete silence. My mom then said 'Look honey, at this state of time I don't want you hanging around alone.' For some reason I felt really insecure at the moment, like something bad was going to happen. 'I didn't tell this to dad. And tomorrow's the charity ball. And I, dad and Suzie are going to Aunt Sylvia's today. Sam's going to his martial arts practice and you have to go with him or come to Aunt Leah's.'

- 'Does that old grandma who came to my eighth birthday still live there?' I remember her trying to tell me to eat cake when she was actually shoving her handbag on my face.
- 'Yes, sweetie.'
- 'Oh god, why doesn't Aunt Leah come to live with us? Why should I go to Sam's martial arts practice?'
- 'Because you need an eye kept on you. I called up Sean from Combat Academy and he told it was fine to have you this evening.'
- 'Who's Sean?'
- 'The one who trains Sam.'
- 'Oh, but mom it'll be too awkward for a girl to go to a place with sweaty guys.'
- 'Oh so now you finally say you're a girl.' I grinned.

I and Sam had a ride to the gym. There was a lot of equipment I couldn't name. A tall man stood at the front and seven guys sat in a row in front of him which included my brother. Sean had given me a comfortable spot at the corner on a comfy bean bag. They were just doing all the normal stuff that we see in movies related to fighting. I sat there, texting Uncle Cody. He was in Paris shooting an action movie named 'Tonnerre' which means 'thunder'.

I heard the door open, in front of the door stood my brand new foe: Jake Martin. He said 'I'm sorry. I got into trouble with the new cops in town.' He dropped his bag and stared at me as if I were an alien from Mars. 'Okay, Sebastian, you fight Martin.' Sean said. 'Come on Sean. Why would I do that? Fighting Martin is suicide.' The guy complained. 'Oh come on Sebastian, don't be such a chicken. Come on buddy.' Jake encouraged. 'Promise me I'll live after this fight with my legs and arms in place.' The guy said. 'I'll make sure you're not dead.' Jake promised. Jake was such a show-off.

They began their fight and Sebastian tapped out. So I guess Jake won.

My brother had to fight this guy who looked very odd out of the crowd. He was as tall as my brother, pale and he had long hair that covered his eyes. And of course my brother was the winner. After everyone had a turn fighting, Sean said 'Okay guys, we'll take ten minutes break.' Everyone knew which door to walk to, and they did. I just sat there with my phone. I got a message from Uncle Cody saying 'What are you doing there? I bet you went there to see shirtless guys.' He mocked.

'Oh shut up Uncle Cody.' I replied.

After three minutes I got a reply saying 'You know I don't like to be called *uncle, Sara Jane Salvatore.'*

I texted back to him saying 'Yeah, yeah, I know. So what are you doing now?'

- 'I'm in my PJ's in the twelfth floor of Salvatore suits eating apple pie.' He replied.

- 'Apple pie?'
- 'Yeah, I missed your mom. No apple pie can taste like the ones your mom makes. What's the secret ingredient, my lovely baker niece?'
- 'Oh I'm not going to reveal that secret because I don't even know it. Even Aunt Sylvia doesn't know the ingredient. Actually no one else knows except mom and I don't bake, I help if I'm bored.'
- 'Aunt Sylvia? Oh you mean my other older sis, Leah don't you?'
- 'Yes, Aunt Leah it is.' After that conversation I got no reply and I wasn't interested in sending another message.

After the ten minute break Sean began teaching all pairs of two some new moves. The only thing I could think about right now was an intense odour of guys who had great physique sweating litters. After the clock struck seven on my watch wrestling school was over. All the guys went into their doors and didn't show up for about half an hour.

The first to come out was the weird looking guy, he didn't give a reaction as he walked out the door with his stuff and his hair hanging over his eyes were split in the middle like curtains.

The next was Sebastian and the other two guys who were always with him. So only Jake and Sam hadn't come out from whatever was behind those doors.

After a while Jake walked out looking at his watch. He had finally put on clothes. He looked at me and said 'I thought you would be in school for the try outs from four o'clock.'

I said 'Well maybe I'm too good for try outs. I'm an outstanding player.'

'Oh you play soccer right, I was talking about cheerleading.' He mocked. I smiled sarcastically. 'I know you're jealous that I won the race. I told you I'd win.'

'Okay we competed at something your good at. Now let us compete at something I'm good at.' He said walking closer and giving me that show-off look.

- 'What are you good at? Chewing gum?' I said folding my arms and giving him the 'bring it on!' look.
- 'Let's fight.' When he mentioned the words my heart stopped. Was he insane?
- 'Jake Martin, did you collect your brain when God was distributing them?' He chuckled and said 'I know you wouldn't accept this challenge because you don't stand a chance winning.'

I got onto my feet and nodded. 'When you know I don't stand a chance winning, why do you want to fight? I thought you owed me one.' He said 'Oh come on, you're a coward.' Yes, the craziest idea I've ever even thought of hit me. I said 'Fine, but there is no guarantee I'm winning. I'm doing this just to satisfy you.'

He frowned and said 'What makes you think you can't win?'

- 'Oh so you say I have a chance to win?'
- 'Well, 1.00001% chance to win.'
- 'Okay then.' I agreed. The next second I felt his fist connect with my gut but he didn't seem to be putting a lot of effort and I went flying and hit the wall. Ouch! That hurt a lot. I saw a hammer through the door to a shelf. I raised my hand and concentrated. The door began to shake the hammer floated out. Jake didn't know that it was happening. With the blunt back of the hammer I hit his head. He rubbed his head at the back and then I slowly began to raise, sparks of fire sprouted out from my body. Jake looked and me and smiled. He jumped up and touched the fire that I produced. Immediately after that his body turned up into flames and he was flying too. He was wobbling, so was I, but I wasn't as wobbly as him. I shot a ray of fire at him. He blocked it with his hands. He flied towards me to hit me but unfortunately for him, he just passed right through me. But then I guess my energy began to fade; I began to lower to the ground. He wacked me in my head and I flew across the room, skidding on the rough floor and banged against the wall.

I felt like I had broken my rib cage and my left leg. Jake came running towards me, he bent down and asked 'Are you alright? I just touched you and it happened.' He was panicked. And what was that I saw in his eyes? Concern . . . . for me!! Why does that sound funny?

'You almost kill me and you ask me if I'm alright?' I said sitting up. I felt that slow chills down my spine and the pull in my gut. Suddenly the room temperature decreased, I felt really cold. Jake blew into his hands and the mist appeared, I rubbed my hands together. I saw a faint reflection of myself on the glass behind. My eyes were changing from grey to blue-ish—white. Suddenly my vision got blurry and tears poured out my eyes. I shut my eyes tight not knowing what was going to happen. My heart was beating really slowly. When I opened my eyes a ray of ice shot right at Jake and he stood like an ice statue, exactly the way he stood seconds ago, rubbing his hands. I felt normal again. My leg didn't hurt. I stood up and walked around the frozen statue of Jake Martin. It was incredible! How did I do that? I knocked on the ice.

It was so hard, how could I possibly get him back to normal? Yes, maybe I'd lost an irritating idiot, but he was a human being like others and there are a lot of people who love him. Before I could melt the ice, the ice shattered over the floor and Jake rose up into the air in flames.

A second later he was standing on the ground; he pushed me against the wall and put his hand on both the side blocking my way out. He stood so close to me that I could feel him breathe on my cold skin. I held my breath. He didn't utter a word, but I knew he was mad at me. His eyes bore into mine but I denied meeting his eyes. He was so filled with rage that if he would have just brushed against me, I would fall apart. Each time I met those eyes it was like coal was melting in my brain. I tried to have a fixed gaze but he stood so close I was losing control of my actions. I looked away. I hoped so hard that I wasn't blushing but when Jake's eyes softened, his frown faded and he smiled that dimple smile and stepped back, I knew I was blushing hard.

He said 'I guess you win' picking up his bag. I said 'No you win.'

'You don't have to have sympathy or anything. I may be a jerk sometime but I'm just. It's only fair if you win.' He said stuffing his hands into his pockets. I nodded and said 'No, you didn't whack my head or throw me across the room when I accidentally froze you. It was my mistake and I am unaware of the incredible things I can do, you understood that and made a wise decision to back off. You win, and anyway, you are the strongest guy in the entire planet earth.' He smiled and walked towards the door. He took out his hands from his pockets of his khaki shorts and turned before opening the door. He bit his lips; he was holding something back that I was supposed to know. He began 'I . . . you . . . um . . . I'll see in you in school tomorrow.'

I nodded. I don't know why, but I think Jake has something called a heart. Sam finally came out.

When we got out Jake was standing in the parking lot. He was on the phone, he said 'But how will I get home then? No way am I getting on a bus!' After a while he said 'Oh come on, have mercy Alley, I know I got into trouble with the cops five times before and because of that you always get into trouble, but I swear this will be the last time. I am your baby brother . . . . No I don't say that all the time . . . . C' . . . . Alley . . . . hello!' I guess his older sister hung up on him.

He sighed with frustration. Sam suggested 'I'll give you a ride home.' So we started the car. I sat in the back and both the boys started talking about boxing gloves. It was a better conversation than listening to mom and her friends talk. Our house was just a few blocks away from Jake's so Sam dropped me first. When I got out of the car, Sam got out too. He said 'Um . . . I guess they aren't home yet. Don't stay up waiting for me or them, we got the keys. Have dinner and go to bed. Remember tomorrow's Friday, we got to stay up long at the night because of the ball. So have a good night sleep okay.' He kissed me good night and hopped back in the car. Jake probably heard the whole conversation and I bet he was jealous. Yes, I know I have the most wonderful siblings in the world!

Chapter 7

The charity ball

$\mathfrak{J}$ picked up my bag and headed downstairs. My body hurt so much I was finding it difficult to walk, I guess it's the after effects of our fight. As usual we rode to school and this time I took a seat which didn't have 'Jake Martin' carved on it. Jake was on my right. Ms. Green took out a bundle of papers from her bag and handed it out to the whole class. It was blank, nothing written in it. After distributing it to the whole class, she walked to the front of the class. She said 'I want you to write down the happiest moment that you experience in this whole academic year. I want you to submit this little sheet that I have given on the last day of eighth grade. It doesn't have to be something related to the school, it could be experienced anywhere, with anyone, but it must happen in this academic year. You see, eighth grade is like the time you bid farewell to childhood and become more mature. Just a little souvenir I'd like you guys to carry from middle school. But one rule, the essay should consist of more than hundred words' a slight smile appeared on her face.

The day was slow and sleepy. It was recess and I brought my tray to the four seated table where Luke, Katy and Jake sat. I banged my food on the table. The whack that Jake had given me on my head still hurt. Jake was also hurt, he had a cold box of orange juice on the back of his head where I hit him with the hammer. I grabbed the box from him and laid it on my head. Ah, that feels good. Jake sighed and bit his burger.

Katy said 'Coach Ryan wanted to see you in the teacher's common room.' 'Coach Ryan?' I asked not understanding. Then I got it 'Oh, you mean Aunt Leah. Why?' I questioned. She shrugged.

I got up and placed the juice box back on Jake's head. He gave a sigh of relief.

I marched to room 23 which had a big board on the door which said 'Faculty only.' I knocked on the door. Mr Neumann, our history teacher, opened the door. He smiled at the sight of seeing me and asked 'Well, what are you doing here?' I said 'Aunt Leah . . . . I mean coach Ryan told me to come here.' He nodded and said 'Well your Aunt Leah isn't here.' 'Here you are,' said a voice from behind me. I turned to see Aunt Leah. She put her arm around my neck 'Come in.' I frowned and said 'doesn't this board say "Faculty Only"?' She pulled me in without an answer. Inside I saw a lot of familiar faces, our home room teacher, Ms. Green, my math teacher Mrs Fiona Lore, Mrs Fells, our biology teacher and many others. When I was looking around Aunt Leah got herself a glass of orange juice. She took a sip and then frowned. The next second when she placed her hand on the glass, mist covered the transparent container of juice. The glass looked like she just pulled it out from the refrigerator. My eyes widened, 'You are the one I got that from.' I said. She asked 'What?'

- 'The whole cold, ice . . . . freezing thing I did yesterday.'
- 'Yeah, I guess I understood you right.' Then she pulled out a bundle of papers and held it out to me. She said 'Give it to your mom.'
- 'What is it?'
- 'Just the manuscript of her next book,' she wanted comments as usual.'

After school I, Katy, Jake and Luke walked home together. For some reason my mom said I'd be safe when I'm with my friend, but she didn't mention which friend. So she just let me walk with them. Luke and Katy were in front of us and I and Jake walked behind them giving them the privacy they needed. After a long moment of silence Jake said 'Heard you're going to the ball today?' I nodded. He said 'I was thinking . . . .' he had begun to blush and I had a bad feeling about it. And he did the exact thing I expected later.

He stopped and said 'You hate me, don't you?'

'No.' I lied. He glared at me. 'Okay, maybe a little.' I agreed. 'Well, even I hate you a little bit too.' He confessed. I nodded. That was no new news. But then he asked 'But . . . SJ . . . . can you come with me to the ball, can you be my date?' I shrugged and said 'I bet there is a long list of other girls who are waiting for you to ask. Why'd you pick me?'

- 'Because you are the only girl who doesn't have a date and doesn't frighten me.' He said as he began to walk again. I giggled and walked by his side. The thought that the strongest guy in the world, who almost has every guy in the world frightened by him, happens to be scared of girls made me laugh like an idiot on the pavement. He asked 'so are you coming with me or not? We haven't got much time. And neither of us have a date. And who can you possibly go with in such a short notice?' I frowned and said 'Just watch.' I went into Simon's Smoothies, where most kids hung out after school and yelled 'Hey, who wants to go to the charity ball with me tonight?' Almost every eighth grader I knew in that place raised his hands. I turned back and smiled at Jake. He said 'But I asked first.' I made a face and turned towards the crowd of guys.

'I pick . . . .' I zoomed around the room with my finger pointed. Before I could make a decision Jake yelled 'Whoever wants to take her to the ball has to get a punch from me.' The whole crowd of guys gulped. They all went around like nothing ever happened; they sat on their chairs and drank their smoothies. I turned to Jake and asked 'Hey, why did you do that?' He caught my hand and dragged me out of the shop. Luke and Katy didn't even know we weren't following them. They had walked two blocks without us. I and Jake raced to catch up with them. I was running in normal speed, like a normal human but even then I was faster than Jake.

I still didn't say yes or no to Jake for the question he asked. He kept asking me for an answer till I reached my house. He asked me so many times that I couldn't say no, but I didn't want to say yes just yet. He stood at my front porch while Luke said bye to Katy at the next house. He said 'C'mon, make up your mind.' I smiled and said 'Um . . . . okay, I made up my mind. I'll go with you.'

'Thank you so much!' He said. He almost hugged me with excitement but he stopped himself. 'I'll pick you up at six thirty.'

'I don't want any trouble with the cops.' I told. He smiled and said 'Don't worry, my uncle is the sheriff, I got into trouble because the cops I met yesterday were new to town. All the other cops know that I drive, and don't worry, I'm a good driver. If you don't trust me ask your brother.'

'Six thirty it is.' I said. As I walked into the house I saw my dad standing right there as he welcomed me with a warm smile. He asked 'Seems like you got a date for your ball.' I nodded. 'Jake's not such a bad guy, in fact he's a really good kid.' My dad continued as I hopped on the couch in the living room and stretched my legs over the table. I shrugged, half agreeing to his statement. 'Do you like him?' Dad asked a question which shocked me. I found the right words and blurred out 'Well, both of us literally hate each other to death. He was helpless so I agreed. And we just have to get along because of Katy and Luke.' My dad took a long breath. He said 'But he's not a bad guy. He's a nice kid . . . .' 'What are you trying to convince me about dad?' I asked suspiciously, interrupting him.

He sat next to me and said 'Well, just telling you he's a good kid from a respected family and he sure didn't mean to hurt you last night.' I was very surprised! How did dad get to know about the fight we had yesterday? Even Sam didn't know about it.

'How'd you know, dad?' I questioned. He shrugged and said 'Tom reads minds, and he can't keep anything from me.' I nodded understanding what had happened.

That evening I got into the dress that mom had got me. I stood in front of the mirror. My dress was red, red silk, it was scrunched up on the top and then straight and skinny all the way down. To be truthful I can't walk on heels so my mom got me cut-shoes so I guess I'll be able to walk. I held my hair in my hand and just ruffled it once and then I thought I looked fine but my mom had to come into my room then and say 'Oh my God! Hon, you have to do something to your hair.' I turned around. 'Well, I think it looks cool. There's nothing wrong with it.' I said. My mom already had begun rolling up the sleeves of her cardigan and I understood that she was going to give me a make-over. 'You wear your hair like that when you have your black leather motorcycle jacket on with worn out jeans and combat boots. I know what I'm going do to it.'

- 'Who cares how my hair looks?' I said putting on my shoes.
- 'I do.' My mom said.
- 'But you never cared how my hair was when I wore dresses before.'
- 'That was when you were a child. And then you hardly had any hair to do something with it. And that was for charity benefits and business dinners or book launches. This is a charity BALL, where you go with a DATE.' I just blinked at my mom. But she had it her way. She CURLED my hair! She made me put on MAKE-UP! But when she was done, I had to admit it was a pretty good job. I actually looked . . . . well feminine. She made me put on a red head band and she said it looked great because my hair was black and it was matching my clothes. How come I never knew that your accessories HAD to get along with your dress? I mean honestly, who on earth is going to notice if your finger nails are polished the same shade as your dress?

When I came to the living room my dad shuddered when he saw me. 'I cannot believe Sara Jane Salvatore actually looks like a girl. A very beautiful young lady. We have done a great job after all Kelly, haven't we?' he eyed my mom. But my mom was too busy asking me to turn around and admire what she had done. What was so great about putting make up on someone?

When Su came into the living room in her pink 'hello kitty' PJ's she was stunned at what she saw. At least I guess she was. Because the first thing she said when she saw me was 'Are you really my sister?' I couldn't do anything but smile. Then came the actual critic, Samuel Salvatore dressed like a gentleman in a tux. He was carrying himself like he was James Bond or something. When he looked at me he went all 'Um . . . you look . . . . I don't know like a girl' he said that like it was a bad thing. 'Do I look bad?' I asked him. His jaw fell open and he was like 'Bad? You look amazing. If you step out like this half of Mid Springs Academy will be behind you.' Then my dad and Sam had this silent conversation and then dad said 'Be home by eleven, both of you.' The door-bell rang clear and loud.

I turned to see the clock slip its minute hand to six, exactly six thirty, what a punctual guy!

Suzie opened the door. I heard my dad and Jake having a conversation at the front porch. Jake looked well . . . . how do you think he looked? He stood in front of my dad with folded arms as my dad patted his shoulder.

When I stepped out Jake was on the phone turned the other way and I saw the car door open so I slipped myself in. After Jake finished his conversation he hopped into the car. He turned to me and his eyes widened. He muttered the word 'Hey' and turned to start the car. It was a long and a silent drive. While we waited for the traffic signal to turn green, Jake said 'you . . . . um . . . look really nice.' I was shocked. I found my voice and said 'Thank you.' He smiled.

Till we reached the ball I was in the shock that Jake Martin, the guy who hated me from the depth of his heart actually COMPLIMENTED me! As soon as we entered the ball we spotted Katy and Luke. Katy wore a pastel blue dress, she looked pretty cool. Katy said 'Wow, you look so beautiful! And you and Jake, we didn't know about it. Plus, we can never imagine you both actually get along for once.'

The three of them introduced me to a couple of their friends. Then Jake brought out the keys to the terrace and said that the four of us could go watch the sunset and that the view was great. At first I too wondered how he knew the huge building so thoroughly then I realized that he probably owned the goddamn place.

It was October and fall was slowly starting its way into winter. Luke narrated an incident for us to laugh over. He said 'Hey Katy, remember once Candice had asked Jake to the homecoming dance at senior high school. Oh gosh, God knows what's up with that chick; we're still in middle school for crying out loud!' Katy and Luke had seen it happen, so they laughed their organs out. Jake glared angrily at Luke.

- 'So what did you say?' I asked Jake. Then Luke finally controlled his laughter and said 'You should've seen Jake's face, oh gosh . . .' he stopped for another laugh 'He stared at her for a few seconds like she was nuts and then he went 'um . . . huh . . . hmm . . . see you later' and then he ran all the way to geometry and told me what had happened. He was sweating and panting . . . huh' Luke began laughing again.

While I was enjoying the joke, I could see Jake at the corner of my eye, he had a fixed gaze, right at me. I ignored the staring and rested my head on Katy's shoulder watching the beautiful sun lower at the horizon. Katy got a phone call so she went to a quieter place. I sat straight and Luke put one arm around me and the other around Jake. Luke was a tall guy, not as tall as Jake, he reminded me of Sammy in many ways. I don't know him too well, but he cared a lot. He loved Katy so much he'd give anything for her and he cared about Jake so much sometimes I even got jealous. Jake on the other hand was the total opposite. He was irritating, irresponsible, immature, and idiotic, the list could go on. But well he wasn't all that bad maybe. Unlike me, he wasn't a great student. But he managed to get B's. He was one of the world's biggest show-offs. Considering the way he was boasting about the architecture of this building when we came in.

He was a really talented guy who was known for good looks and strength. [When I said he had good looks, it's not like I thought he was good looking, but most girls in school like him, except me . . . and Katy, but Katy likes him like a brother . . . you get what I mean don't you?]

After a while Luke went searching for Katy. Jake drew close to me and put an arm around my shoulder. I felt really awkward but Jake didn't seem so. He said 'I would've made things better if I had a second chance.' I frowned and asked 'What?'

- 'You know what I mean, like a second-first impression.'
- 'Sure you could do that?' I asked looking up at him
- 'I would try my best.' He almost said that with sincerity.
- 'Okay then, you got your chance. I know nothing about you. And I'm meeting you for the first time.' I said.
- 'Oh c'mon, that can't happen. But I want to say something.'
- 'What is it?' I asked crossing my legs.
- 'Look, I know you think I'm a complete moron and I'm not smarty pants like you alright. But that's just the moronic side of me. If you really knew me, the other side of me, even I could say you would've thought I'm not a bad guy.

And . . . . I'm . . . . so . . . sorry for being such a moron to you and the fight, I hurt you real bad. And I still owe you one.' I was surprised that he actually apologized. But the word sorry got out of his mouth so quietly I could hardly hear it. I guess he doesn't apologize much.

- 'Well, I should apologize too. I'm sorry for being rude and for freezing you the other night. And you don't owe me one anymore.'

- 'How do I not owe you one anymore?' He asked in surprise.

- 'Well, I think that freaky guy, I think his name is McCarthy, he's not approaching me because you're always around me. I've just been to school for two days and he's always around just gaping at me all the time.' He chuckled. I could see the sun kiss the horizon in Jake's mirror-like eyes.

- 'McCarthy isn't a bad guy. He's pretty nice, but he's just awkward. Actually his whole gang is awkward, I get the whole Goth thing . . . . but he is weird and a bit freaky but he plays nice ball though. He's a mid-fielder.' I nodded. 'And freaking scared of me.' Jake continued. 'I try to be nice to him but he always looks at me like he's going to soil his pants or something.' I giggled. Jake didn't, he just looked at me with an expression like 'Thank God you're glad' and another expression like 'That wasn't supposed to be funny.'

After a long moment of silence Jake said 'I think you look really cute when you smile, you know the deep dimples.' I had two thoughts in my mind, why was he being so nice to me? And 'OMG!!'

While I was still awe-struck Jake requested 'Please say something. Break the silence.' I smiled and thanked him.

After the clock struck half past seven we hit the dance floor. Jake pulled me into the dance floor and I was the worst dancer in the universe. 'I don't know how to dance.' I complained. He held my hand and whispered in the quiet crowd 'Just follow me.'

'Take your right leg back when I place mine in the front . . .' He told me instructions as we danced with the slow rhythm of the music. I danced! Can you believe that? ME?! SARA JANE SALVATORE had danced! Well of course I couldn't have done it without Jake. And I bet I wasn't such a great dancer because I was feeling cold. I was shaking. But Jake pulled me closer when I felt something really different. It wasn't like I was in love or anything like that because Jake did smell really nice. It was different . . . . supernatural. Suddenly this blanket of warmth just covered me.

After a long time of dancing, we decided to go get a drink at the bar. When we sat at the table, the bar tender said 'Aren't you guys under age?' Jake rolled his eyes and said 'All of us here are under age. I want a fruit punch. What about you?' I told him I'll get whatever he got. Both of us sat there drinking punch, watching the couples dance.

Jake gulped down his punch; I bet he was really thirsty. Suddenly I heard a female voice say 'There you are!' from behind Jake. When Jake heard this, his eyes widened and then he bit his lips creating dimples in his cheeks. He did that whenever he was nervous or scared. A tall girl with blonde hair and blue eyes approached Jake. She kissed him on the cheek and Jake, disgusted, wiped her lipstick of his cheek. He looked . . . well . . . disgusted. She looked at me and smiled an evil smile. I smiled back, sarcastically. She held her hand out and said 'I'm Candice Firm' so she was Candice. I said 'SJ Salvatore' as I went to shake her hand she drew it back. I just drew my hand back too. 'Sports secretary, the new striker for soccer team, the girl who gets A's, I know.' She said.

She ran her fingers through her blonde, wavy hair and said 'So Jake, how's the team doing?' putting an arm on his shoulder. I sucked punch from the cup with a straw. Jake replied to the series of question that she bombarded him with. After a while even she got sick of asking so many questions without a proper reply. She just wandered off. Jake sighed with relief. While I and Jake shared a debate over Messi or Ronaldo [I was on Messi's side and Jake was on Ronaldo's] Sam and Alison appeared. Alison was a girl with straight dark brown hair and calm eyes which were golden-brown and she was Jake's older sister. She said 'Wow, you look amazing.' I shrugged and smiled. 'Jake, you're a lucky guy.' She added. I could feel my face warm. 'You look good too. I like your . . . . . shoes.' I said.

I was actually searching for something that I could comment on. Even if they weren't my type, they suited her legs. Sam and Jake looked at me in astonishment when I had said that comment. She thanked me. And told me that she had designed it herself and about how she designs clothes, shoes, accessories and all that. It was so boring but I had to stay up and listen. The one thing I noticed were Sam's eyes narrowing to me and then to Jake and back again. After she finished explaining that, while the two of them were leaving back to the dance floor, Sam whispered something in Jake's ears which made him smile.

After their departure Jake said 'To be frank, you shy yourself a lot and also blush a lot.' What kind of reply should I be giving for that? I didn't know if he was just saying it or was complaining. 'But you look really pretty when you do.' He finally said. I looked down at my feet and thought of the last sentence he'd said. He put his finger below my chin and raised my head, 'Like right now' he said. I denied meeting his eyes but his eyes shot right at me. It was like melting charcoal. Someone beside us cleared their throat and a male voice spoke 'Am I interrupting any romance?' Both of us turned to see Luke.

'Um . . . you got to start school you know. It'll help you a lot.' He said.

- 'School?' I asked.

- 'Weekend power school. It's the place where we go every weekend and learn how to gain control of our ability and how we can use it and stuff. We have loads of fun.'
- 'Cool! But shouldn't I be filling some kind of application form for that?'
- 'No, you just have to walk into Harry's office and say your name. Go to the locker room and get picked by your flower. That's it!'
- 'Picked by your flower?'
- 'Hey, I ain't going to tell you everything, you have to come and see yourself.'
- 'Okay . . . I'll think about it.' The ball was up till twelve but my mom called and reminded I should be home by eleven thirty, which was generous of her because my curfew was eleven. On the ride back home, I was really tired and didn't talk much. But Jake couldn't keep his mouth shut just like Sam. He said 'I had a wonderful evening, thank you for coming along.' 'Actually, I should be thanking you for asking me. I had a wonderful time too. And thanks for teaching me how to dance.' I said. He chuckled.

Jake chuckled in a cute sort of way. I mean, it was . . . well cute. I really liked his chuckle.

He walked me to the front porch and before he left I asked 'Um . . . you know Jake' I said. 'Yeah . . . .' he looked up at me 'We should, you know like-' I couldn't complete. I regretted even starting the sentence. 'I know, we should do stuff like this more often.' He said. 'Stuff like what?' I asked.

- 'Be friends.' He said. His hands were in his pockets.
- 'Yeah, and knock out the fighting.' I said. He nodded with that cute chuckle.
- 'I'll give you a ring after I come back from Weekend school. We could hang out.'
- 'Yeah, sure do.'
- 'See you later.' He said. Then when he was on the way out the gate he turned back just once and gave me that 'take care' look.

I walked into the house. A small guy about thirteen with curly and bushy hair, who wore spectacles but I couldn't miss the gleaming golden eyes underneath them, was sitting near the fire place. A guy with blonde wavy hair and bottle green eyes was there, Mathew, Karen and Suzie were there too. I waved and asked 'Hello! Well, who are you guys?' The kid with the blonde hair said 'I'm Leom McQueen, Luke's brother.' I shook his hand. The other guy smiled and said 'I am your date's brother.' At first I didn't understand what he said, but then I got it. 'Alexander Martin, Jake's brother right?' He cleared his throat and said 'Don't ever call me that, just Alex.'

I ruffled his bushy hair. I patted him and said bye to all five of them.

Before I left the room Mathew said 'You look pretty, way better than my sister.' I turned back and looked at him. All I could do was smile at the kid's comment.

Chapter 8

I meet my lost family

'This tastes really good.' Sam said as he dug his fork into a big plate of pasta. My brother was a big fan of pasta, especially the ones mom made. My mom cooks only once in two days, so we try to enjoy that one meal to the core. Mrs McClellan usually does the cooking. We were sitting on our dining table for lunch. Everyone seemed to be so into the food that no one uttered a word but Sam. And anyway, Sam can't keep his mouth shut even while playing hide and seek. The phone rang and mom picked up. 'Hello . . . hi . . . um . . . okay . . . yeah, yeah I understand . . . . Oh c'mon it's not at all a burden . . . . okay the three of them will be happy to hear this . . . . they'll have loads of fun . . . . sure . . . . okay hold on a sec.'

Mom asked 'Ben, Tom and Julie got some issues and need to leave to Ottawa tonight. You don't mind if Alley and Alex stay for a while do you?' Dad nodded a no. Then mom again spoke into the phone as she took her plate and walked into the kitchen.

After lunch I got a call from Jake.

- 'Hello.' I said.
- 'Hey, this is Jake.'
- 'Hi!'
- 'I and Luke are off to Katy's now, you want to come?'
- 'Yeah sure.'
- 'And we'll drop by at Simon's Smoothies.'
- 'Alright. I heard your siblings are coming to our place to stay.'
- 'Yeah, I'm staying with Luke . . .'
- 'So . . . See you at Katy's.'
- 'And . . . err . . . I hate you.'
- 'Aww . . . me too.' With the last words I hung up on him.

I went to Katy's and knocked on the door. Jonah opened the door with a huge textbook in his hands as usual. He looked up from his book and was surprised to see me. 'Hello SJ, What a surprise?' I said hello and walked into the house. I saw Jake's car parked in the driveway. When I got in Jonah said 'Their upstairs, in Katy's room.' I put my hands into my pocket and double stepped up the stairs. I knocked Katy's door and her voice said 'Come in' and I entered the room. 'You actually knocked!' She exclaimed. 'Yes I did.' I agreed. Wasn't that perfectly normal?

Her room was in different shades of purple, from her wall paper which had purple fur, I guess we call that wall-fur, to her pillow, everything was purple. Luke was lying on her bed watching a DVD of a horror film. Jake flung open the door with a big bowl of popcorn in his hands. 'Coby's here with the popcorn. Gimme the bowl, dude.' Luke said. 'Coby, Is it a new nickname?' I asked. Jake stared at Luke like he was yelling at him with his mouth shut. Luke finally said 'Yeah, I call him that sometimes.' Jake turned to me with a bright smile and ruffled my hair 'Hey smarty pants' I knew there was something they're not telling me, but I'll eventually get to know it anyway. 'Hey tough guy' I said returning a big bright smile.

While we were watching the movie Jake suddenly laughed and Luke and Katy didn't react like it was unusual. He laughed again and said something I couldn't hear. I looked at Katy with a question mark on my face. She said 'That, well, you see his dad can read minds, he can also communicate with people very far off with his mind.'

After watching the movie, we went down town to Simon's smoothies. We got ourselves a corner table. A gang of four, two boys and two girls entered the cafe and all four of them were dressed in black. They wore long coats, heeled boots, and curved hats. 'They are the Sterlingtons. The girl with curly dark hair, she's Annabel Sterlington. And the guy with blonde hair is Ethan, the green eyed girl is Emma, and the guy with dark hair, he's Aaron. They live three blocks away from our place. They don't talk much to anyone. They're pretty private all the time. Only Aaron and Emma say hello sometime.' Katy introduced.

I looked at the girl with curly hair. Her blue eyes shot right into mine. For a second, I thought I'd approach them and have a conversation, but I knew I wouldn't do that. Jake sucked the last few drops of his smoothie as his eyes met Aaron.

Aaron approached the table right after the siblings had a small conversation.

Even under the dim lights I could see the grey shade swirling like a tornado in his eyes. He said 'Sara Jane Salvatore, the girl of the century.' For some reason I knew he and I had the same grey shade of eye colour. 'You should start coming to school. It's not healthy to keep yourself stiff. You need to expand and relax, and if you don't take control of yourself soon, it'll take control of you.' He said. 'Sterlington, the four of you look familiar, and your names sound familiar too.' I confessed. 'Where's Aunt Kelly?' He asked. I blinked. Aunt Kelly? Was he talking about my mom? I asked 'Who are you, how do you know my mom?' He chuckled and said 'I'm your cousin, your mother's dead sister's son, her nephew.' My eyes widened in surprise. He was talking about my aunt who had died when I was nine, Aunt Sabrina Ryan, who later on became Sabrina Sterlington. 'You mean your Uncle Bryan's son?' I asked.

'Yes.' He said in a whisper. The part of the family I never knew and was always curious about was found. My jaw dropped open and my hands fell over my mouth.

I dashed open the door and yelled 'Mom! I found the Sterlingtons!' My mom and Mrs McClellan came out from the kitchen in their aprons. I was followed into the house by my lost family. My mother dropped her spatula and her hands fell over her mouth.

That evening the four of them and mom and dad talked about incidents I never knew.

I came out to the back yard where Jake, Sam, Luke and Katy were hanging out. I sunk down on a chair. Luke got a phone call from his father, he was ordered to come home ASAP. It was getting pretty cold. I pulled my coat tight around myself.

Jake was lying on his deck chair, eyes shut. He looked like a five year old kid. Luke got up to leave, he was about to wake Jake up but Katy said 'Don't! He'll get mad; you know he can't sleep too well lately. Let him sleep.' 'He can stay, mom wouldn't mind, anyway Alley and Alex are here.' Sam said. 'Alright, I'll leave with Luke.' Katy said and rose.

Alley came out to the back yard and saw Jake sleeping. She said 'I thought he was at Luke's place.' She sat next to Sam. I asked 'So . . . how did your date go?' 'What?' They asked in unison. 'I mean the charity ball.' Sam cleared his throat and asked 'First, you tell me how your date with the tough guy went?'

- 'I asked first.' I said frowning.
- 'Jake never asked a girl out on a date ever before, but he asked you, so I want to know.' Alley whispered. I blinked.
- 'Well . . . nothing much, we just danced and talked.' 'You danced!' Sam exclaimed. My mom opened the door and said 'Kids come for dinner.' Sam left, the aroma of the chicken pie was dragging him towards it as, Alley followed him.

Jake seemed like he hadn't slept in weeks, just like Katy had said. I stood next to the chair, staring at him. I reached out and ran my fingers through his soft, silky hair. You know the feeling that you get when you pull your hand out of water and when the air touches your skin it get really cold and the water seems warmer? That's how I felt when I withdrew my hand from Jake's hair. He hadn't eaten yet and it was growing cold. I patted him on the shoulder and his eyes slowly opened. I said 'Come inside have something to eat and then sleep.' He just rubbed his eyes and sat up. 'Seems like you haven't slept well lately?' I said. 'Yeah' was all that he said. 'SJ! Jake!' I heard my mom's voice call. 'Hurry up for supper!' He got up and stood. 'I thought I was staying at Luke's.'

'I guess you're stuck here till tomorrow.' I said as I stood up.

We had supper but Jake went straight to bed. Sam carried him THREE floors to the guest room. My brother should join the weight lifting competition at the Olympics.

'He doesn't weigh as much as I thought he would.' Sam had said. 'Is he that light?' Alley questioned. 'No, I mean he's not that heavy but he is not light.' Sam replied.

I lay in my bed trying to sleep. That was Aaron, Anna, Ethan and Emma I just met. I couldn't believe it. My mom had said that after my aunt died they moved back to England. Their dad was British, you see.

At 3:05 am, I heard noises come from the back yard. I woke up and made my way to the backyard, following the sound. I saw the four of them, the Sterlingtons, stand there in a circle. But I remembered them leaving after dinner. In the middle, a ray of golden light shot down from the sky. They were whispering something to each other, but it sounded more like summoning. I heard a cold, blood shot, voice which sounded so familiar say 'don't worry, he will find you. And help you go through the situation.' It was a girl's voice. I walked towards them and asked 'What's going on guys?' The four of them turned, their eyes were blood-shot, red, dark blood red. I stood there in astonishment. The light flickered and vanished. Their eyes changed back to normal. Annabel walked close to me. She drove her hand towards me and I woke up with a start. It was dream. I was panting and sweating. To my surprise, I found Jake on my couch. I gasped. 'Oh, Jake you scared me.' He said 'couldn't sleep, I guess you had a bad dream.' I nodded. 'Same here, something's happening, I can't sleep and when I do I get some horrible dream and wake up with a start.'

I told him 'Oh God! What's happening? Things have been growing really weird since I came to town.'

- 'It's okay. You should come to school. Things will get better; it'll make you feel good.' He said as he sat next to me.
- 'BTW, what are you doing in my room?'
- 'I told you I couldn't sleep. I felt this kind of sensation which was very strange but it drove me to your room somehow, I just entered the room few seconds before you woke up.'
- 'Am I supposed to believe you?'
- 'I swear it is the truth. To be honest, I haven't slept well since you came to town. Before that I kind of had bad dreams but I could sleep a while. Things have been changing since I met you the other day. I've felt really strange things, so indescribable, both pain and joy.'
- 'Yeah, things have changed for me too, since I moved into town.'
- 'I think you should go to sleep SJ. Good night, sleep tight.' I laid back on my bed and pulled my sheets up as Jake slowly shut the door behind him. I thought of what he had said and the words sunk in like needles. What if I was the one who didn't belong here or stuff grew wrong because of my presence?

Chapter 9

Weekend Power School

I went into a fresh pair of clothes after my morning shower. I raced downstairs and sat on the kitchen table where Mrs McClellan made our favourite caramel waffles and maple syrup for breakfast. Alley sat next to me with a mug. The telephone rang and dad picked up. 'Hello . . . Good morning Mrs Hedges, is it so . . . . Yes, yes, tonight? Okay . . . . art gallery . . . . Dublin, alright. You got my tickets? You did, thank you. I'll be waiting for the cab . . . . alright, goodbye.' He put the phone down and sat on the kitchen table. He said 'We have to go to Dublin tonight, Kelly. And there's an art gallery, I guess you would be interested to go. I have to buy a good spot of land to get the Salvatore suits there, I'm planning to buy some place near Mack Splash, that way I don't have to move place to place to take care of my business in Dublin. Our flight's at 7: 30 pm.' my mom hesitated before she replied. 'Do we really have to? I mean, the kids have just moved into town, I don't think they'll be able to take care of themselves.' I reached for my mom's hand and squeezed it 'its okay ma, c'mon you've always wanted to go to Dublin. And I want you to get something for me if you stop by at a charity benefit.'

'Oh honey, are you sure?' My mom reassured. I nodded. She said 'Okay, I'll drop cash in the drawer near the fire place. And you got all emergency numbers, right?' I nodded. 'Don't worry; no one would dare to sneak into our house when Jake's in here.' Dad said. Alley smiled and joined the conversation 'Jake and Sam would be an undefeatable team.' 'SJ's pretty good herself.' Mom said with a wink.

That's when Sam and Jake came downstairs. My dad delivered them the news of flying to Ireland. Sam nodded. Mom said removing her apron 'Sam make sure SJ doesn't blow up the house and SJ make sure Sam doesn't blow up the house. And both of you together take care of our guests, and also of Su. And no parties! Do you understand?'

Jake was getting ready for going to school. I asked 'Can I come along?' He turned and said 'Of course, I'm glad you want to. You need to, actually.'

We waited outside Katy's house for a cab. Katy stood in the pavement with a bag slung over one shoulder as she tucked a strand of brown hair behind her ear. A cab flew past us, I pointed and said 'Hey, we could've got that one.' Jake took a long breath and said 'I mean we got to get the right cab, which is sent from weekend power school for students.' I nodded. I was getting frustrated; standing there for a long time bored me. 'Don't you guys take anything to school, I mean, books, pencils, erasers, anything?' 'We don't need to SJ. It's like having Phys Ed for one whole school day at weekend power school. We just have fun learning, we don't have desks and chairs and stuff. Just open area with extraordinary stuff.' Jake replied.

All of a sudden an apple green cab fell from the sky. Actually it looked more like a cab was thrown from the top. It was like any other cab you'll see except for the odd green color and it had a big sign on it of an owl's head. The letters 'WPS' were printed. A guy with tanned brown skin peeped out of the window and said 'Ride's here.' Jake, Katy and I walked into the car. He opened the door and let Katy in. I signalled him to get in before me but he said 'After you, Ms. Salvatore.' I hopped into the ride and the car was pulled up into the atmosphere. We were floating in the air at high speed. I asked 'Why can't we travel by land?' Katy replied. 'So normal people can't see us, and to not give in the location of our school to our enemies.'

'Who's the new mistress?' The driver asked. 'It's someone everyone knows . . . Sara Jane Salvatore.' Jake introduced. 'SJ, this is Chad, he drives us to school every week.' Jake introduced.

- 'But, can't people see the cab fall down from the sky when it lands?' I asked.

- 'Of course not, that's why Master Sillvius Spark created the magic mist with his brother.' Chad replied.
- 'What's the Magic Mist?' I asked with curiosity.
- 'Well Master Spark has the ability to control the seas, so he created the magic mist with his brother Charles, which covers the things that mortals do not have to see, for example this cab. Only people like you Ms. Salvatore can see through the Magic Mist.'
- 'Who's Master Spark?'
- 'He is one of the oldest people you would ever meet, his ability is pure and strong, the more generations pass the weaker the power gets, and it drains away. He is one of the leaders of our kind, the one who knows all about who we are, and why we were made. He knows the answers to the disturbing questions that pop up. He is my Master who gave me life and I promised him I will serve him till the last breath of my life.'
- 'He gave you your life?' I asked
- 'That's another story. I was a born slave in the household of the Cyrus family. My grandfather had lent some cash from them and passed away, my father was too poor to pay it back. Cyrus kept my father and mother in his house as slaves, once my father tried escaping and got caught by the family's guards. That night my parents were tortured the worst torment anyone could go

through, that night my mother had a dream. In that dream it was declared that I would be born and I would bring them out of that nasty place, and I did. I mean, with Master Spark's help of course. I couldn't have done it without him.'

- 'Wow, your childhood might've been living hell.'
- 'Yes it was. By the way, how is Ms. Sylvia Ryan doing?'
- 'Aunt Leah is doing fine.'
- 'And my buddy Cody, how is that guy? I didn't meet him since college.'

'He's rocking; he's enjoying his life, that man. He's in Paris, shooting a film.' The cab landed with a thud, in front of Luke's house, which I guess was also designed by Mr. Martin. 'Is it your dad's work?' I asked to Jake. He gave me that moronic smile like a total show-off and said 'Isn't he talented?' with an eyebrow raised. When Luke came the four of us got squeezed in the little car.

We landed with a big thud again when we reached our destination. All of us fell on each other.

Katy was on me. I exclaimed 'Katy, get off me!' 'You guys mind getting off my ankle, it doesn't hurt But it's pretty irritating.' Jake said looking at Luke. It was something like this: Katy was on me and I was on Luke and Luke was on Jake's ankle. Luke tried standing up, leaving a little space for Jake to pull away his ankle. Katy hit her head on the roof of the car. 'Ouch Luke!'

she cried rubbing her head. Jake got out but Katy yelled 'Jake mind helping me, my leg's stuck.' Luke opened the door and all three of us fell outside. 'That hurts.' Said I. Luke pulled Katy up. Jake gave me a hand, I just remembered the first time I met Jake Martin. He was holding his hand out apologizing. I ignored him that time. But this time I reached out and he helped me up. He put his arm around me and all four of us were walking to I have no idea where.

WPS was something like this: It was a huge campus in the middle of the woods. The surrounding smelt fresh and green. The campus looked more like an office on the outside. 'My dad designed this too.' Jake said adjusting his hair. He and his attitude! But that attitude suited him anyway. The inside of the building was marble-tailed and smelt like oak trees. There were many people roaming around-talking to each other or on the phone, shuffling through books, polishing weapons, etc. We entered the elevator, a man in a purple and green T-shirt asked 'Which floor shall I take you?' Jake said 'We want to go to Harry's cabin.' The man punched a few buttons. It wasn't numbers exactly, it was signs. Some resembled animals, flowers and alphabets. We shot up straight then we moved horizontally. The smell of jasmine and jazz music blaring made me feel even sicker. We stopped with a jerk in front of cabin no.23. It said 'Harry Stevens.'

I heard an unfamiliar voice of a middle aged man say 'Come in' when Luke had knocked.

There was a desk in front of us, a chair which had its back on our side. There was a smell of burning cigar and on the walls hung photographs and portraits of unfamiliar faces. It seemed like a normal office. The chair turned slowly. A guy with curly brown hair and sea blue eyes turned. He had a cigar in his mouth; he was probably around Mr Neumann's age, 26 to 28.

He said 'Good morning kids. Who is checking in?'

- 'Hey Harry, we present to you Benjamin and Kelly Salvatore's beautiful daughter.' Katy said pointing her polished finger at me. He leaned over his desk, staring right at me. Staring is bad manners. And I didn't like the way he stared at me. 'Here's your application form. Take her to the choosing area, Katy. And boys, Billy's waiting for you.' Jake and Luke showed me thumbs up and strutted out of the room. Katy shoved a pen at me. I picked it up and turned to the application form. It was like a normal application form just like in any other school in Black Fury. It had that sign of the owl I had seen on the taxi. It had weekend power school in big font, it was in green print. I filled it and handed it over to Harry. He smirked at me after reading the form. He said 'Um . . . you definitely filled the form better than your brother.'
- 'You know my brother?' I asked

- 'Of course I know your brother, Samuel. And your cute little sister, what's her name . . . yes, Suzie.'

I and Katy had another elevator ride to the choosing area. We entered the choosing area; it was like a gym, in a school. There were rows of tables which had the following flowers—sunflower, marigold, daffodil, lily, tulips, roses and my favourite white orchids. I said 'If this is called the choosing room, which means I got to pick a flower? I'm not such a big fan of flowers, but for some reason I got the girl instincts a little bit and I'm really fond of white orchids.'

- 'See, you are a girl, deep inside.' Katy mocked. 'I wouldn't pick the orchid if I were you. It is the last level and it's pretty tough. And don't worry, you don't pick the flowers, the flowers pick you. This is the way things work. Most of us here start from the sunflower. It's like the level 1. But some of us here directly get to go to some other level. And the white orchid is the last level. You have to go on two incredibly hard quests when it picks you, SJ.'
- 'Which level are you in?'
- 'Me . . . lily, the fourth level. Okay now let's get you into the actual choosing area.'

Katy took me into a room, which seemed more like a locker room in Mid Springs Academy. The seven flowers appeared in front of me. Katy said 'I'm gonna have to leave SJ.' I nodded.

All of a sudden the lights went out, and seven big tall flowers appeared in front of me. The sunflower bent over, it was such a weird situation. I kept glancing at the white orchid. The sunflower went back to its position. One by one each flower bent over. Now the lily bent over, it went back to its place too. The tulip bent over. I expected it to move back to its place too. But instead it ran its petals over me. Now I was stuck in a tulip's petals and no matter how hard I pulled back nothing happened, yeah great, that happens to everybody every day, right? The whole room started growing darker and darker. I took my one last glance at the orchid. For some reason I felt like the flower was looking at me too. It became pitch dark.

When the lights came back I was in the gym. I was holding a tulip in my hand and I didn't even realize it. Jake, Katy and Luke were standing in the end of the gym. I ran in full speed towards them, took just a second to reach.

Katy smiled and said 'One level ahead of me huh?' punching me on my shoulder softly. 'Yeah I guess.' Katy grabbed the flower from me and said 'Next year I'm gonna be the one holding the tulip.'

We had to take another elevator trip to Harry's room. I was kind of sick going on this flying elevator now. Luke opened the door and all of us entered. Katy placed the flower on the desk and said 'Tulip.' He noted it down and said 'Wow, no one has been picked for the fifth level at the first try.' Jake cleared his throat. 'Except two months ago, Martin did. And Jake as you joined in the end of the previous year; you're stuck in tulip this year too.' Harry added. He said 'Alright kids, go to training and drop your new friend with Trish.' 'I think she needs to get the pep talk first.' Jake said. 'Alright then, don't waste time. And by the way, welcome to weekend power school Ms Salvatore.'

Chapter 10

Getting trained

Jake took me to the actual school. It had a lot of rooms and lockers. On the last door in the entire corridor hung an old wooden board saying 'Hamilton.' Jake accompanied me. He said 'Have a nice day.' He pulled out a tulip from inside his jacket and said 'You left something of yours in Harry's cabin.' I took the flower from him. He knocked on the door and opened it. 'Hello sir! Sorry to disturb. We got a new student who I think needs your encouragement.' said Jake. The teacher turned and said 'Oh Ms Salvatore, we were waiting for you. Harry said you'd be coming. And Martin, how are you my son?'

'I'm fine.' Jake said with his dimple smile. His eyes were sparkling 'I'll catch you later.' He whispered in my ear as he left. The teacher started 'Hello my dear children. My name is Patrick Hamilton. Well I'm going to give you advice or say the 'pep talk'.

This power that you are having is a gift: a gift which you should use to save the world for good. All of you might know the story of Cyrus. He is even more horrible than what you've heard. When I was your age I lost my parents because of him. I could've saved them if I just had the right training. You kids should utilize this opportunity. You know, I always thought that I am going to be a big loser in front of Cyrus. I underestimated myself. But now I realized that I have more important things in life that Cyrus doesn't have. I have a family, friends who love me. I have people who love me and care for me. But Cyrus doesn't have all that.' I rubbed a petal of the tulip. Mr Hamilton continued 'Cyrus possesses strength, but he doesn't have love, wisdom and self—respect, which we possess. We are here to learn how to use and control this power of yours.'

'This whole session we are having is for you to realize how important your responsibility is . . . .' He continued for about fifteen minutes then said 'Today's session ends with this. Thank you children, you have a lot of learning to do out there.' There were only twelve kids including myself.

I looked at this card which Harry had given me. It said 'Sara Jane Salvatore, tulip, locker 209.' I searched for locker 209 and found it. I opened it only to find nothing, emptiness. I shut the door and stood in this unfamiliar place not knowing what to do or where to go. I stood there holding a tulip and a small card. The bell rang and the corridor was filled with kids, my age, most of them younger, and some older. I spotted Sam from the crowd. When I started walking towards him, someone knocked me down. Both of us fell down with a big thud. Oh not on the first day of this school too. I turned and saw Jake next to me. He said 'SJ I'm so sorry, I was . . . don't get mad.' I chuckled and said 'Just like the first time we met.'

'Yeah, just like the first time I met smarty pants.' He said as his features relaxed. I smirked at him. He said 'So how was it with Mr Pat Ham?' 'It was fine.' I said picking up the tulip. He looked at the tulip; I could see the corner of his lips curve to a smile. He continued staring at me for like thirty seconds. I felt very uncomfortable so I just looked away pretending I didn't notice him staring.

Jake told me we had to get moving so both of us started. We saw a huge metal door with big block letters saying 'TULIP'. We opened the door to find trees. There was a forest inside the school? No actually the school is in the woods. There were just nineteen people, including myself. All of us lined up, it actually reminded me of military school. A woman about Ashley's age walked in, she was in black clothes. She wore a long trench coat, which seemed pretty thick, and it wasn't winter yet. She wore thick shades above her eyes, and boots for her feet. She said 'Good morning class! I'm sorry for my absence yesterday, I was unwell. I hope all of you have enjoyed your hols because now it's time to face tougher quests. So how many of you are new? Please step forward.' I stepped forward with seven other kids. She looked at all of us and said 'I know you, you and you . . . . but you?' She asked pointing at me. 'Happen to be Ms. Salvatore, who I haven't seen before, in the campus.' She finished. I nodded. She asked 'Do you know any kind of defence, other than running away?' She asked and giggled to her own joke. I stood confidently without a smile and said 'Yes, I do.'

- 'Name them for me, will you?'
- 'Archery, I'm good with swords, daggers, knives, even guns.'
- 'Prove it.' She said. 'Let's see whether you can actually beat anyone here, let me think . . . . Martin!' Both Alley and Jake stepped forward. 'I called Alison.' She said. Jake stepped back and apologized. 'Bring two swords; let's see whether she is telling the truth.'

Alley looked at me hesitantly and ran into the shed. She brought two swords and handed one to me. I took it.

Both of us raised our swords. She got the first move; I tell you it was unexpected. She went for a stab on my shoulder but I stepped aside. I couldn't get close enough to hurt her, for a while our swords just clanged each time one of us defended. In the back of my head, I didn't want to fight with her, I didn't want to hurt her, but I had no option. When I lost my concentration she hit the hilt of my sword and my sword went skidding away from me. Before I could move towards it, her feet went into the middle of mine and I fell with a thud. My hand was just a few centimetres away from the sword. Her legs were tangled around me and the tip of her sword pointing at me. She whispered 'Sorry, SJ.' I broke free and whacked her head as she fell, I said 'Sorry Alley.' In return I took my sword and she was up too. I tried hard thinking of all the moves Ash had thought me. Finally I got the perfect one at the perfect moment. She had taught me a way of clanging the flat end of my sword on the sharp tip of the opponent's weapon. That way the weapon would slide out of her hand and I'm strong enough to tackle her. I got a scratch on my shoulder and she had a scratch on her arm. I hit her sword and it flew really far, I pushed her against a tree, my blade really close to her neck. I looped my arms around hers, and we were tangled. There was no way she could escape unless she wanted her neck sliced. She couldn't break free and quit.

Everyone clapped their hands in applause. The lady said 'You're not bad. Where did you learn all these moves?'

I said 'Back in NY, I had a trainer.' She asked 'May I know his or her name?' I said 'Ashley Jerkins.' She was surprised when I said the name 'Ashley lives in New York?'

-    'You know her?'

- 'Of course I know her, she's my sister. We had this argument and she left home. Okay anyway, those are personal issues, let's get back to class.'

All of us stood in the line. I apologized to Alley for the fifth time and she smiled and said 'It's okay SJ, it's just a game.'

Jake whispered 'I never knew you could do that.'

Our trainer said said 'Let me divide the groups, four groups of five, Hermine, Helen, Hera, Hillary.' She took out a scroll and read aloud 'Jake Martin, Madison McKenzie, Linda Embry and Peter Heckley, Annabel Sterlington. You form the team Hillary, you decide your leader. Sara Jane Salvatore, Aaron Sterlington, Emma Sterlington, Alison Martin and Nicholas Jackson You form the team Helen.' When the last name was told I noticed Jake's hand close into a fist as he winced. Nicholas Jackson, wonder who he is. And I hadn't realized that the Sterlington's were here, a flash of my nightmare twinkled in my eyes.

The last group was mentioned 'Leo Camber, Ethan Sterlington, David Barton, Rick Richards, Maria Antonia, you are group Hermine.' Leo, the guy with blonde hair muttered 'Awesome, we got to wear green for the rest of the year' sarcastically, under his breath.

I asked Jake 'We have to wear a uniform?' He nodded. 'And why are we given these names, I mean something's got to be behind it.' He took a moment to recall and said 'Helen, Hermine, Hera and Hillary are the four sisters who were the first holders of life; the four of them could control each element of life: the seas, fire, earth and air. They together with the chosen two opposed Cyrus. They lived for another hundred and thirty years and opposed Cyrus with the chosen two again. Then the Spark brothers showed up from France. They inherited the ability from the four sisters. They have done a lot for us and are well remembered even today. I think you should start reading the books on the last shelf in your library at home.'

- 'Books on the last shelf? Why?'
- 'They explain the answers to all your questions. You got pretty interesting books on your shelf. I saw the SJ carved on the desk. I bet no other teenager in the world would have a thousand dozens of books, really, what's with the paranormal research stuff?'
- 'You read all those books?' I asked, embarrassed. He nodded.
- 'You think I read books? I just flip through them. I only read books about our kind, because even I can sometimes die out of curiosity, now answer please?'
- 'That's just some dumb thing I, Sam and Su did two years ago. But the experience was thrilling. The Ouija board thing was an amazing experience but nothing really happened.'

- 'C'mon, you never told me you're a psycho path, genius.'
- 'I'm not a psycho path, maybe a little bit of the genius part.'
- 'Oh please, I saw your certificates too, you are a human encyclopaedia.'
- 'Thank you.'
- 'Um . . . you're welcome, but that wasn't supposed to be a compliment.'
- 'BTW, what color does team Helen have to wear?'
- 'Purple, and team Hera has to wear blue and Hermine has to wear green and Hillary has to wear red.' He replied even if I hadn't asked him all the details. But that would've been my next question anyway. He smiled showing his pearly whites.

The lady finally remembered to tell her name 'Yeah, for those who do not know my name, Trish Jerkins. You'll get your uniforms next week. Now, go to the stables, new comers, you got to pick your horses. As today is day two, just spend quality time with your horses. Go for a nice ride, but don't get lost.'

Alley led me into the stable. There were many horses and most of them were stallions. There was dried grass everywhere. Shit, I literally mean that the place smelled of nothing but shit. Alley opened the stable and said 'Here's mine, I call her Tinker Bell.' She said patting the white stallion. I heard a horse gallop, I peeped out to see Jake on his black stallion hooting and riding it out the stable. 'Tinker Bell, are you kidding?' I asked. 'I named her when I was four; cut me some slack, alright.' She said 'I'll show you the new horses. Can I help you pick?' I nodded.

She led me into a tunnel which opened into another stable. This stable was smaller. She said 'Look around, pick the best before others.' I walked around the stable, looking in. Most of them were either black or white. At the last few stables I spotted brown ones, with really silky and smooth fur. That minute I knew I was going to pick one of them.

When I was zooming through, one of the horses broke out of its stable. It ran around like crazy and then stood next to me patiently. For some reason when I touched it's mane, I had a strong sense that this was the one I was looking for and I was sure of nothing as much as I was sure of this in my life ever before. 'You want to pick him? He's new.' Alley said. 'Yeah, I'm going to name him . . . . Oscar!' I said. The horse lowered expecting me to hop on and I did. I went around into the woods; I didn't know where I was going or how I'd be able to find my way back. But I simply knew that it was the best horse ride I'd ever had in all the years of riding.

Jake Martin

Chapter 11

My chat with the Salvatores

That night after SJ had spent her morning at WPS, Mr and Mrs Salvatore were leaving. At the doorstep stood SJ as her mom kissed on her forehead and said 'You're in charge of the house. Remember all the things that I've told you.' SJ chuckled and said 'C'mon mom, it's not the first time you're letting us off alone. I know what I'm supposed to do.' 'List them for me.' Her mom insisted. 'Remind Mrs McClellan what you told her to make for meals, tell her where the ingredients are. Take care of Suzie, make sure Sam doesn't blow up the roof. Got to make Leonard trim the grass, water the flowers and dry clean the laundry. I got your numbers and the cash.' Her mom patted her on the shoulder. Her mom and her dad kissed Su till she had her mom's lipstick all over her face. She hugged Sam and told him to take care of his sisters and she said goodbye to the rest of us. And that was the last I saw of her in a week.

I hadn't talked to SJ since we returned home as she had got a little sick because of the car ride and the elevator. The only thing I knew was that she had a pleasant ride with her new horse. But before I could ask her how the day went Sam pulled me to a corner. 'What's up?' I asked. He gave an expression like he was going to piss his pants right there. 'Dude are you all right, do you need to use the toilet?' I mocked. He ignored my statement and said 'I got to tell you something bro . . . . I got my scar.' He kind of said that like 'I soiled my pants in front of hot chicks.' My eyes widened and said 'Cool! So soon you're stuck up with some chick for the rest of your life.'

- 'That's not the issue. I know who 'the chick' is.' When Sam mentioned the words I got curious.
- 'Who exactly is the chick?'
- 'You wouldn't believe it.'
- 'C'mon bro, break the suspense.'
- 'Well . . . it's . . . um . . . Alley.' After making sure I heard him correctly I said 'That is so cool! Why are you so worried about that?' I wanted to jump up and down like a little kid. Sammy is my bro, now isn't that fantastic news?!
- 'I'm not worried I'm nervous. I can't be the same with your sister. I don't know how I'm gonna tell her it's me, over all that I don't know how I'll tell SJ.' Okay, a guy being nervous to ask his girl out, I totally got that. But a sixteen year old guy who is nervous to tell his sister he met his soul mate, that's crap! 'Okay bro, don't worry about SJ. Leave her to me, SJ's easy to handle.

Just relax and focus on telling my sister.' Instead of doing what I told him, he frowned 'How should I be reacting when a guy tells me that my sis is easy to handle . . . that can also refer to a word called seduction? Yeah leave you and SJ alone, giving you all that privacy . . . blah . . . blah . . . blah' It clicked only then; he took my sentence totally in a wrong meaning.

- 'I didn't mean it that way.'
- 'Oh yes you did.'
- 'No I didn't' I argued on till I couldn't fight anymore. He may be a good friend of mine but he just likes to see me being pushed around sometimes.

I searched for SJ everywhere possible, but yet she was nowhere in sight. When I was passing through the dim lighted corridors, I found Suzie struggling to get something form the highest shelf in the library. Suzie, I didn't know at all, I came to a realization that I haven't talked once to her. My brother had a little something for her, so let me go check out my bro's first crush.

I entered the room and asked 'Hey Suzie, need help?' She turned to look at me as she smiled. Her smile was so calm and her face glowed. Her eyes twinkled as she spoke 'I didn't know that you knew my name.'

- 'Of course I know your name, how can I not know. Alex talks about you a lot.'

- 'Does he?' Her face lit up with that child-like innocence and charm.
- 'Yes he does. Seems like you need a hand.'
- 'Yeah, can you take that box over there?'
- 'Sure.' I put my hand up and pulled out a box with pink fur over it.
- 'Thank you bro.'
- 'My pleasure. You're a nice little girl, you really are. What's in it?' I asked even if I wasn't interested the second I saw the pink fur.
- 'It's my art tools; I got it from my Aunt Leah on my birthday. She gifted it to me when I was six; she said it was for angels of art. Even after growing up, even after realizing I'm not an angel, I'm yet so fond of art. She gave me the push to realize my talent.'
- 'Now who told you that you aren't an angel?'
- 'Well, no one did. SJ always called me an angel. Mom and dad called me their princess and Sam always told me I was his doll. Being called with so many names, I came to a sinking realization that I'm really not any of them. And I'm twelve now, I think I'm pretty grown up.' I bent down on one knee, she was just two years younger than I but she wasn't really tall—as I said 'Well now I'm telling you, you really are my angel.' Her lips curved into a smile when I said the words. She said 'Maybe I am an angel, but not your angel.'
- 'Why not?'

- 'Because you already got one.' With the last words the kid walked out the door. I sat there thinking about the last words she had just said. Only later I learned what she meant.

I went to bed that night a little early. I laid in my bed just thinking of the conversations I had with Sam and Su. They were blood related and so similar in many ways yet so unique.

It was 4:58 am when I still rolled in my bed trying to sleep. I had music blaring in my ears but even that didn't kill my boredom. My stomach growled from hunger as I had neglected my meal.

I went downstairs into the kitchen and to my surprise the lights were turned on. I found no one in the kitchen table but heard someone beside the refrigerator. I saw SJ slumped down in her PJ's with coffee in her hand having a far off gaze. She hadn't noticed my presence. I said 'SJ, are you alright?' She turned to look at me; her eyes were like liquid steel as usual, ashy and steamy. She didn't react much. I sat down beside her and asked 'C'mon smarty pants, tell me what happened.' Instead of replying she did something unexpected. She hugged me and tears began to fall from her eyes. I was too shocked to say anything. I found my voice somewhere deep in and asked 'Who died?' She wiped her tears and said 'I guess I'm going to.'

- 'Don't say that. Why?' I wiped her wet cheeks.
- 'I had a dream,' oh, this was my story 'the most painful thing I've ever felt. I fell asleep in the library, I had a dream about Cyrus, and it was so real, so painful.' She said the last word so deep from her heart I felt it. 'I don't think I'll ever be able to sleep ever again. I'm beginning to fear one of the most needed activities for a human. I fear sleep.' This was something common between I and SJ. For the first time I knew exactly how she felt.
- 'I've gone through it too. But don't worry, you're not always gonna have dreams like this. And you really need to sleep. Don't make these stupid nightmares bring you down. C'mon, you're 'SJ Salvatore' you can't fear anyone. You are the one who should be feared. You do not know how much power you possess. Cyrus's strength isn't even a dot in front of the capability you have. I promise I'll always be there to help you, right by your side.' I stroked her hair and her grip on my shirt loosened. I admit that was a pretty good lecture. I have no idea where I got those lines from. I let the words sink in for a while.

Her hand still clung on my shirt but now I relaxed. And I also sensed her body relax beneath my arms. I always had this weird faith that she wasn't like other girls. She was different and even if I wouldn't admit it if the whole world asked me, the reason she isn't like other girls is the reason I'm so fond of her. She looked at me stunned and said 'That's really sweet of you. Thank you, you make me feel better. How come only the two of us get such dreams?'

Her question sunk into me like daggers. I came to the sinking realization that what Grandpa said was becoming true. Only the both of us got the dreams. I didn't think of it before, it's just too fast. Time was passing faster and fate would begin to twist, world is going to spin faster and soon we'll have to stand up against Cyrus. I had the fear buried deep within me. I looked into SJ's eyes not knowing what to tell, all I could think of was Is it me and SJ?

She broke the silence asking 'Do you know the answer?' I nodded a no. 'I'm hungry.' I said when I had come back to my senses. SJ smiled and said 'I'll make you a sandwich.'

I sat on the kitchen table hogging on my chicken salad. SJ stood in the balcony watching the sunrise. I gobbled down the last part of my dinner in the early morning and asked 'Can you make me a promise?' She turned looking stunned. She thought about it and nodded. 'Like the way I promised you, promise me you'll always help.' She frowned and cleared her throat. 'Do you remember that I was the one who helped you first? Firstly, you'd never need me; I'll be the one who'll need you. But anyway, I promise.' The lines she said flooded through my brain. I knew that she wouldn't need me in a few days and I'll be the one who needs her hand to stand up straight.

If I was right, the prophecy fell on me and her, so she has to cooperate with me and she has to grow out of her fear. What could I possibly do for that?

The night of Halloween came by the next weekend. It was a beautiful Saturday afternoon in Black Fury. I, Luke, Katy and SJ had just got down from our school cab [we can't say school bus, so we call it school cab]. In WPS today we had loads of fun. The Helen team had to fight against Hera and Hillary against Hermine. Though Hillary lost, it was an awesome battle! We lost because most of the members in my team were new; their defence skills were still a bit low. But the main fact was that they didn't know where they needed to use their supernatural ability and where they didn't need any supernatural defence. Helen won anyway. All because of SJ, she's learning pretty fast. She's got really nice moves and she just knows where she should use what. We got our uniforms today. Tomorrow I'm planning on combining forces with team Helen.

Everyone decorated their houses with pumpkins, bats and the super market was filled with people who came to buy candy. By the time we went to Jenkins super market the candy section was empty, not one piece of candy left. That's when we went to Mack Splash where there was a lot of respect for us just because we went along with SJ. The chocolate store was damn crowded. I thought it was Halloween and not valentines. But SJ found her father's friend and told him she needed candy. In half an hour we got two huge boxes of candy for Halloween.

I, Su, Sam, SJ, Alex and Alley had been putting up bats and pumpkins and owls and spiders, Alley drew, painted and cut out a huge picture of a witch in a broom stick which was our masterpiece. I had to admit my sister was good at art. I hung one of those spiders and climbed down the ladder. I went into the kitchen and pulled out a bottle of water from the refrigerator. I saw SJ standing by the window again and thinking of something unpleasant and I knew that instant, that it was about the dream she had last week. 'SJ, I told you to get your mind off it.' I said. She turned to me, her hair was still tight in a ponytail, and she had her usual athletic look. She said 'I wasn't thinking about it, Uncle Cody said he'll be here for two weeks in Black Fury, he promised me and yet he hasn't showed up.' I picked up her cell phone and said 'Give him a ring.'

- 'He's probably really busy. That may be why he hasn't shown up yet.'
- 'Oh c'mon, give him a ring at least.'
- 'No, I got to go see Mrs McClellan; she's down with a cold.' She strutted out of the room with a tray of apple pie. I asked 'Can I come with?'

I knocked the door and a girl who was probably as old as Alexis, Katy's eldest sister's, opened it. She said 'Oh, what a surprise!?' SJ smiled politely and said 'Hello Margret, I hadn't seen you in a long while. How are you and Toby?' The girl smiled and said 'I got engaged with Toby few months back. His parents want him to get settled and then get married. So, he's searching for a bigger place and he got a promotion so more salary.'

- 'How's your job going on?'
- 'Uh that, I'm planning of joining Mid Springs next fall. I'm sick of running my own day care. C'mon in.' the girl hadn't even said hello to me yet. And SJ was such a polite person to everyone but me. I don't know why she's so fond of arguing with me all the time. Okay . . . . fine, even I loved bossing with her. It just is fun.

My house was more modern and trendy but SJ's was more old—fashioned.

My dad was a designer sent from heaven. It was like those houses you see in the country side. Mrs McClellan sat on the coffee table with a rose nose and a box full of paper towels. SJ placed the tray on the table and they had a chat . . .

I and Luke were sitting on the stones near the sea shore and threw pebbles in the water and watched the ripples. Luke asked 'How's it at SJ's' I nodded. I hadn't talked much with Luke in the past week even though he had spent the whole week right next to me. 'Let's have a sleepover, the two of us like old days. My place welcomes you.'

- 'Your place welcomes me, but your father . . .' I didn't have to finish that sentence. Luke thought about it.
- 'I'll talk with dad. C'mon one sleep over.'
- 'What about SJ and Katy, wouldn't they feel left alone?'
- 'Leave the girls buddy, I want to spend time with you.'
- 'We are spending time right now.'
- 'C'mon, you used to love sleep over's, all of a sudden you've changed.'
- 'Okay dude, sleep over, tonight.'
- 'Not tonight, tonight's Halloween. The four of us can spend time in the hills. It's packed during Halloween and dad made reservations for the four of us.' That's when Katy came running, totally destroying the boy atmosphere. She asked 'Did you hear Cody Ryan's in town?' I said 'Oh you mean SJ's uncle; yeah she was disappointed that he didn't show up early in the morning.'
- 'Hey, guys wanna go get some ice cream?' Luke asked. 'Sure.' I said. Luke got on his feet and said 'Race to the parlour.'

I ran behind him while Katy crossed her arms with a chuckle and followed.

Sam was sitting in Flakes Diners with Micah Delve, the captain of our soccer team as well as the son of our coach. I licked the last bit of ice cream and walked past when Sam spotted me and waved. He signalled me to come in and I did. Luke followed me inside. Katy had already left for home.

'Hey Jake what's up?' asked Micah. 'I'm doing well, what about you?' I replied. 'Never felt any better.' He said. Micah had broken his arm in a fight with Reed Jackson, Nicholas's older brother. Reed was the kind of guy who doesn't go to college nor did he ever work. I don't think he got a diploma. He just roamed around hitting people and creating commotions wherever he went. He got into trouble a lot that the cops around knew him very well.

I got a call from SJ's number; I picked up the phone and spoke into it: 'Hello smarty pants!'

- 'Hey Jake remember me?' Instead of hearing SJ's voice I heard a grown up male voice.
- 'Um . . . who is this?'
- 'Oh don't tell me you don't know me.' It finally struck me.
- 'Cody Ryan?'
- 'Yes, you guessed it right! Long-time no see!'

- 'How do you know me?' I asked, but was still debating in my mind whether the question was rude.
- 'I knew you since you were in your diapers.'
- 'Well . . . I never knew that.'
- 'I wanna talk to you right now. Fury cafe, see you in 5.' The line went dead.

I raced all the way up the town to go to Fury cafe, I think I should've flied but it was day so I couldn't. When I went there Uncle Cody (I just got the habit of calling him Uncle Cody from the Salvatores) waved at me so that I could spot him. I sat across the table with him as he ordered coffee. 'Hey, why'd you call me here?' I asked. He looked at me from top to bottom.

- 'Not a bad choice, SJ has good taste. You work out a lot, huh?'
- 'Sorry, I don't get you.'
- 'Nothing, you'll get to know some time soon. Just wanted to check you out and what's up with my favourite niece?'
- 'She's alright. She's a girl, they have delicate times.'
- 'No she ain't good. There's something she's hiding from me. And Sam's been annoyed that she hasn't told him what's bothering her, that's why he's been holding back his scar thing.'

- 'Bothering her,' I thought of the dreams and I told him about them. I reassured it was nothing to worry about.
- 'No it's not the dreams. It's something else she's bothered about, something that worries her. She was alright when I got there, but after she'd gone upstairs to her room and came down again, something changed.' Uncle Cody said. For some odd reason I couldn't concentrate on his words. He just looked so odd, skinny jeans a really flashy jacket; he looked like he just walked out of a fashion magazine. And so many people around were just staring at us I couldn't help but notice.
- 'Don't you feel so odd, like your always being watched by everybody?'
- 'Oh I'm used to that. Five years of my acting career and I'm already this famous. Thanks to my directors, they just have a perfect story each time.'
- 'Uncle Cody, how old are you?'
- 'I hate it when my own niece calls me uncle, call me Cody, I'm just 27!'
- '27! So is Aunt Jess!'
- 'Who's Aunt Jess?'
- 'Never mind she's my mom's irritating sis. Let's come down to the matter anyway.'
- 'I need you to find out what's happening to my niece.'

- 'Why me? I think you should appoint Katy for that.' Before he could reply I heard a familiar voice say 'I know why she's upset. Because she saw what Leom saw.'

I and Cody turned our heads at the same time. Alex stood there with his iPod in hand. You see Alex is really attached with electronics, he has the ability to make them do what he wants and he's really good at handling them. He could hack anybody's computer.

'What did Leom see, Alex?' I asked. He turned towards the window and gazed for a long while. Then he said the words which made my blood cold and soul tight 'Dad's going to die tonight.'

Chapter 12

Halloween!

'**I** saw him die. I just saw him die, right in front of my eyes and I couldn't help him. I saw it twice.' SJ spoke, her voice trembling with fear of what was going to happen. 'I, you, Katy and Luke were together in this place, crowded place, I don't think it was this part of town. There were a lot of kids our age, and older. When it grew late in the night only a few people remained and suddenly a blue light covered the place. It was suffocating. Out of nowhere, a big flash of golden light passed through your dad and . . . . puff . . . . he was . . . burned to death. And I assume it was liquid fire, it smelt like something was burning. It all happened so suddenly I couldn't notice much. We ran up to your father but when we reached, he was already . . . dead.' Pearls of water began flowing down her cheeks; she was so scared like she had done something wrong. I gulped. 'But dad's not here right?' Alley said.

Sam entered the room with his head hung down and said 'Your dad and mom are coming home tonight.'

'Darn!' was the only word I said. All those beautiful days I had with dad flashed upon my inward eye as though he was already gone. The days he would leave our car somewhere and I, him and Alex would walk halfway and hitchhike the rest, our perfect dad-son adventures. 'We have to do something about it, a master plan.' Alex suggested. All at once we turned to look at SJ.

She wiped her tears and asked 'What?' 'C'mon you're the one with the mega mind. Sort the brilliant plan and please tell me something like a grown up would to make me feel better.' I suggested. She chuckled even when I knew a part of her was already feeling sorry for me. 'I think we could sort something out of my brain, but I need all your help there.' Luke rolled his eyes and said 'Of course all of us will contribute for helping Mr Martin. He's way better than my dad.'

Leom cleared his throat. 'Don't you dare tell that to dad or mom.' Luke threatened. Leom just nodded like a good little brother. 'First we got to find the location. Did any of you have any plans for hanging out tonight?' Luke nodded. 'Hanging out where?' SJ questioned like an investigator. I could tell her brain was functioning really fast. Her brain wasn't like ours; her brain was the kind of brains that have a superfast computer stored in them with access to all files. I wonder whether she had brains only under her skull or everywhere in her body. She probably had brains instead of muscles.

'At the hills on the other part of town my father got tickets for the four of us for Halloween.' SJ sat quietly for a long time while all of saw the hands of the clock ticking. My father, my dear father was going to die and I was sitting in my friend's house simply, with no plans in mind to save him. 'Can we go visit the place, right now?' SJ asked. All of us sort of nodded not knowing what she was going to do.

The ten of us, Cody, Alley, Sam, Luke, Leom, Katy, SJ, I, Su and Alex took three cars of the Salvatores' driveway and rushed all the way to the other end of town above the hills of Halloween. The Hill of Halloween is a kind of amusement park or a ghost house or a freaky place where teenagers hang out to soil their pants on the night of Halloween.

In the car I drove with Leom, Alex and Suzie in the back and SJ sat next to me. She was looking out the window profoundly thinking. I said 'Thank You for being helpful to save my father.' She turned to me and said 'I haven't done anything yet. And after you hear my plan, I bet you wouldn't be thanking me.' I just chuckled. I asked 'Do you remember the time we spent in the charity ball?' When I mentioned the words I saw a slight and faint reflection of her lips curve into a smile. 'Yes' she said 'I do remember, it was a beautiful day.' Some part of me inside told me to quit the topic and shut up, but my heart told me to go on. 'Indeed it was a beautiful day. That day I learned there is a girl out there prettier than my mom.' She still denied turning and looking into my eyes, but I knew that she was smiling and blushing as well.

When we reached the bottom of the hill the cars lined up in the parking lot. It was being put up and made ready for the grand opening tonight. The Hill of Halloween opens its gate only during Halloween and sometimes on the night after Halloween as well. We stood outside the gate when a man came out and said 'I'm sorry kids, it's not open now, come at five thirty.' All of us folded our hands and cleared our throat, and Cody cleared his throat more loudly. The man looked at all of us. We were the off springs of the eight most richest and well-known people in Black Fury. And of course everyone knew about Cody Ryan.

That man just nodded and said 'Please, I can't let you in, I'm sorry.' SJ said 'Sir, please let us in. I promise we will never touch a thing. We just want to look around. I'll give you the cash.' The man nodded and said 'Please don't touch a thing' and opened the gates for us. SJ handed him a $50 bill and said 'That's all I have for now.' We went inside and I said 'I'll pay you back when we get home.' as we all walked in.

- 'No, you don't have to.' SJ quoted that in a very firm voice.
- 'Of course I will. It's for my father and I know you get $100 a month and you just spent half of it on my dad.'
- 'How do you know that?'
- 'My parents are similar. Yeah we might be rich, but our parents talk about responsibility and

how to save and not to get spoilt and how money is not everything in the world.'

- 'Yeah, my parents use the exact words. And you missed accountability; my dad's glued to that one.'

- 'Oh so is mine or was.' I said in a slow tone coming to the realization that all of this was true. My sweet father was going to die, MY father! She squeezed my hand as a bead of tear ran down my cheek. 'Jake, are you crying? Jake Martin is crying. That's breaking news!' SJ mocked. The last thing I cared about was SJ teasing me. I just wiped my tears and said 'Just don't tell anyone.' She squeezed my hand again and said 'I know you really love him. And crying was something sweet that you just did.'

She observed the surroundings trying to find the exact place where she saw my . . . . I can't say it, I'm sorry.

Leom yelled 'Guys! Here's where I saw it happen.' All of us ran to the spot. Luke held the piece of paper in which Leom had drawn the surrounding and it was a perfect match. SJ looked around and nodded. It was the place where my father had his last stand. Alley had broken into tears and Sam held her. He kissed her gently on the cheek and that's how I knew he had already told her about it. I asked 'SJ, did you know about that?' She just slowly said 'I knew it before he got his scar.'

SJ strutted around thinking of what to do. Then she came up with an idea. The most important role was of course played by me but if Alley screwed up I have no part in the play. She told us about the plan and I had to admit it was brilliant. But it was all about the source, identifying the source and blocking it. SJ, Sam, Alley, Su, and I were the only ones who were doing the action part. After plotting the plan and telling each one of us what to do, SJ wanted to go to the stables at WPS and spend some time with her new horse, Oscar. I didn't know why but I gave a ring to Chad and he picked her up, anything that made her feel better.

I sat all alone reflecting on the plan and what I had to do. Cody sat next to me and said 'Cheer up dude. I got good news. I mean it's not so great but I guess it'll cheer you up.'

- 'What is it?'
- 'Just like SJ had directed I went to the future, I tried mid night and one and two in the morning but the clock didn't turn.'
- 'What?'
- 'I travelled to the future and there was nothing but emptiness. Fate has yet not decided what has to be done.' Those words made me feel glad in a way but still deep inside I couldn't concentrate on anything.

Then we heard a big thud, it was probably SJ. Cody looked at his watch, it was nearing six. He said 'C'mon let's get moving.' I drove in the car quietly and SJ didn't have much to say either. She was afraid too, but she was afraid to show her fear. It was her plan she had to be more confident about it than anyone else. Alex sat with his hat covering his tears. Suzie, my little angel, just kept her hand on Alex's shoulder as he inhaled. Leom tried consoling Alex and told him everything thing was going to be alright. He was just in fifth grade but talked more like a grown up. And Alex was very close to Leom. Even if he was three years older, those guys grew up together.

SJ sighed and said 'I'll try all I can.' I didn't react to that much because I didn't want a conversation to begin. I just wasn't in a mood to talk, even if I met my father right now, I wouldn't be able to talk. I would just be too afraid; what if I spoke something wrong that would hurt him and that would be our last conversation?

There were so many such questions floating through my head. We gave our passes and entered the hill of Halloween though the kids couldn't come in, we got them a place elsewhere to keep on track of what we do and help us if we needed it. Somehow, we found a way to sneak Suzie in.

When the clock struck one in the night I saw a faint shadow of my father enter in. All of us got into our positions. SJ signalled us our spots. Alley stood invisible following my dad with an invisible shield around him. We'll just have to protect our father for as long as possible. When my father entered the area of his death, I guess he spotted me, the boy with loud thoughts. 'Jake, where are you, your thoughts are pretty loud boy.'

Sam signalled me to show myself to dad. But before the blue mist showed up I heard someone crash down.

All of us turned our attention and saw Aaron Sterlington lie on the ground, his arm on fire. He put the fire out; he had bruises all over himself. SJ said 'I knew it would've been you from the beginning.' Aaron slowly stood up trying to balance himself. Suzie rushed to the spot, she was fast.

- 'What did I do?' Aaron managed to ask.
- 'You work for Cyrus don't you? You and your siblings?'
- 'No, of course not. Why would we do that?'
- 'Spit out the truth. I've seen it. The four of you summoning someone. You tried to kill Mr Martin, why?'
- 'Look SJ, I am your brother. And why would I try to kill Mr Martin? I swear I didn't do anything. I swear on my dead mother.' SJ came to a sinking realization that she had just ruined her plan by herself because of false accusation.

Unfortunately, the blue mist covered the place. Before I even digested the fact, I saw my father flying in the air and hit the wall with a loud bang! I raced up to him but before I caught up I felt something twist my leg and pull me down. I fell down. I saw a hot orange ball coming to my father. I couldn't get up and the tight grip just tightened the more I struggled. But just before it hit my father, SJ made a thick shield around him. Fire was continuously shot at her and I knew she couldn't hold any longer. In the meantime the grip tightened over my whole body. I couldn't move a muscle and my whole body felt numb. I couldn't even blink. Water flowed down my eyes, my eyes were burning. Sam passed through things trying to find from where the attack was being made and I couldn't see much of anything because tears filled my eyes and blocked my view.

I tried breaking free and the more I struggled, the loser the grip became. Whoever it was was losing his strength and finally I heard the words which gave relief, not physically but emotionally from Sam 'I found him!' I finally broke free. Even after that I couldn't move much. SJ got drained of energy and fell on the ground. Slowly I got control of my body and stood up. My whole body felt like it went through an oven and got baked and crushed in the food processor. I dragged myself towards Sam. He held a tall guy by his collar staring at him with disbelief. He spit out the words that surprised me 'Micah, what's wrong with you?' Yes, it was Micah, but not our captain Micah. I mean, his eyes were blood shot and red and he looked like he was possessed by something. The red colour began flickering in his eyes. Slowly the brown shade returned to his eyes. Sam shook him and asked 'What happened to you?' Micah looked around like he wasn't supposed to belong here. He looked around like he'd just woken up from a trance and said 'Where am I?' While Sam answered his questions and asked a few I raced to my father. I wasn't exactly running. I would've run if I could. My legs were barely stable, I walked wobbling to my dad and fell near him. I held his wrist and checked his pulse. He was still alive! 'He's alive! Dad's alive!' I yelled. Suzie smiled a smile that faded soon. And I learned why she had. SJ was hurt. Hurt really badly, worse than my father. She had bruises all over and she was even burned.

Chapter 13

The Sleep Over!

Dad held my hand. He had broken his leg. Katy sat next to him healing him. I bet it must've been so painful because those small bruises that I had, when I was getting healed it was one of the worst kind of pain I've ever felt. My mom stroked my dad's hair and spoke some consoling words. Dad's tight grip tightened around my wrist. After my dad got fixed Katy went by to SJ's place and wanted to know what was going on.

SJ could heal herself. She was just too afraid. I heard her yelling for life while I stood out in the front porch of her house. Her crying was so full of pain and I felt like everything was my fault. I didn't have the guts to enter her house when I heard the yell. It was so loud that I heard it from the front porch even when she was yelling from her bedroom. Luke came out and sat next to me. He rested his hand on my shoulder and said 'It's okay buddy.'

- 'What happened to her?'

- 'Don't even ask. Her whole body is broken, Katy just replaced all her bones back in place and fixed them together. That poor little thing, she's being tortured. I mean cure tortured.' I just held my head and sat there. I could feel the pain she's going through. I literally mean it.

After it was done Sam told me he'd given her some pills to keep her sleeping so she wouldn't feel the pain. I went upstairs to her room. She was wrapped in a blanket. She slept so deeply she couldn't even notice the chilly wind coming through the window. The strong winds have begun and soon snow would begin to fall. Even after the pain she had gone through, yet she just looked so beautiful like the girl I took to the charity ball. Her hair so perfect even if there was nothing she did to make it that way. It had some glow radiating, so soft, so silky. I sat beside her.

- 'I wonder how Micah's feeling. He got controlled by Cyrus, man that would've been painful.' Sam said. I nodded stroking her hair.
- 'It's all because of me she had to go through this right?' I asked. The guilt was killing me.
- 'No, she would've done it for anyone.' I looked at Sam for a while then he said 'Yes, she did do it for you. You know she cares about you. You just are special to her.'
- 'You're not kidding right?'

- 'Of course I'm not.'
- 'Why?'
- 'I have to admit, I don't know. She just likes you. I mean, what's not there in you that a girl wouldn't like?' I chuckled.
- 'You know each time I look at her, the earth beneath me starts shaking. It's like it's not gravity that's holding me to earth but it's her. All that goes through my head is SJ, SJ and SJ.'
- 'Well, that's what people call love, bro.' Sam said and winked at me.

That afternoon Mr and Mrs Salvatore had arrived. Before I knocked the door to the living room I heard Mrs Salvatore saying 'I told you guys to look after each other and not to burn down the house. That also included breaking yourselves. And SJ, I told you to be in charge and you yourself having proved to me that none of my kids are worth of taking care of themselves. Sam, you are the oldest and the only son, don't you think you have any responsibility? Suzie is a kid and both of you have set a bad example. You guys have grown up; you should be a role model for your sister.' Before I had second thoughts of knocking I heard Su's voice say 'Mom, you don't know what happened. I would tell you that both of them have showed me that saving others' lives is very important. They have also showed me that sometimes you have to sacrifice one thing to get the other. You have to give up for the ones you love. They have shown me the meaning of true friendship and love and care, it was such a noble act. Only if you listened to the whole story you would understand what your kids have done. They have done such a nice thing that your heart would overflow with joy when you hear it.' I guess her mom's writing genes have got to both the sisters. They just know how to put it into words.

Before I knew it my dad opened the door and said 'I'll tell you what happened, Ben and Kelly.' I didn't even know my dad was there.

He narrated the whole story. He summed up the whole thing with 'You have such wonderful children.' It actually hurt me in a way but I just kept quiet and stood with my father. My father patted me on the shoulder and said 'You have not done any less, son.' I smiled. SJ sat on the swing with her blanket around her. She looked so tender. I walked up and sat next to her. 'How are you feeling?'

- 'I'm fine, I just can't move right. Did you go to school?' I nodded a no. I had totally forgotten about WPS.
- 'Hope you get better soon.'
- 'Don't worry tough guy, I'll be walking down the school hallway tomorrow, I'll be just fine.' She rested her head on my shoulder. We sat in complete silence for a long time. Just being with her made me feel that she was fine. My dad came by and thanked SJ once again. She just smiled

and took her head of my shoulder. I helped her in and set off to my place. In the car I and dad had a conversation 'Can I stay at Luke's place tonight?'

- 'Sure. Son,'
- 'Yes dad.'
- 'How did you feel when you knew about it?'
- 'About what?' I knew what he was talking about but I needed time to think of an answer.
- 'About my death.' I took some time to reply.
- ' . . . . I felt the way you would've felt if you knew you would lose me.' I guess I nailed it.
- 'Hmm . . . . SJ's a nice girl.'
- 'Yes she is. Dad I got news for you.'
- 'What is it?'
- 'Alley and Sam, the new couple. The brand new soul mates fate has marked.'
- 'Is it so?' I could see my dad's eyes twinkle with joy.
- 'Yes it is.'
- 'That's awesome! I mean, Sam is a wonderful kid.'
- 'I agree until you wouldn't pick him over me.'
- 'Don't worry, both of you are the same to me.' That afternoon at lunch all of us sat quietly. My mother broke the silence 'I'm proud of you guys.' Alley said 'We couldn't have done it without the Salvatores'.' Then the room grew silent again. After lunch all five of us saw

a movie together in our living room crushed in one four-seater couch. Just like old times.

That evening I drove to Luke's place. I rang the bell and Mr McQueen opened the door. He looked at me, his green eyes so fierce. I bet he would've been popular among the ladies when he was younger. But to be honest, I don't like him too much. 'Hello Martin'

- 'Good evening Mr McQueen!' I said.
- 'Luke said you'd come by.'
- 'He did.' 'Rob, Robert! Honey who is it?' I heard Mrs McQueen's voice from the kitchen. She came to the front porch wiping her hands in a dish towel. 'Jake! How are you?' She asked. I like Mrs McQueen. She was friendlier in nature than her husband. Though Mr McQueen doesn't torture or abuse anyone, he's just not happy to see any of the kids. 'I'm good.'

She invited me in. Mr McQueen was an auto-mobile engineer. But he didn't look like the cool hunk of any kind. Yes he designed totally cool cars with extraordinary features but he always wore a suit. And Mrs McQueen is a nurse; I don't exactly know what they would have in common. But I knew one thing, Robert hated me. Who knows why? I don't like him either.

I raced upstairs to Luke's room with my things; I wanted to get as far as possible from his dad. You see

Robert [I'm just used to calling him Robert] isn't the kind of person who gets along with me. I opened Luke's door to find him sitting on his desk, untangling the wires of the joystick. When he saw me he smiled and asked 'Hey what's up?'

- 'Nothing much, bro.'
- 'How's SJ holding up?'
- 'I guess she'll be fine by tomorrow.'

'I'm gonna ask you something and just be honest alright.' He said as I hoped into his bed and switched on the TV so we could play video games.

- 'Okay.'
- 'You really love her, don't you?' He let that sink in for a while. I thought about it.
- 'I don't know.' I finally said.
- 'How can you not know?' He asked as he shoved popcorn into his mouth.
- 'You and Katy were best friends since childhood; did you ever even think you'd fall in love with her?'
- 'Of course no. But I was a kid. And you're not and I have a strong feeling you're falling in love.' He said in between his chewing.
- 'I'm not, I'm really not. I just care about her a lot.'

- 'Care about her a lot, why do you?' I thought about his question. I really didn't have a good lie for that.
- 'I don't know what I'm feeling, what I'm doing. I'm just so messed up after yesterday.'
- 'Okay buddy, relax. I think we could get back to normal life after tonight.'
- 'I can't, maybe you can.'
- 'Why not?'
- 'Because I'm already marked for the job Luke. Fate has chosen me and my mark is my identification. The prophecy is on me and SJ.'
- 'How can you say that?'
- 'I knew the night she cried on my shoulder. I have been destined to do this, I have no choice. Time's running, the day I get my scar, it's no time to waste for me and SJ. Most of the time no one gets past twelve years, we're fourteen, we just have minutes left, maybe seconds.' The second I said that I regretted it.
- 'Okay bro, chill. It's gonna be fine. C'mon lets hop out for a swim.' I raced downstairs and when I walked past Robert he frowned at me. When we got out the back door I whispered 'What's up with Robert?'
- 'He's my dad; you don't call him with his first name.'
- 'Oh yeah, Robert!'
- 'Jake . . . .'

- 'Yeah, yeah, Mr McQueen.' I said rolling my eyes. Luke tossed his shirt on the floor and jumped in. I removed my T-shirt. That's when Luke said the words which made my throat dry 'Dude, you got something on your arm.' I turned to look at my left arm to see a mark of Cupid firing hearts. Darn! I was marked.

I jumped into the cool water and swam around for a while. Luke patted me on my shoulder and said 'It's okay. Don't be so shy and stop blushing like a girl. Race you to the end!'

After a while Mrs McQueen came with towels and told us to come to the table for dinner. When I got out of the pool and grabbed the towel she held out for me, she spotted my scar. She asked 'Oh my God! Who's the lucky girl?' I just chuckled. 'It's SJ.' She answered the question herself. 'How do you know?' I asked.

- 'Well Leom told me. He even told me more about it. I mean your wedding and kids after the wedding.' I stared at her in disbelief. My best friend's mom is talking about my wedding and my kids. Yeah that's not awkward at all!
- 'What . . .' was the only word I could manage to say. How else can a fourteen year old guy even react to his best friend's mom when she talks about his children and married life?!

- 'I mean, you're going to have three children: two boys and one girl. The oldest is Ryan and then Alice and Noah. Okay Jake, stop blushing.' My mouth was open the whole time. The only thing I understood was that I'd live long enough to have children. 'And I know how many grandchildren I'll have too.'
- 'How many does Luke have?' I got excited.
- 'Twins. One girl and one boy, Leo and Lizzy.' I couldn't stop but laugh. The whole thing just sounded funny. 'Luke, I got twin niece and nephew, bro!' I mocked. 'What about Leom?' Luke asked. 'One girl child.'

'I can already imagine your Lizzy coming up calling me "Uncle Jake, Ryan's breaking my toys." 'I said and laughed. Luke stared and said 'Stop making fun of me.'

- 'Oh, look who's shy now, huh?'
- 'Stop talking 'bout my kids.'
- 'Wow, Luke, you're already talking like a dad.' Luke gave me one stare before entering the dining.

Chapter 14

Flakes Diners

One week had passed by and I still kept the news with me and didn't tell SJ. It was Friday morning, our first hour was history. Mr Neumann told us the history of Black Fury. 'Do any of you know how Black Fury, our little town got its name? I mean, Salvatore, you're new to town, don't you think this name is kind of awkward?' SJ looked up and nodded. That was the second time he's addressed her. In every class Mr Neumann would address SJ at least five times. Yeah, he was getting on my nerves, to tell you the truth. I mean, he's twenty . . . . something and SJ's turning fourteen next month. Why can't he look out for older girls and leave my girl alone. I would be lying if I told you that I hadn't fallen in love with SJ over the week. Yes I liked SJ Salvatore the only girl in the whole school [exclude Katy] who doesn't have a thing for me. And all the other girls who would go nuts for me, I just didn't like.

But to get back to class for the first time the name "Black Fury" actually sounded odd.

'Thousands of years, way before any of us were born; this town was so beautiful, full of nature. But this man who happens to be a stranger to everyone till today set his foot into the town. After that there was complete chaos in this town, so many murders, so many thefts, robbery, etc. People in this town years ago had a lot of superstitious beliefs. They believed that this man was bad luck and decided that he had to leave the town for the betterment of the town and its people. They did, but that man got furious. That night a black layer was gradually pulled down from the sky which brought with it clouds. It rained and showered for so long in the month of June. June is spring time here, so the plants didn't grow well and the beauty of this town vanished. The black night, they called it. And that's how Black Fury got its name. Black, which refers to the night and Fury which refers to the man.' Right when Neumann finished the bell rang. All of us got out and went to our lockers. I looked at my schedule and was happy to know the next class was Phys Ed. SJ dumped her books into the locker. She looked frustrated. She twisted her hair into a small, spiky, cute pony tail. She took a deep breath. She moistened her lips in a way that was so cute. I asked 'What's wrong?'

- 'Nothing, it's just that I have a lot of work. We got a big game on Tuesday and this whole party thing that Katy's arranging for her sister and fiancé and the essays and the homework and the

147

articles that Mrs Griffin asked me to write for the school newspaper. There's just so much work left and no matter how fast I run there isn't enough time to get all the work done!' She exhaled with frustration.

I patted her on the shoulder and said 'It's okay, take a break. After martial arts training the four of us can hang out at Simon's Smoothies.'

- 'I don't think I can.'
- 'Why not?'
- 'Because after soccer training I'm planning on heading home and finishing of the articles. Then I'll race to the florist and order the flowers and then the baker and order the cake and then I'll come home and have dinner and go to sleep. I don't think I'll have enough time for hanging out.'
- 'I'll help you. You work on your articles and I'll order the flowers and the cake and I guess we could hang out at Simon's Smoothies then.'
- 'Are you sure?'
- 'Yeah, I'll do it.'
- 'Thank you that's really sweet. And I guess I'll have time to finish my essays too.'
- 'Okay, I'll pick you up. It's a Friday night, so how about dinner at Flakes Diners? The four of us, instead of Simon's Smoothies.'

- 'Sounds great!' She smiled and walked towards the gym. I went to the boy's locker room and changed. I saw Micah there, sitting in front of his locker with his head in his hands. I asked 'Yo Micah! Anything wrong?'
- 'No man, it's just that since Halloween I'm kind of getting this odd headache and noises in my head.'
- 'Did you visit a doctor?'
- 'No, but I don't think a regular mortal could deal with this. I have a feeling this is not a normal headache that normal people get.'
- 'Then I think you could drop by at Mr Robinson's house. I think he can help you.'
- 'Thanks buddy, I'll think about it. Is Jonah in town?'
- 'Yes he is. He's got big exams coming up so he's stuck in his room with the books. You could tell him hi while dropping by his house sometime.'
- 'Yeah sure. And . . . Jake,'
- 'Yeah?'
- 'I want you to become captain. I talked to dad about it.'
- 'Are you sure? What 'bout Sam?'
- 'I asked Sam, he recommended you.'

Mr Evan Delve, our coach entered the room. 'Boys! Get on the field! Be fast, the gals are faster than you. If you maintain this speed, there's no way we'll get the championship mastered.' I put on my shoes and jogged to the field. Luke was standing in the corner of the goal post, fixing his gloves.

Luke whispered in my ear while we did push—ups. 'Did you check out that goal SJ put? I feel sorry for the goal keeper.' And rule number twelve was, no talking during gym. So I and Luke got a punishment to run around the field sixty freaking times! 'I hate you!' I kept saying that when we ran around the field.

After the whole day ended, after I had gone to martial arts training my body was broken. I swear I couldn't move a bone and my mind just kept telling me that I have to make the proposal special. I mean, my first girlfriend was my only girlfriend and I can't screw it up can I? But I also had to order the flowers and cake and pick SJ up. My hand slowly moved into my pocket and pulled out my cell phone. I called SJ and asked her what kind of flowers to order and what cake. She instructed everything clearly to me but I was a broken down loser who couldn't get up from his bed. I slowly sat up on my bed and that seemed to take all my energy.

SJ had asked me once more whether or not I could do the job and I'd put the burden on myself. And now, I'm regretting it. My dad opened the door and asked 'Are you alright son?' I cleared my throat and asked 'Do I even look alright dad?'

- 'Yeah, you look . . . . well . . . damaged.'
- 'Yeah, that's the right word.'

- 'What are you worrying about? I mean not the ordering cakes and flower stuff, something else at the back of your mind not so clear to me but I know it involves SJ.' I know I couldn't hide anything from dad. Even if I did, like I said before I'm a boy with loud thoughts, he'd figure it out anyway. I told him about my scar and all that stuff. I said 'I just don't happen to find any place special.' My dad rested his hand on my shoulder and said 'Why do you young boys these days search like crazy for the solution when it's right in front of you.' He let that sink in and I took some time to understand it. If you didn't understand, how do you think my damaged brain could? And right now even my body was damaged. My dad said 'My designs make up the town. And the best building I've ever designed is our home. I think the backyards the right place. And by Sunday your mom will finish her decoration in the back yard and she's been really excited about it. You know your mom is talented enough to put up the most beautiful designs. Leave the pressure on us; just plan the part about asking her.' The minute my dad said that I just knew that it was going to be the most beautiful moment for the both of us.

I called up Katy and asked her to heal me. And she did and my body was so numb I couldn't feel the pain.

Then I ordered the flowers and the cakes. I knocked on SJ's door right at seven. Her father opened the door. He excitedly said 'What a surprise! C'mon in my boy, SJ's upstairs.' I went upstairs to her room and knocked the door. To be frank, I don't knock on anybody's door except SJ's. I never knock Katy's door and she just gets pissed off about it and that's what makes it fun. Others like Alley, Luke, Sam, Alex and Jonah and all don't ask me to knock on their door, so I just don't. SJ opened the door, she said 'You didn't have to knock.' I guess she joined the don't-knock-on-my-door club . . .

I entered her room, I guess she had just had a bath, her hair was wet and her towel sat on the floor and her bath robe was on her dresser. 'Sorry I took so long to open the door, I was changing.' 'It's okay.' I said. Her laptop was open on the bed and papers were dumped on her desk. Her closet was wide open and she opened up another shelf pulled out a pair of socks and was putting them on.

I saw a white sundress or whatever you call it hang there. I said 'You'd look really beautiful in that.' She hopped next to me putting on one sneaker. 'Oh that one, Aunt Leah got that dress for me to wear on Sunday, at the party.' She said. 'By the way, thanks.' She smiled and bent down to tie her lace.

She picked up the towel and the robe and said 'Sorry my room's such a mess.' And that minute I knew something was up with her. She would never say anything like that to me. I mean, we usually fought most of the time. It was so unusual that she treated me like a guest. Both of us had changed the way we spoke to each other after Halloween. And both of us knew it.

She took a few minutes to clean up her room and then we walked out of her house. I guess she had a haircut because her hair was up till her chin the last time and now she had hair only long enough to fall below her ears. And it was more spiky than usual. I ruffled her wet hair and asked 'Did you have a haircut?' She nodded.

We had a long drive to Flakes Diners and on the way she asked 'How's your dad doing?'

- 'He's doing fine.' I replied. She started looking out the window like usual. But this time she had something in her mind she wanted me to know.
- 'Jake . . .' Her sweet voice said. 'I've got to show you something.' She turned and pulled up the sleeve of her left arm. And that second I was a 100% sure that I was looking at the angel with whom I'll be in love, forever and always. I could hear a violin and birds fluttering around. On her fair and flawless skin was the mark of cupid firing hearts, the exact one on mine. I said 'Cool, who's the guy?' I didn't want her to know now that it was me; it would just ruin the surprise. She shook her head as drops of water splashed around. She said 'That I don't know. I'm curious I'm really very curious. But I just don't happen to find him.' I couldn't just spit out 'It's me, idiot.' But I really

wanted to. I drove in silence for a long time. She leaned on the window and asked 'Sometimes don't you look out the window and simply think who it might be?' I said 'Yes, I used to. But my dad used to tell me that don't go searching for things a lot because sometimes you just find the answer right next to you. We just have to wait with patience.' When I said that she looked at me in a weird way but then she just turned back to the window.

When we reached Flakes Diners Katy and Luke were already there. Katy hugged SJ when she saw her. She said 'You look so cute with the new bangs!' SJ rolled her eyes and said 'Sometimes I think you should've been born in my place. My mom would love to have you as her daughter. You're girly my mom's way girly, I think you guys would get along fine. My mom compelled me into cutting the bangs.' She rolled her eyes.

Luke punched me on the shoulder and said 'Did you tell her?' I nodded a no and told him about my plans. We had dinner and talked about a lot of stuff. Katy, the chatter box always came up with something. And today she stuck it to me. She told 'SJ, did Jake tell you his real name?' Darn she got on my nerves. 'What do you mean, "Real name"?' SJ looked at me curiously. A tiny drop of white sauce stuck on her lower lip. I said 'Jacob . . . Jacob Martin. Though I never use my real name, I use them only while filling applications.' I wiped the cheese of her lip and licked my finger.

The three of them got involved in a topic about chemistry and Luke's strength just happened to be chemistry, that's why he worked it up a lot with Katy. And of course SJ, the brainy loved every subject so she and Luke started talking about electrons and protons and whatever "—trons" are left. And Katy, the chatter box, will always find a way to get involved in a conversation.

I sat there digging my mac and cheese when I smelt an essence of danger. I looked at the next table and right there I spotted my biggest enemy in the world, Nicholas Jackson. I thought that jerk was still in England. He had his gaze fixed straight at SJ. And that gaze was not a good one. I whispered 'Move to the corner, we'll exchange sides' to SJ. She turned her head to face me and then I realized how close we were. SJ pulled back. She asked why but I just told her to do it.

Luke and Katy whispered to each other and then giggled. SJ looked at them for an answer and they signalled the table next to ours. I smiled sarcastically at Nick, he gulped and turned away. SJ said 'I guess there's something else you're not telling me.'

- 'I don't want to talk about it alright.' I said. SJ kept quiet and didn't pester me like Katy would've done. Katy got a call from her going-to-be-brother-in-law. They talked for so long and I guess Katy got another person who talks as much as she does. The party was on Sunday and I had planned to ask SJ after the party. The ride back SJ just cuddled in the seat with her jacket wrapped around her. I reduced the air conditioner but SJ was still pale.

In a few minutes she fell asleep. That's when I learned she'd not slept the whole night before and the day and sacrificed her time of sleep today just for me. She looked like a little girl in her blanket, so delicate and tender. I didn't want to wake her up because I knew she hadn't slept so well lately. I carried her to her front porch at ten. I rang the doorbell and Mrs Salvatore opened the door. She smiled and said 'Hello! Thank you for dropping her and, of course, carrying her till the front porch' in a whisper. I said 'My pleasure, I'll drop her in her room.' I went upstairs and when Sam saw her in my arms he said 'Hmm . . . . what's up?' I said 'I'll tell you about it later.'

- 'I already know.' He said.
- 'Leom?'
- 'Yeah and your dad.' My dad couldn't keep anything from Mr Salvatore and the whole family got to know I learned later. I tucked her in her bed. Her fingers clutched to my jacket. I slowly took her hand and placed it on the bed. Mr Salvatore came in the room and removed her shoes. 'I'm gifted to have such children.' He said. And I knew he meant me, Alley and Alex too but I said 'SJ is a charming girl.' He then said 'You are too, son.' That's when I realized that Mr

Salvatore had always addressed me with 'my boy' and now it became 'son'.

- 'Thank you, Mr Salvatore. That's really kind.'
- 'Well, I'm just saying the truth.'
- 'Can you do me a favour?' I asked after a gap of silence.
- 'Of course, what is it?' he said standing up and putting his hands into his pockets.
- 'What kind of flowers does SJ like?'
- 'Well, I doubt whether she is a big fan of flowers son, but I know she adores the white orchids.'
- 'Anything else she loves?'
- 'Well, she just happens to love a lot of things.'
- 'Anything I can gift her.'
- 'Well . . . . she's been asking for a sword.'
- 'Thank you. What's her favourite colour?'
- 'I don't know which colour she adores more but I know it'll be red, black, white or blue.'
- 'Thank you for the info.'
- 'My pleasure son.'
- 'And . . . Can you stick to the "my boy" till I tell her about it and then you can call me son.'
- 'Okay "my boy". Have a good night.'
- 'You too, *dad!*' I hopped out of her room as her father ran his fingers into the hair of the most beautiful thing he's made. I stopped by when I saw Su. She said 'All the best bro.' I said 'Thank you, my little angel' and ruffled her hair.

Chapter 15

We fly a car into a castle

'Surprise!' Alley said. I rubbed my eyes. It was a Saturday morning and I was asleep and Alley just ruined it by opening the curtains and yelling like she's gone mad.' What's wrong with you? Can't you let me sleep? Get the hell out of here, you moronic jerk!' Her smile faded. But it was EIGHT and it was SATURDAY! She said 'I spent two weeks designing this suit just for you. I wanted it to be a surprise for my baby brother.' My sister was sensitive. If you yell at her she'll cry right there. 'I'm sorry I yelled at you. It's just that my body hurts.' I said. She said 'I'll give you a massage.'

- 'You really will?' My sister never offered to help before.
- 'Yes, just relax.'
- 'What do you want? What's the catch?' I knew she wanted something from me.
- 'You have to wear this suit to the party tomorrow.'

- 'Give me a reason.'
- 'To show Cody Ryan one of my exotic designs and ask him whether he'll be my star model.'

I looked at the suit. It looked fine and anyway I didn't even think about what I was going to wear.

- 'Fine, deal.'
- 'Deal.'

After my extremely amazing massage I got a call from Chad, he said he'd be picking me up in five minutes and if I wasn't downstairs by the driveway, he'd just leave me and go to the next stop. So I raced into the restroom and had a shower, put on some dry clothes and waited down. Just like he'd promised, Chad was at the driveway with Luke in the passenger seat next to him.

On the way to SJ's and Katy's I told Luke and Chad about my talk with Mr Salvatore and asked Chad where we'd get an extraordinary sword. Chad said 'Jake, I have to tell you something I overheard Master Spark say.'

- 'Well, what is it?'
- 'Master Spark was talking to someone; I don't know who it was. He said the chosen one will come after his sword. He said the sword's blade was made of a mixture of elements which only the maker of it has knowledge of. It is immortal weapon I guess. The only immortal sword that

exist for now. He also said the one who creates swords like this one would also come and seek the sword. He said whoever comes first the sword belongs to them. But I have a strong feeling that sword needs to be in the hands of Ms. Salvatore.' I took some time to reflect on it. No mortal weapon could hurt Cyrus so we needed an immortal one. So now if the maker gets to him first then SJ and I wouldn't really have a shot at killing Cyrus.

- 'So . . . let's go get the sword.'

- 'Are you insane, no one can meet Master Spark without an appointment? There is no way you are getting past the guards. And I also overheard him say that something was not right with it.'

- 'C'mon we're not stealing anything; we're just going to ask for what belongs to us.'

- 'Yes I know Jake, but really you shouldn't risk meeting Master Spark as a visitor. And I personally think the sword is not worth the risk.'

- 'This Spark guy is really getting on my nerves. Yeah maybe he is the oldest of our kind and yes he is respectable because he has served for us and fought many wars with Cyrus's army. But seriously, what is this guy's problem?'

- 'Oh do not say that about Master Spark, child. As I told you before, he is a very generous man.'

- 'We are meeting Mr Spark and getting the god damn sword right now. Pull over, let's get to his house.'

'Castle, Jake. Not house, that old guy lives in a castle, which is probably way older than him.' Luke said. 'How do you know?' I asked. 'I've crossed by the castle a few times; I never dared to even glance at it for longer than a second. The beasts guarding the gates are like hellhounds.'

Chad was still flying to our next stop. 'Chad, buddy,' I said. 'Do you mind giving me the controls?'

- 'I told you Jake, I'm warning you.' Chad said. I didn't listen to him. I signalled Luke to take the car for a ride till I toss Chad on the back seat. Luke took hold of the steering wheel, and without an effort I pulled Chad's arm and tossed him back and leaped to the front seat. 'Oh no Jake, do not do this. Do you even know how to fly this thing?'
- 'Look buddy, you didn't take me to the place I wanted to go so I'm driving myself.'
- 'Jake oh Jake, don't do this. Master Spark will get mad at me and he has helped me so much I cannot do this to him.'
- 'You're not doing anything. We threatened you and you are our victim. Just tell him that we . . . . um . . . knocked you out. And when you woke up you found yourself in the castle.'

- 'He's not going to believe that and I am not going to lie to him, Jake. Stop the car if you ever respected my friendship with you.' Okay now that was the kind of stuff that people say and make you stop doing what you want. I hopped into the back seat and Chad leaped in front. I said 'If you're not going to help I'll do it myself.' Chad sighed and said 'Jake, you do not understand.'
- 'Look, you are the one who doesn't understand. The whole world will get destroyed if we don't get the sword. It's an immortal weapon and we really need it.'
- 'Jake it is not the only immortal weapon I said it was the only immortal *sword*.'
- 'You mean there's more.'
- 'Yes, remember the four sisters, they had immortal weapons too. The arrows of Hillary, the spear of Helen, Hera's dagger and the knife of Hermine still lay in the castle protected from the hands of the evil. The sword isn't exactly Master Sparks' own sword, but the brother's together have protected it in the castle. It was Jenifer's sword, the chosen one hundred and thirty years ago.'
- 'But SJ wanted a sword.'
- 'Jake, I promise you I will get the sword to you somehow. But now is not the right moment. You have to go to school.'

- 'What if the maker or whatever gets there before us.'
- 'Be patient my friend. Patience is virtue.'
- 'Damn the virtue.' I muttered. Luke chuckled. Chad dropped the car with a great thud; I would be lying if I told you it didn't hurt. SJ and Katy hopped into the ride. SJ sensed that both I and Chad were annoyed and asked 'Yo Luke, what happened before you landed. And why were you guys late?' I was stuck between two girls who smelt like designer perfume. I mean it wasn't SJ, it was Katy. Luke didn't give SJ a very clear response; he just said something like 'silly fight'. SJ looked at me with curiosity. She was curious to know everything; you see she hated it when she didn't know things. She always read or surfed on the internet about stuff, I tell you she is wise but a little too wise. To be frank she was one of the only girls in senior middle school, who had beauty as well as brains (here I include Katy, even she doesn't have brains.)

When we got to school instead of running to class, I stayed back in the parking lot. I needed to get that sword; it would make SJ so happy.

Thankfully, no one spotted me hiding in the bushes expect Sam and Luke. Luke just knew I would do that, you see your best friends can predict your mind set. And of course Sam knew because he could just see through the bushes. He smiled and winked at me, I mouthed I'll tell you later, so he just wandered off with a smile.

When the bell rang and no one was around I slowly crept to Chad's car. Chad was right outside school, eating a hot dog. The keys were in the car (the drivers don't need to take their keys, no mortal would come here to steal the car and why would any of us do it?) I jumped into the ride and before Chad found out I turned on the engine. I heard a knock on the window and that minute I knew I was doomed. Fortunately, when I opened the window, I found Mathew Robinson, Katy's brother, standing there licking ice-cream. He said 'Wherever you're going, take me with you!'

- 'Or? What will you do, Matt?'
- 'Everyone in school will know your real name, I'll tell them you were named after Reed Jackson's dad.'
- 'Hey, I was not named after that brat's dad. You suck Matt, hop on.'
- 'All right bro, don't worry, I won't tell anyone.'
- 'You'll be busted if anyone gets to know. And we are going to a place of a very respectable person, you must not tell him about the stealing and stuff. By the way, we are not stealing, we're borrowing.'
- 'You're going to meet Sillvius Spark right?'
- 'How did you know?'
- 'Respectable person, duh, it was Mr Spark.'

- 'Okay, hold on!' We shot into the sky and we were on the way to the castle. The feeling was amazing. The wind gushing through my hair. The air smelled so fresh and new.

Luke had told me it was nearby school and only flying taxicabs were aloud. Within thirteen minutes we reached our destination. The guards were big, furry, brown monsters who we fought at school. We trained with them. But these guys were twice as big and twice as nasty. I got out of the car and looked at the guards. They were hellhounds, I mean, I've never seen hellhounds, they just looked really scary. There was tiny little door bell and I rang the bell. The sound was so huge Mathew fell off his feet. The guards sensed our presence and turned towards us. I smiled and said 'We're just here to meet Mr Spark; you don't want to pick a fight with me. I'll go in and come out without any harm.' I put my hands up in the air. One of them had a broken horn. He bent down and sniffed the both of us. They looked like furry bulls standing in two legs.

I heard an old, broken, cold and calm voice say 'Let . . . them' he coughed 'inside . . .' The beasts opened the huge gates and we walked into the castle. A big, blue, old palace with a big pond or maybe a lake in front of the house lay there. The building was so old I thought it might break down any second. Mathew was holding my pants the whole time, he was so scared, even after we entered the castle and the giants were far away.

When the doors flung open by themselves, both I and Matt got a heart attack. I gasped! The whole castle was blue; of course, Sillvius Spark had the ability to control water. Two young boys, maybe a little older than me, in white came down the spiral staircase and said 'Our master awaits you.' I and Matt slowly crawled up the staircase. The building smelt of fresh rain. Inside the room, a man, faced back, stood nearby the window. His cold voice said 'Please have a seat. 'He hadn't turned to look at us. The two guys pulled big comfy sofas and placed them behind to sit down. I sat down and pulled Matt into his seat. The old man had grey hair and wore a baby blue suit. He turned to us and that was the day I saw the face of Sillvius Spark. It was so fragile and wrinkled. He had sky blue eyes. He had a long white beard. He said 'what do you seek young man?' He was talking to me. He had his eyes fixed into mine. I said 'Hello sir . . . I'm . . . . I'm . . . Jake Martin. I came here . . . . for the . . . sword.' He smiled and said 'I don't think you are the chosen one or the one with crafty hands. Who are you, my child?'

I gulped 'Sir . . . I'm here instead of Ms. Sara Jane Salvatore.'

- 'I see that, child. But who are you?' A big lump formed in my throat when I said the words for the first time.
- 'Sir, I am the protector of the chosen one.' Instantly I felt the responsibility on my shoulder.

- 'I see . . .' he said stroking his beard. Then he relaxed a smile and said 'I've never seen any boy before come here for his loved one.' I didn't react much. Mathew sat with his mouth wide open for a moment, then he mouthed 'when did that happen?'. Spark asked 'What do you seek again?'

- 'The sword sir. Your sword, it is the immortal weapon which is needed. And sir . . . someday it has to come into SJ's . . . . I mean Salvatore's hands.'

- 'Yes I know that, but what is the need of it now? I didn't get any information about Cyrus harming anyone. I don't think he has found all his parts yet. And the sword, it's the most powerful sword which exists on earth but its power is reducing. I personally want the black smith to get it because it had to be remade, but I do understand you son.'

- 'Sir, indeed he has. He tried killing my father last week, by God's grace I saved him . . . I mean Salvatore saved him.'

- 'Come to me with your loved one, Jared'

- 'Jake.'

- 'Whoever you are, you should be grateful I am wasting my nap time for you. Now go, and come with the chosen one. I want to see the girl myself.'

- 'But sir . . . I want it to be a surprise.' I didn't know whether a man like him would ever understand what I was trying to tell because it had meanings in a romantic sort of way.

- 'Surprise!? You are a charming young man. But I cannot give you the sword; the sword must be first touched by the chosen one.'
- 'Sir, please understand. I need the sword by Sunday.'
- 'Why Sunday?' Yeah he was a good old guy who understood my reason when I explained. Mathew's jaw was still down and he hadn't closed his mouth.
- 'Well then . . . . I shall want a favour in return.'
- 'I will do anything sir.'
- 'Seems like you have great love for her.' I blushed.
- 'Yes sir . . . I love her with all my heart.' I wasn't ashamed to tell the truth.
- 'I heard the girl's really wise.'
- 'Yes of course. She is wise.'
- 'I need you to pour this into the river Rapplyn, tonight. A faint glow will appear it can be seen only by a person with perfect vision. When it appears say "the perfect one's found". That's all.'

He handed me a small vial of blue liquid, and then he pulled out the sword. It was wrapped in a velvet cloth. He said 'The power works only when it is touched first by the chosen one. Make sure no one touches it but her, now be gone.' I thanked him and strutted out of the castle.

Oh don't make me explain what happened when we got to school. We got caught red handed. And everyone was mad at me and not Mathew. That clever dude slipped off into the crowd. Yeah to be frank I got my butt busted. Nothing really mattered, they can't put me off school but I apparently had to clean up toilets after school. While I was scrubbing the floor in the men's room, someone opened the door and came in. I turned to see SJ in a pair of plastic gloves. She said 'I think you need a helping hand.' I stood up and said 'No SJ, don't do that.' But before I could say anything she said 'Why do things the hard way, Martin?' She stood at one place and moved the mop, the brushes and everything else. She said 'Work can be done the easy way.' Within seconds the whole washroom was clean and shiny. I said 'Thanks.' She said 'you could've done it yourself, tough guy.' She punched my shoulder.

When we came out of school campus, Chad was waiting for us in the parking lot. I knew he was really mad at me. 'I'm sorry' I said as I climbed into the car. We had a long drive back home. I held her hand the whole time and she didn't seem to notice. She said 'I had a dream last night.' She had told me what Chad had told me, about Mr Spark and sword and stuff. She said 'I have to get that sword.'

- 'Don't worry, we'll get it.' I said. The sword was inside my jacket. I felt the soft cloth on my skin. I had to hide it. She just kept quiet after that.

Chad had a permanent scowl on his face. I bet he was so freaking mad at me. After we dropped SJ, I hopped on the front seat next to Chad and apologized. I told him what had happened and nothing was his fault. And, Chad isn't a hard nut to crack. He melts like butter. So anyway he accepted my apology.

When I got back home my mom and dad stood at the front porch with their arms crossed. Oh darn, I just got myself into trouble. I sat calmly and explained how I'd done everything just for SJ and my parents softened. My mom ruffled my hair and said 'Don't ever do that again. If you want anything, just come to us and we shall grant your wish.' My dad nodded, agreeing to my mother's statement.

I went upstairs to my room. I reflected on the conversation I had with Sillvius Spark. I was glad he understood the modern mind of teenage boys. I wonder how old he is, maybe a hundred plus.

I pulled out the potion he had given me and thought of the favour I needed to do.

My mother entered the room and handed me a box. I asked 'What is it?' My mother smiled and said 'Give it to SJ, and look up to the sky tomorrow night. I and Kelly have put something up. Good luck, son.'

Sara Jane
Salvatore

Chapter 16

Candles float in the backyard

'Hi!' Katy exclaimed when she saw her sister and her fiancé. Her going—to—be sister's husband was an anaesthetist and her sister was a teacher in med—school. The whole Robinson family was here and I felt awkward there. But Katy had her fingers laced into mine so I had no choice but to stand there, and pulling away would be mean. I looked at Jake and Luke standing by the corner, Jake mouthed 'enjoy!'. I grinned at him and turned. When Alexis saw me she was stunned. She said 'Sara Jane Salvatore?' I nodded. 'Just SJ' She said 'You've grown so much.' Here it comes again.

- 'Yeah, I couldn't help it.' She hugged me and then turned to her family. Finally Katy unlaced her hand from mine and I ran over to the corner to accompany the boys. Luke said 'So, did you have fun talking?'
- 'We hardly talked. 'I muttered. Jake wasn't . . . well . . . wasn't really paying much attention to

me since yesterday evening and I've been upset about that for some reason. I know he didn't do it in purpose but I just felt that way. Katy turned and called Luke over so he left muttering something. So that left me and Jake alone. I didn't want to start a conversation, let him begin with something. I scratched the scar in my arm. I know it is Jake. I've had my visions, but the future can change. I doubted whether he had got his scar yet. Maybe he didn't, I thought. But yet I couldn't satisfy myself.

He didn't say anything but when all of them came our way, Jake put his arm around me and pulled me closer. I just looked at him but he denied meeting my eyes. He was just doing it to avoid conversation, I told myself.

After we reached Katy's house, all of them were having a blast already. I raced down to the chocolate shop and bought the chocolates. When I was coming outside I saw Luke with the cakes in his hand. Jake was beside him with flowers. I came out with dozens of boxes in my hand. Jake saw me and smiled. And that moment I was happy to know he noticed. He said 'Give me that, I'll take it.' I gave him the boxes and took the flowers. They were a huge bundle. It weighed so much I was almost going to drop it when he gave them to me.

I zoomed through the separate bunches, sunflowers, tulips, lots of roses, lilies, daffodils, and when I spotted the white orchids I froze. I didn't tell Jake to get the white orchids. They were so beautiful and so unique among the whole bunch. Jake asked 'Are you alright?'I tried saying something 'Uh . . . just . . . . flower . . . nothing, I'm fine.' He looked at the orchids and smiled. I just followed them to Katy's place.

Planning the party was pretty nice. We could've got professionals and other servants to do the work but when you do it yourself, it just feels better. And I had the catering business lagging in the back of my mind.

I came out of the washroom with my bathrobe on and I found mom, Aunt Leah and Cody sitting on my bed sharing a laugh. I asked 'What are you guys doing here?' My mom smiled and said 'To give you a makeover. Go check out your sister, she looks like an angel.' Cody tossed his hair and said 'Oh I'm not here for that. I don't give people makeovers, I'm the critic.' I rolled my eyes and said 'Oh c'mon not again. The last time you gave me a makeover everybody . . . .' I came to the sinking realization that everybody told me I was pretty. My Aunt smiled and said 'I guess your mom finally left me and got two little angels to torture.'

- 'Oh you are so right Coach . . . . I mean Aunt Leah.' I said.

'You two, will you stop it! I will give her a makeover and all of you will be as stunned as you were when they saw you in the charity ball.' My mom said. I took out the white sundress and put it on. My mom gave me shoes. Fortunately she couldn't do anything to my hair. I bet she put on some make-up, or whatever it was. I think you call that eye shadow. My mom said 'I just gave you a slight touch of make-up. Don't worry, it's not too much.' I rolled my eyes.

After she was done I looked at myself in the mirror, and to be true I had to admit I did look stunning. And this time the reaction was not so different. Sam was the first to spot me. When he saw me he froze. I mean literally froze. He just stood there blinking with no motion.

'Are you alive?' I asked. He exhaled and gasped for air. He rubbed his eyes and just walked with no comment. I had to admit Suzie looked really beautiful. She looked at me and smiled. I smiled back at her and said 'You look like an angel.' She thanked me and walked by. I went downstairs. After Cody fixed himself, which took around an hour, we left to the Robinson's next door as a family.

By the time I got there the place was packed. I thought we would be first because her house was right next to mine. Loads of people were there. I looked around the decorations I put up. You see, this was supposed to be a surprise party but Katy can't keep her mouth shut.

I couldn't find my friends at all. Someone patted my shoulder and I turned. It was Mr Martin. I smiled. 'There, at that last table.' He said. 'How did you know

I was . . . ?' I began. He smiled and said 'Even if I'm not listening thoughts pop into my head.' I walked over to the last table. When I stood there the four of them—Robin, Alexis, Katy and Luke, were shocked. 'Not again.' I said. Alexis said 'you look . . . . amazing.' I thanked her. Her fiancé's name was Robin Flitch and he was a pretty cool guy. I sat down and asked 'Where's Jake?' Luke said 'He's gone to get a drink.'

While we had a chat, Jake was approaching the table. When he saw me he said something like this 'you . . . . uh . . . buh . . . huh.' I smiled and said 'Hey, tough guy.' Instead of calling me smarty pants he gulped. He stood looking at me for so long I began feeling awkward. 'Jake, sit down.' Luke said. Finally he took a seat between me and Luke. Jake dragged his chair next to me and whispered 'You look even prettier than I'd imagined in this dress.' I could feel his breath on my neck. He tucked a strand of my hair behind my ear.

I don't know why Jake gave a dimple smile after that, either I was blushing or he thought of something funny but I'm guessing the first one. He leaned over to Luke and whispered something. Luke patted his shoulder and said 'Just relax.' The whole night went pretty well. I had loads of fun and for the second time in my life I danced. Sam came up to me and said 'You aren't such a bad dancer.'

Jake didn't concentrate on anything much. He was nervous about something, I don't know what it is but

I knew he was nervous. Alley pulled Cody and brought him to Jake. She said 'This suit you see, I designed. How is it?' Cody looked at it. He told Jake to stand up and he went around him thinking hard. Then he smiled and said 'Yes, I will be your model. So when's the next show?'

Alley blinked in disbelief. 'You really will?' She asked to reassure. Cody nodded. She jumped around up and down; she ran to Sam and kissed him. I smiled at Cody, he winked back at me.

While I was making sure everyone got their dinner and all that stuff Jake came to me and asked 'Hey, can you come with me?'

- 'Where?'
- 'Well . . . some place you've never been to.' I nodded. He smiled and said 'Um . . . . hop into my ride.' He led me out of the Robinson's house and we sat in Alley's new porche. While he drove I asked 'Can you tell me where you're taking me?' He smiled and said 'Just wait for it.' I just kept quiet and waited for whatever he was going to show me. I looked at my arm and I realized the scar was fading. I didn't know why, but I really didn't want to ask.

When the car finally stopped Jake opened the door for me. He said 'Welcome to my world.' He held his hand out and I took it. He led me to a big gate. The security opened the doors and I almost felt like I saw paradise.

The lawn was so big and so beautiful, flowers lined by the path which led into a beautiful house which stood in the middle. What I was seeing was the true meaning of art and design. It was way better than my house . . . so indescribably amazing. He said 'Well, this is the best dad could do.' He walked me through the whole house and he kept apologising to me when we got to his room. I loved the house. It smelled of fresh roses. Every table had flowers, everything around was scented with musk just like in my house, everything around was just perfectly set. I asked 'Do your parents really let you have a flat screen in the washroom?' He shrugged with no reply. When we'd seen the whole house, he said 'Um . . . this one will surprise you.' He opened the back door and I saw the most beautiful backyard anyone could've ever seen. 'This is so . . .' I stammered. There were no words to describe, it looked so . . . indescribable, and it surely did have the X-Factor. He squeezed my hand and said 'Not prettier than you.' I blushed again.

It was one of the most extraordinary designs I've ever see. Candles floated in the sky, brightening the yard. Many beautiful flowers also floated around, even if I wasn't a big fan of flowers I liked the way they were. They were sparkling and shiny they looked more like stars than flowers. The moon gave it an extra beauty effect.

Jake looked at me and said 'You've ever tried flying without burning?' I was confused. I was always lit up on fire when I flew. I asked 'Is that even possible?' He said

'Watch this.' He put his arms around me and magically both of us lifted in the sky. I felt some kind of force beneath my feet push me towards the sky. When he let go of me I began to float. Looking down at the backyard, it looked like I had a glimpse of paradise. I said 'This is wonderful. Your mom is a very talented lady.'

He said 'You know I always like to do stuff different and special but some kind of stuff we just have to do it the way Romeo and Juliet did it.' My jaw fell open. Then he said the words I had been waiting for since I had my vision. He knelt down in one knee (and it was kind of awkward because we were floating in mid-air) and pulled out white orchids. He said 'It's me; we are destined to be together. So, Ms. Sara Jane Salvatore will you be mine forever?' I was too shocked to react. It was practically the best moment of my life. You know people say that they have this moment when they hear the church bells ringing and the world around swirling, it was something like that, only I had butterflies in my stomach. Then I realized he was nervous too, sweat trickled down his forehead, and he flashed a smile that he usually gave when he was nervous. I said 'Get up Jake.' He was shocked. He gulped and stood up, I mean floated straight. He asked 'What . . . ?' But I didn't let him finish. I said 'you have no idea how long it took for you to ask me. At least you could've assured it was you.' He blinked and asked 'Is that a yes or no?' I smiled and said 'That's a yes silly.' He smiled with relief. He hugged me so hard I felt like I would dissolve into his arms. And then he bought me down. He motioned me to sit on the chair. He took out a box and said 'I got you a gift.'

- 'Oh come on Jake, you've already done so much.'
- 'This one's from mom and dad.' Before I could protest he pulled out a platinum necklace which had a diamond on it. He put it on me. I just stared at it for a long while. He pulled a chair close to me and sat down. 'It's my mom's, my dad's mum gave it to her.' I touched his face and asked 'Did you do all of this just for me?' He nodded.
- 'Do you love me that much?'

He took my hand and kept it on his chest. I felt his heart beating.

- 'I would do anything for you.' He pulled me into his arms. His body radiated some kind of warmth which felt nice because I was wearing a dress on a cold night, without a jacket. I said 'You know, for some odd reason I always feel safe and secure when you're with me.' He blushed and said 'I'm your protector, that's the way you are supposed to feel.'
- 'Can we go on a date tomorrow?' He asked.
- 'Jake, you see I can't . . .' It was too fast. I mean I would love to but not this early. 'I . . . Maybe

after two days. I just need space to breathe.' He nodded and said 'I understand.' We spent a lot of time chatting and the weirdest part was when he mentioned the fact that we'd have three kids and stuff, and he said their names. I bet I was blushing so much he couldn't avoid but mention 'You look so pretty when you do that.' He blushed too. After a while when he opened the back door to get back home both of us froze. Outside stood Sam, Alley, Mr and Mrs Martin, mom, dad, Cody, Jake's aunt Jess, Aunt Leah, Alex and Su. I shrunk behind Jake and he was big enough to cover me. Alley said 'Aww . . . they look so cute together.' I don't know who blushed more me or Jake.

My mom smiled at me. So did Mrs Martin. But what I noticed was some kind of conversation passed through Mr Martin and Jake. Jake smiled at his dad like they'd just shared a private joke.

My dad said 'I think we're running late, you've got school tomorrow' looking at his watch. After the crowd was clear, we finally got an "alone time" to say goodnight. He held my hand and kissed it. He said 'Goodnight, I'll see you at school tomorrow.' Even if I couldn't see her but I felt Alley's presence, maybe she was waiting to see if her brother kissed me on the front porch. But I knew very well that neither of us had the guts. I said 'I'm sorry about the date thing. Let's just be single for two days, we won't get that opportunity back. You are going to be stuck with me forever.' He thought about that and then nodded. 'That's actually a pretty good idea.'

I went back home and got into my PJ's, and the minute my head hit the pillow, I fell asleep.

Chapter 17

Jake fights with Nick

I woke up to the noise of the television. There was no one in the house. It was dead silent and very cold. It wasn't normal when it was this cold during October. I searched all over my extremely large house, but still no sense of presence. I even came out of my house but yet there was no one around. The whole neighbourhood was so quiet. I knocked on Katy's door. No one responded. I pushed the door slightly and the door flung open. That's when I realized there was no one in her house too. Where was everyone? Why have they left me behind? I had almost begun to panic, when I spotted a headless guy on a couch. Yes, I recognized him. It was Cyrus; this was the second time I got a dream from him. His cold and evil voice said 'So Ms. Salvatore, you think you and that little brat Martin can get away and lead a happy life? Oh, I'm not making it easy for you.' I was too shocked to respond. The last time he just threatened me, showing me visions like I was going to lose the war against him. Now he was talking to me, directly. I shivered. He said 'I know you can hear as well as see me Jane.'

- 'Cyrus!' I gasped.
- 'So you know my name?' He said with mocking laughter.
- 'How do you know my name?'
- 'Because you are my enemy. You and that filthy Martin are the chosen ones this century. Of course I'll do my homework before I attend the test. You still didn't answer my question. Do you really think Martin and you are gonna live happily?'
- 'I and Jake will live happily after we destroy you and throw you back outer space, this time another galaxy.'
- 'You young lady, have a lot of courage.' He said that like it was unhappy news.
- 'I am my father's daughter, if you are braver, why don't you show me your face?'
- 'How can I? I don't have my face with me; it is probably in another planet.'
- 'How do you do this?'
- 'How do I do what?'
- 'Connect to me in my dreams?'
- 'You think this is your dream? This is my mind reaching you.'
- 'Why are you showing me all this?'

- 'Because I want you to back out from the fight now.'
- 'What makes you think I would do that?'
- Um . . . you're still a child, it'd be good for both you and I if we could combine forces. I'll give you half the share, it's a massive deal, and you can think about it, take your time.'
- 'I don't need any time, even if you ask me now or tomorrow or whenever, the answer is NO.'
- 'Well, then, I pity you. Losing all you have at such a tender age. Oh SJ, remember, there will be loss, betrayal, anxiety and abandonment. You will be late to save what matters the most but only to you.' He vanished within a second. What did the words mean?

I woke up with so much confusion.

When I reached for my locker, I heard Jake say 'I didn't give it to her, she couldn't digest everything she saw, and it'll be my next surprise.' Luke's eyes widened when he spotted me. He waved. I smiled. Jake turned and I knew he didn't want to tell me what it was with the look on his face. He said 'Hey, smarty pants.'

- 'Morning, tough guy.' I replied. In a way I was really glad he still hadn't changed from his annoying self.

I told Jake and Luke about my mysterious dream and how Cyrus had actually spoken to me and how it wasn't him appearing in my dreams and it's his mind and thoughts connecting to mine. And both the boys looked as confused as I was. 'Maybe we can talk to Trish, Billy and Harry about this.' Jake insisted.

Suddenly I heard a cold voice say 'Are you Jake Martin?' Jake turned to reveal a girl with curly blonde hair and deep sky blue eyes. I had a really bad feeling about her, for some odd reason.

'Yeah,' Jake said. The red lipstick she wore stretched like elastic over her pale face when she smiled. She said 'I'm Lisa Brown' and held her hand out for Jake to shake it. 'Hey' Jake said as he shook it.

'I want to join the school hockey club, guessed you could tell me who I should consult.' She said. Jake frowned and said 'Well, who told you I knew?' The girl hesitated and then said 'I saw the posters on the walls, of the big game and you were the new captain for the team, so I guessed you'd have known.'

After that night when Cyrus had used Micah to kill Jake's dad Micah wasn't doing too well. He wanted Jake to be the captain and lead the team through the league. I guess the power which was over him was too much for his body to take, he was recovering very slowly. Katy goes by his house and gives some encouraging words and tries healing him, but he's mentally ill and not physically but Katy does some acting for his satisfaction.

Jake said 'I'm sorry Miss, but I ain't in charge of the sports club and all. Here's the girl, Sara . . .'

- 'Sara Jane Salvatore, secretary of sports clubs for girls, yeah I know. Everyone knows who she is.' She said that like it was kind of a curse. 'I think you could consult Coach Elvis, you can find him in the third floor in room 105.' I said, I had no idea how I'd remembered it so easily. Before if girls came asking me stuff I'll have to shuffle through the papers to find out.

She smiled at me like it was the hardest thing for her. She leaned over to Jake and said 'I'll meet him after school.' She smiled at Jake in a flirty way. Jake stepped back and then all of a sudden smiled back at the girl. Oh, I knew what he was up to! Before I could say anything he said '2 days, muffin.' I knew he wanted to annoy me, but that didn't mean he could just hang out with another girl. I choked back my curses as he put his arm around her and walked her into class asking her whether she was new to school. I walked next to Luke who had been watching the whole scene. I cursed in French so Luke wouldn't understand. But unfortunately he said 'Okay, maybe you should curse in another language. Gosh the way you curse makes me feel guilty.' 'Sorry,' I muttered 'You know French?'

'I lived in France for two years.' He said. 'You did.' But right now I wasn't interested in his history. Katy came out of class with her text book in her hand. 'Wow, what's up with Marshmallow?' she asked. Before I could tell her, Luke said 'Don't you dare curse that girl again, and if you want to curse do it in Latin or Greek so I wouldn't understand.'

'I'm done cursing her.' I said. 'I don't know Latin or Greek.' Luke told Katy what had happened and she said 'Oh I'm so lucky to have you Luke. You're so not like Martin.' And they kind of kissed so I moved away giving them their privacy. I felt sort of like the third person. And for once I didn't have Jake by my side pestering me. Just a few hours ago, I lay in his arms in his back yard, looking at the sky, falling in love and today, here he is, putting me off. Yes, we hardly got along but this . . . . this is horrible. Before I broke into tears Luke came over and put his hand on my shoulder. 'Its okay sis, Jake will come back to his senses. The kid's just having fun playing with you.' 'But . . . . he did so much for me yesterday and today he just gone off with another girl. That's . . . . that's . . . .' I couldn't finish my sentence. I was so full of anger.

I knew he was just playing, but if it was any other girl, I wouldn't have felt bad. I hated Lisa the minute I saw her, why her?

Katy gave me a hug and said 'its okay, Jake's just toying with you, don't become his victim.' That's when I saw my perfect chance to annoy him. Nicholas Jackson, the one Jake hated form all his heart walked into class. He's not bad looking I mean he is good looking. He had wavy brown hair and sparkling golden-brown eyes that reflected everything like a mirror. Okay, maybe not as cute as Jake when he runs away from girls and as hot but yeah, he was good looking. But his looks were the least of my concerns at the moment.

When the bell rang I ran into class and sat on the desk right next to Nick. Lisa sat right in front of me next to her sat my boyfriend or destined soul mate or whatever you call it. Katy sat behind me and next to her sat Luke. Both of them were curious to see a girl fight a girl on a Monday morning. But sorry guys, I got to deal with a new guy to get my old guy.

Lisa kept holding his hand and talking to him and Jake was pretty much involved in the conversation too. When Aunt Jess, I mean Ms. Green entered the class everyone grew silent. Aunt Jess was always casually dressed and she was just so pretty even when she didn't do anything about it. She was so natural and she always had this faint glow when she smiles, and I've been having strong suspicions about her and my Uncle Cody. She wore a white blouse and jeans, not like any other teacher in school.

She called Jason Lace, one of the guys who was the best friend of the back row and slept a lot and asked him to read a poem written by Shakespeare. He read the poem so horribly I knew that moment that English just had a heart attack. You see sometimes I have these writer instincts, it's hereditary. Ms. Green just told him to go back to his place and read the poem herself. She explained what everything meant and how beautifully Shakespeare has described stuff in it and all which I totally understood.

She told all of us to summarize the poem as homework and write a report on old man William Shakespeare which wasn't going to be tough because I'd done loads of research on that guy.

Few minutes before the bell rang, Ms. Green let us off. I turned towards Nick and flashed a smile. I said 'You're Nicholas Jackson right?' He nodded, surprised why I'd asked him such a question or maybe why I even talked to him. 'SJ Salvatore, it is. You have an oddly unique style in combat, been observing you since I came from England.'

I didn't exactly understand whether that was a complement but I just smiled. I asked 'So why'd you go to England?' When I asked that question his face darkened and his smile faded. 'Well . . . .' he said 'The only other person who is blood related to me other than my brother is my Grandpa and he passed away. That's why.' I patted him on the shoulder and said 'I'm very sorry about that.' He just sighed and said 'What's up with Martin?' Even he happened to be surprised when he saw Lisa sitting on Jake's desk. I turned back to Nick, gulping down all the evil words and said 'Can we not talk about that stupid guy and the blonde?' Nick kind of chuckled and said 'If you don't want to, it's fine with me.'

I didn't exactly get why Jake hated Nick so much. There wasn't anything bad about him; I mean he was a pretty cool person to hang out with. During recess, Nick and I were talking about hanging out in Fury Cafe today, and I was sure I wanted to go, and I knew Jake will be there too, at least to keep an eye on me.

When I had agreed and Nick wandered off to his next class, Jake banged me towards the wall in his softest manner. He had literally lifted me with just one hand. He said 'You don't weigh much at all. You really need to put on some weight.' I made a face at him. Then he turned to serious mode and asked 'Do you even know what you're doing? Nick? Are you serious?'

- 'Well, muffin' I said coming back to my feet again 'If you can hang out with Lisa, why can't I hang out with Nick?' Jake hesitated.
- 'But . . . . Nick is dangerous. He could talk you into doing anything. He has the ability to convince anyone into doing anything.'
- 'I know, he's told me about it. And I happened to inherit the power from him.'
- 'Aw, unfortunately you can't use your powers over me, I'm your protector.'
- 'Sadly, I don't need to waste my powers over you.'
- 'Are you really going to hang out with that guy? I mean you're going on a date with him even before you're going on a date with me?'

- 'You're the one who started the thing with Lisa not me. And it's not a date, we're just friends.'
- 'Oh c'mon, you're the one who asked for the two days.'
- 'I thought you understood, Jake-'
- 'Well then maybe you're just very possessive and you always want attention. Lisa's a friend and I bet she's way better than you.' He shouldered his bang and walked away. I'm possessive; I mean seriously, am I? The words he said broke my heart into a million pieces. I caught up with Jake and said 'You really meant that?' He was really mad at me like it was my entire fault. 'Yes, you are being possessive.' He said. Wow, hold on a sec, he's not the only one who's got head weight. 'Think straight, don't be foolish. Do you understand that you're hurting me? Don't you understand me; you said it was too much to digest for me just this morning. Gosh, what you did for me yesterday, it was the most amazing thing. And what you just did today, that was the worst thing that ever happened to me. You suck; for once I actually thought I loved you. You're so heartless; you seriously need to make up your mind.' He stopped and looked at me and said 'Just get the hell out of my face, SJ!' I sobbed and ran back home, quitting school after lunch.

When I reached home, I ignored mom's questions and ran upstairs to my room, still sobbing. I didn't know why I was crying, I didn't know if I loved him anymore. I just felt like crying. I had my own reasons, and he's the one who started the whole thing. Why am I the one who's crying and not him? He's probably happy with Lisa, He's Jake Martin, and he has thousands of other girls as an option. But me, yeah maybe I always got the spot light, but I never wanted it. He was the first guy I fell in love with and my love already shattered.

About an hour before I went to Fury Cafe, Cody entered my room. He placed his hand on my knee and asked 'Why were you crying, hon?'

- 'I . . .' Tears flowed again.
- 'You know you can tell me anything.' I looked at him. His grey eyes were determined, and I knew he really loved me and cared for me. I sobbed and told him everything that happened back in school. He thought about it for a long time and then said 'Do you want to know how Jake feels? He's probably crying too. C'mon I'll teach how to teleport.'
- 'I'm not interested. I got to go to Fury Cafe in an hour.'
- 'So you really are going to on a date with Nick even before you go on a date with your real boyfriend, fiancé, stop me before I go beyond

that.' I punched him on the shoulder and said 'It's not a date, we're just hanging out.'

He held my hand and said 'You're denying it, but deep down you really want to know how he feels, SJ.'

I looked at him for a long time and after a state of time I actually read his mind. "C'mon SJ, come with me. I'm doing it just to help you." I nodded. He held my hand and said 'As soon as we go there, you turn me invisible.' I nodded. In a fraction of a second, before I realized, we were in Jake's room and I turned myself and Cody invisible. As usual the room was a mess and almost hundreds of potato chips and fries cover were lying here and there.

Jake sat on his bed and Luke stood beside his bed. Jake was bending his dagger with his bare hands. And Luke was shooting hoops with Jake's basketball. 'You know, to be frank bro, what you did was wrong.' Luke said tossing the ball into the basket. 'You shouldn't have been so harsh with the girl.'

'You know how much I hate Nick.' Jake said. 'And I never expected her to do that. I cleaned up toilets for her and I even flew a car into a castle and put so much work on my parents to fix the back yard, and she just always wants to be in the spot light, she just wants all attention.' Yeah, and I was the girl who gave her worthless life to save his dad. I didn't know I was that worthless. He threw the dagger at my direction and it just passed through me. I was just feeling worse, now. 'She gave her own life to save your dad.' Luke said. 'Dude, are you seriously taking her side. She's the girl who popped in town yesterday and I knew you since you were in your diapers and yet you pick her over me.' Jake yelled. 'I'm not taking sides. I'm just justifying the damn problem. Both of you are wrong in one way. You should just make up already!' That was the first time I actually saw Luke getting mad. 'You yelling at me, I thought I was your best friend.' Jake said. Luke said 'That is why I'm yellin' at you. Because you are my best friend and you're doing something wrong. I'm a true friend who's just correcting you, if you don't like it, it's not my problem.' Jake sighed. 'I'm sorry bro.' Luke sat down again and put his arm on Jake. He said 'Apologize to her. Girls are very fragile, I mean generally. And I think you should apologize.' I was just thinking how lucky Katy is, and how lucky I am to have a bro like Luke. 'Ain't apologizing to anyone, if she wants me, let her apologize to me. And anyway, I'm not even sure if I can ever face her again, she said I was heartless after everything I did for her.' Jake muttered. Luke said 'You called her possessive, first.'

I couldn't stand it anymore. I was feeling worse the more he talked.

I teleported back home, 'You just made me feel worse.' I said. Cody sat next to me and said 'I'm sorry; I didn't know it would end up like this.'

-    'It's okay; you were just trying to help.' I said putting on my sneakers. He combed my hair for me which was like a nest. My eyes were swollen from crying so hard. And yet I still wanted to cry more.

'Why are we paired up? We don't even get along with each other. Why does the fate have to ruin my life so much?' I asked. Uncle Cody just smiled and said 'That's what makes you both a perfect pair. You are just so perfectly imperfect for each other. I mean, he's tough and you're brainy. That's an odd setting but yeah, you guys look like a nice couple.'

- 'Don't make me cry again.' I said. But I knew sooner or later I'll start crying again. And I sure did.

I went to Fury Cafe and swung open the door to search for Nick. A voice behind me said 'You're Salvatore aren't you?' I turned to see a bunch of guys my age. He said 'I expected you here with that guy . . . . what's his name? Martin, what happened? He didn't show up, eh?'

I wanted to punch him that moment but I said 'I don't know who you're talking about.' I agree that wasn't intelligent but, I was so tensed I didn't know what to do. 'Oh c'mon, you were the girl dancing with him at the charity ball.' The guy said. I observed him. His jeans were so tight that even Cody wouldn't wear it. His face was full of acne, he had blonde hair and the bangs fell on his forehead covering the acne. He wore a brown jacket which smelt like ladies perfume. 'Oh him, he's a heartless fool who I do not enjoy talking about.' I said.

- 'Oops, seems like there's been a break up. Want to join my club? You're one heck of a chick and I'm one heck of a guy.' I was already frustrated enough. Did I need more nonsense? I wanted to blow an air bubble inside him and burst his body or just vaporize him. But I walked to one table and sat down. I ordered coffee. Then I heard a familiar voice say 'We'll take this seat.' It was Jake's voice. Once, my Jake's voice, who I loved so much I'll do anything for him. Jake and Lisa sat at the table right next to us. I sipped my coffee. I didn't want to start crying. Then again the freak with tight jeans came up and sat on the chair across mine. He said 'Oh my, SJ's heating up. A hot new couple sitting next table. Someone's getting mad. I'm giving you a last chance chick, you could be mine. And I won't leave you like him.'

I turned to look at Jake, who shifted uncomfortably in his seat, but he held Lisa's hand and they shared a giggle on her joke. Tight jeans freak reached across the table and took my hand. I pulled it away and stood up, 'What is your problem? I don't even know you. And you're not supposed to ask for love this way. You're supposed to feel it. It's something two people feel for each other, it makes them bond together. I've been through it once but I don't think I can fall in love ever again. And I'm not apologizing to anyone.' I slipped cash on the table and walked outside. I sat on the steps and began to cry. I hope I said that loud enough for Jake to hear it. I even heard Lisa comment 'Someone's got an angry girlfriend.'

I felt someone put their hand on my shoulder. I was hoping it would've been Jake but a different voice said 'I'm sorry I was late.' I looked up to see Nick. 'Why are you crying?' He asked. I told him about the freak inside. He said 'Come on let's go in.'

'I don't want any trouble.' I said. He nodded.

When we got in the guy said 'I see . . . Salvatore leaves Martin for Jackson. Bad choice chick, worth leaving Martin for me would've been a wise choice.' I rolled my eyes. Nick sighed and said 'Jonathan, what is your problem?' Eventually he punched the freak called Jonathan and said 'Just wait till I get home to turn you into a corpse, you jackass. And those jeans don't even fit you.' Jonathan ran away crying like a baby and his group followed, I mean his running was more in slow motion. It would've been breath taking for him but he ran so slowly. 'I'm sorry about my step brother, he's a freak. Settle down.' He made me sit on a seat. I felt Jake's temper building. I guess I just knew him too well. Jake said 'Some people just think their big heroes.' I looked at Nick. He smiled and said 'At least I'm not dumb enough leave a wonderful girl like you for someone else.' He took my hand and kissed it.

I was too shocked to respond. I knew that minute Nick just got himself into trouble. Jake got up from his chair and punched Nick so hard; he fell on the ground bleeding. It was a face punch, that tight punch on your nose when the whole world starts swirling, that kind. Jake began 'How dare you . . . ?' I didn't let him finish. 'How dare he, what, Jake? You hate me right? Then why do you care? You're the one who said I was possessive. And yeah, maybe I am but at least I'm not like you. And I'm not apologizing, to anybody. Not even to you. I guess I made that clear.' Jake just stood there staring at me. When I went over to the other side, Jake held my hand for a second. At that moment when he looked into my eyes I knew for sure that both of us were still in love. But that moment only lasted a second. He released my hand and sat on his chair muttering 'I'm sorry, Nick.' Nick just sat up wiping his blood. I bent down and healed him before anyone else saw him hurt. I said 'I'm sorry about that. It just didn't go as I planned.' Nick smiled and said 'It's okay; it's not your fault.'

Both of us walked home and he made it clear he didn't want to talk and I didn't want to talk either. As soon as I reached home I cried and cried just like I had said. I had cried so much my pillow was soaked with water and I got so sick I could hardly move. My mom told me to stay back home and she didn't push me too much asking questions because she knew I would tear up again.

The next afternoon Katy came to my house. She sat on my bed and healed me. I was so drained of energy

I couldn't heal myself. Katy just told me everything would be fine.

I felt a little better after she left. Even Luke came by and told Jake would come back to his senses, but I had lost hope. He loved another girl and they were having a good time together. And Su even told she saw them in the park today, but she didn't know she was adding fuel to the fire.

Alley and Sam were having a chat and I was kind of eavesdropping. I could see through the wall. Alley said 'The weirdest thing ever had happened yesterday.'

- 'What is it?' Sam asked stroking her hair.
- 'Jake . . . . Jake actually cried.' In one way I was so happy she'd said that.
- 'Jake, are you serious?'
- 'I'm not kidding. He just came to my room, put his head on my lap and cried and left the room.'
- 'Let's ask SJ.' I wiped the last bead of tear when they came to the room. I couldn't tell them anything, I would just cry again. Sam kept asking me, I just said 'Please don't make me tell you what happened, I'll just tear up again. Cody's updated, ask him.' When Sam went up to Cody, Alley sat next to me. She put her arm around me and said 'Your eyes are swollen, Sam told you got sick. What happened?' I just began crying again. It was too much for me to take. 'Jake . . . .' I sobbed. 'Does he still love me?' I

asked. Alley giggled and said 'Of course he loves you. Why do you doubt that?'

- 'He hates me. He loves Lisa.' I said. Then Sam came back with the whole story and tried to comfort me. That's when mom entered the room with the phone in her hand 'You have to leave to WPS, right now. Pack up kids.' I frowned and asked 'Why? It's not the weekend.' My mom said 'You got a battle to fight. Trish called; she said everyone's going to have to stay in WPS. Get well trained, and she also mentioned some news for you SJ. Sam, Alley, go get your things packed. New pair of clothes and all in bag packs.' Sam and Alley left the room. My mom sat next to me and said 'As soon as you go to school, you'll have your quest readied. If Cyrus is here, you know what you have to do. Just promise me one thing sweetie, please come back home alive.' My mom cried. I patted her shoulder and said 'I promise, I will come back home after I kick Cyrus' butt.' My mom hugged me and stroked my hair. She said 'Just remember, I love you and I'm proud of you.' 'Mom, don't worry. I'll be fine.'

I packed up a new pair of clothes and other necessary stuff. I put on a new pair of clothes and boots. I was pumped up to kick some ass.

Chapter 18

The president wished me luck

'Your dad will definitely have an eye on you.' Cody said. We were sitting on the front porch. I said 'How exactly will he do that?'

- 'Your dad is a member of the council leaders. Of course he'll keep an eye on you.'
- 'I'm going to miss you.' I said hugging him. He's been with me the whole time I went through the Jake problem, even right now.
- 'Take care, goodbye.' He said when Chad's ugly cab landed. I and Katy approached the cab. I talked Katy into sitting in between Jake and me. We flew with complete silence. 'What's happening!' Jake asked Chad. Chad sighed and said 'They got news that Cyrus's army has been roaming around. His army is forming and soon they will rise. Cyrus is growing stronger by the hour. I'm having a feeling they've signed a quest for you and SJ.'

- 'Luke and Katy, be prepared, you're coming with us.'
- 'This is threatening me in a way.' Luke said.
- 'C'mon, just a bunch of ugly beasts to battle.' Jake said.
- 'Bunch of ugly beasts with the immortal Lucifer Cyrus. Yeah, sounds fun.'
- 'Be confident guys. We're about to face a huge problem.'

'And the two most powerful creatures have broken apart. Yeah seems like Cyrus has already won war.' Katy said. 'It isn't my fault.' Jake muttered. 'Not mine either.' I said. 'Oh please don't start again.' Katy and Luke said in unison. 'Cyrus probably wanted to break you guys apart. You guys have fallen into a trap.' Katy said.

- 'How do you know?' Jake asked.
- 'Lisa . . . Lisa works for Cyrus.'
- 'What?'
- 'Leom saw a vision of SJ and Lisa in a battle. He said it was in some kind of building. He said he heard people yelling and swords clashing. He saw the mark of an eagle in her wrist.'
- 'Maybe she is, but I'm not apologizing.' 'Neither am I.' I muttered. 'He's the one who went off with a girl who works for the enemy, not me.' Jake didn't hear it but Katy did. When we landed, my stomach wasn't feeling so well.

I went to the nearest garbage can and began throwing up. And it wasn't only me; it was also Katy and Luke doing the same. Jake handed me a paper towel and said 'Maybe I'm not that heartless.' I took it from him and muttered 'Thanks.' He didn't wait for me to say anything else, he just walked away.

We had an elevator ride to Harry's office where Trish and Billy were also there. Harry said 'We signed you a quest, but it hasn't yet been approved by the council leaders. They're pretty busy trying to track down where exactly Cyrus' army is forming but no luck. So as usual quests, let's begin with, the two people to go along with you. 'That'll be us.' Katy and Luke said. They kind of said that like it was a huge burden we put on them. Trish said 'It would've been nice if your brother told us any future about the quest.' Luke's eyes widened up. He said 'Yeah, he told me something about him getting a vision we were in San Francisco. But he didn't remember anything else.'

Trish said 'Then you guys should head first to San Francisco. And Billy keep in touch with Leom, we have to get updated. And none of you are carrying any electronics are you?'

- 'Why not?' I asked.
- 'Because, Cyrus is partially still in the outer space. He could track you guys if you use anything.' I

205

pulled out my phone and gave it to Trish. She said 'A fancy phone you have.'

Harry chewed on his cigar thinking hard. Then he got a call, he picked up. Trish said 'Under any circumstances, do not travel by air. Travelling by air just brings you closer to him and please, try and stay alive. Use all the skills you've got. Good luck. The only news we've got is that it would take Cyrus a little more time to regenerate but his army is building.' Harry kept his phone down and said 'The council leaders want to meet you. Off to the main hall the four of you. And good luck.'

For the first time I actually went to the fifteenth floor in the building. When we entered their room, there were thirteen chairs arranged in a semi-circle, all of them huge and royal. The room was big; the sealing was so high that the amazing glass chandelier which hung from it would take hours to fall. The floor was marble tiles. The rest of the room was lighted with candles. There were many portraits of men and women; they all were old, fragile and wrinkled, except the portrait of the four sisters: Helen, Hermine, Hillary and Hera. Their faces were bold and beautiful and ageless.

The thirteen seats were filled. The one in the middle was filled by an old man, probably Sillvius Spark. The other seats were filled with middle aged men and women including my dad, Jake's dad, Katy's mom and Luke's mom.

Harry breathed in and said 'Here are the four who are readied to go for the quest.' Spark put on his spectacles and kind of winked at Jake. They looked at each other for a long time and some kind of understanding passed between them. All of a sudden Jake was nodding a no. Spark said 'Then now is the time.' Jake rolled his eyes and reluctantly removed his bag and pulled something covered with blue velvet. Surprisingly he drew close to me and handed me whatever it was. I took it in my hand, not daring to meet his glittering eyes and un-wrapped it to find a sword. It had a silver hilt with engravings of bronze and gold. Leather was stripped around the handle, and the sword was made of pure bronze which reflected everything clearly and in some positions it was hard to look at it.

And then something odd happened. I felt this cold feeling run down my spine and there was this pull in my gut. Suddenly I found myself floating in the air and I was radiating a blue wave of light. A blue light covered over my eyes and I was risen up in the air and then I fell down with a thud.

Everyone around looked as shocked as I was. But I knew one thing, I felt stronger. Spark coughed and said 'I have given you my power which made me survive all these years. It is great responsibility when you have control over nature's elements.' He coughed continuously he was drained of energy and said 'I will die soon. For what kept me alive I have given.'

A man I hardly knew had given all the power which he had, the power which kept him alive for all these years, to me. He trusted me enough to give his own life and yet I wasn't sure if I could even succeed to destroy the army of Cyrus.

A man in a black suit with silver stripes stood up and said 'We approve of what you demand but we want you to destroy Cyrus' army before it rises completely. The more number of people joining his crew, the stronger he gets. Cyrus won't be descending towards our planet for maybe three months or so. So we still have time before the war begins, but you have to reduce the number of people and prevent people from falling into Cyrus' traps. We need some time to think of what has to be done and the children will have to stay in the campus and train hard. There may be plenty of kids like you who have been misled. Bring as many youngsters as you can possibly get. It would help them as well as you.'

All of them were just so sure we'd win this thing, but I didn't have the confidence.

The fact that I should defeat Cyrus' army gave me the creeps, but the fact that someday I'll have to defeat Cyrus himself . . . . was a nightmare.

Old man Sillvius stood up from his chair, just a minute ago he looked so strong and powerful and in just a few seconds now he looked so week and fragile.

Before I headed out the room, my father approached me. He said 'Your mom told me about the crying, I don't want to know if you do not want to tell me. And don't worry, child. You're my daughter, you'll never fail. Just think of it as another simple test in which you want to score an A+. Be brave and use your mind. Use all the skills Ashley and Trish have thought, you are a great fighter, the power is within you. I'll try contacting you with Tom's help.'

- 'But how?' I asked with curiosity.
- 'Well mind readers can not only hear thoughts, they can put thoughts into people's minds, and they can connect one person's thought to the others. But connecting minds can be more easily done if you're sleeping. So I'll talk to you in your dreams.'
- 'You won't tell mom all the freaky fighting part will you? About the ten feet tall monsters and all, she'll break if she knows about it.'

My dad chuckled and said 'I won't tell Kelly alright. Good luck, honey.'

'Thanks, dad, I'll miss you' I said.

After we came back downstairs, all the trainees who trained in WPS were there waiting for us. For the first time I noticed that there were so many rooms in our school. I'd never noticed the dorm rooms. Each dorm had two bunk beds, which are four people in one room. Before we went to San Francisco I talked to my siblings. Suzie hugged me and said 'I know you can do it, sis.' I hugged her back and said 'I'll do everything I can.' I actually sounded more confident than I was.

Sam pulled me to one corner and said 'You are coming back alive and well. Kick some ass for me, will you?'

- 'I will bro, I will.' I said.
- 'Don't be scared, and even if you are don't show your fear. You're the leader of the quest. Just like the captain of the soccer team, it's the same job here. Defend and protect your people, help them win. If you win, you'll get the credit. But remember, this is a greater deal. There are millions of lives on the line. And just talk it out, with Jake and stay united. You can't do it without each other. Love you!' He gave me a warm hug.

All the kids around wished us good luck and many of them I didn't even know. We strutted out of school. Billy said 'So now, you guys are on your own. You got to figure a way to head to San Francisco yourselves.'

Katy came running out of the building and said 'There's a train going to Washington DC in eight minutes. It's the only train moving today. We got to get moving, fast.' The four of literally ran to the railway station not knowing why we were going to DC. And yeah, I got there in about three seconds or so. Katy, Luke and Jake came running inside the station three minutes later. They stood there panting. I said 'Guys, c'mon, we got no time to waste. Let's get moving.' We reached the platform when the doors were just about to close. We pulled Katy inside at the last second. All four of us stood there panting hard. We looked around the train. I was shocked at the fact that there was no one in the damn train. It was school time so no one really travelled a lot in this town, I thought. The four of us sunk into our seats. That's when a shocking thought struck me; I said 'Guys, we never got the tickets.'

Katy moaned something under her breath. She couldn't talk because she was breathing too hard. Luke's eyes widened, he said 'You can turn us invisible, can't you?' How come that thought never struck me? 'That's a great idea!' I said. After a few minutes of travelling, a man with a black coat and a black hat entered our coach. 'Here comes the ticket checker.' Jake mumbled. The four of us made a circle connecting each other. I focused hard, making myself disappear, that was easy, but making three other people disappear, that took a lot of effort. I felt that same feeling that I had felt the first time, the time when I had seen through the cards. Then when I opened my eyes, the man was standing there looking around, searching for us. He mumbled something like 'A minute ago, right here, and four kids, gone' and went to the next bunk. I let go of their hands breaking the circle. Jake just grinned at me. I looked away, out the window. Katy was the peace maker, she flipped open a map of the United States and said 'So here's the way we're going. So now we're on the way to Washington DC. From DC we'll go Nashville and from there we'll have to catch another train to

Oklahoma City, over there there's a train connecting to Phoenix and from Phoenix we'll take another train to LA. But unfortunately, there is no train connecting to San Francisco this week so we'll have to take a long drive.' Jake said 'Wow, hold on girl. It'll take forever if we travel like that. We don't have time Katy. We got to move faster.' 'We can't travel by air, then how can we move fast?' Luke questioned. That minute the craziest idea struck my mind, I said 'We can teleport right away to San Francisco.' Luke stared at me like I was the craziest person he'd ever seen. He said 'Teleporting all the way across the country by yourself would take up all your energy. You want to take three others with you, forget it.'

'I can do it somehow. Maybe we could take Katy's idea but one change to be made. Teleporting right away to San Francisco would take up all my energy. So first the four of us could teleport to DC and we could follow Katy's route. That would make us reach our destination faster.' I said. All of us looked at Luke like he was the one leading the quest. He said 'Why are you guys looking at me like that? I'm not leading the quest, you guys are.' Jake leaned backward and thought hard about something. He seemed to be in a very pensive mood. After a long moment of silence, Jake said 'Teleporting so much would kill her.' 'Like you care . . .' I muttered under my breath. Katy elbowed me and I asked 'Owe, why did you do that for?' Katy gave me a look which said you know why. 'Anyway, we can't let her die, I can't let her die.' Jake said. 'Aw, how sweet of you . . .' Katy said. Jake rolled his eyes and said 'I'm her protector, if she dies, I die with her. But if I die she doesn't die. We're interconnected with each other.' He said. Okay, so he hated me so much he would let me die if he wasn't my protector. Yeah, that makes me feel so great.

I looked at Jake, he also looked at me. I don't know what exactly happened but we stared at each other. I was just thinking about punching him but he's just too strong. And I know he still loves me, I just have to push him to apologize. I really didn't want the topic to come up again but Luke just had to bring it up. 'You guys are fighting for a very silly reason.' I rolled my eyes and asked 'Silly reason? If Katy leaves you for a guy who is Cyrus' minion, wouldn't you get mad?' Jake asked 'If Katy went out with your biggest enemy before she even went out with you, her real guy, wouldn't you get mad?' Katy waved her hand between us and said 'we're a happy couple, we love each other, don't try to break us apart.' Luke smiled. 'He's the one who started.' I muttered. 'I didn't make the issue serious, she did.' He said. 'Can he just stop blaming me for everything, any way I'm going towards the days of my own death, at least for these few days can't he keep his god damn mouth shut! Can we just come to conclusion and decide whether I should teleport or not?' For the first time in my life I've yelled so much at someone. I was always kind to people, I've never wanted to break their heart but Jake was getting too far.

Katy held my hand. Everyone kept quiet, even Jake. Katy and Luke kept exchanging looks for a very long time. Luke said 'I think we should teleport. It's our only option. SJ, you should get some rest, we need to keep you fully charged. By tonight we'll reach DC, from there we'll start the teleporting.' I went to the other seat leaving the three alone and dropped my weapon. I had my sword polished and my shield spiraled into a bracelet. I dumped my backpack on the floor and leaned against the window. The minute I closed my eyes, I fell into a deep trance.

In my dream I was in place which looked like some kind of historic museum which was shut down. There were tall statues of people in Greek robes and some were even in armour. They wore helmets which had skulls on it. All of them were standing in different poses, like they were fighting in a war. Whereas, the other statues in robes had sad faces—full of worry and grief. I heard a familiar voice say 'So you decided to come after my army.' I turned to see Cyrus, in his headless body. For the first time I realized he didn't have one feet and three fingers in his left hand. He wore a robe which fell on the ground and rolled half way in the floor. It was in a pale shade of cream and brown.

I said 'Yes, I have.' He laughed so loudly one of the statues cracked. He said 'Do you think you even stand a chance?' I said 'Yeah, we're skilled, we're brave and we're fighting for good.'

- 'Alas, you shall die fighting my army. Such a pity that your dying even before you have seen my true form. Even before you've met me in battle.'
- 'Oh please, I'll take down your army with you. I ain't going to die before I kick your butt.'
- 'Yeah let's see if that happens . . . no let's see if you survive long enough till I return.' He began laughing again. His laughter echoed through the marbles. When I woke up I saw an image of myself with make up on! Oh my God, I was still having a nightmare. I had mascara on with eye liner and there was this shade of light pink above my eyes and I swear I don't know what you call them. And the most shocking thing, I had lip gloss on which tasted like strawberry. I muttered 'I'm still dreaming.' That's when my vision grew clear and I saw my image in the mirror, with make up on clearly. Katy took the mirror away and said 'You look fantastic.' Oh my God, I wasn't dreaming, it's all real!

'Katy, what have you done?!' I exclaimed.

- 'What, you look really good.'
- 'You put make up on me!'
- 'Yes I did and you look great. And I was bored.' Jake walked in yawning and stretching. He turned towards me and blinked. Then he turned away. I wondered what that meant.

That night we reached Washington. There was one place I had to visit before I left here. I dragged my friends to Twenty-third Street, West Potomac Park. There was big lake in front of the memorial, which reflected the moon light in its waves. I saw my own reflection Katy by my side. She asked 'Why'd you bring us here?' I didn't have an answer. Something told me I had to bring them here. 'I just felt like I had to.' I said. She just put her arm around me and said 'Alright. Anyway, I and Luke will sort out a place to stay, so that leaves you and Jake alone.' 'No Katy, you can't leave me alone with him.' I protested. She said 'Sis, he's the safest person you can be with. Even with me or Luke you won't be safe, but with Jake you will.' I tried protested but Katy had her opinion. I couldn't protest when she said 'I want to be alone with Luke.' I sighed and let her go.

I climbed up the stairs and Jake walked reluctantly behind. The building was in the form of a Greek Doric temple. There were thirty eight Grecian columns surrounded around a statue of Mr. Abraham Lincoln seated on a ten foot high marble base. He was surrounded by engravings, inscription of the two well-known speeches by Lincoln himself. Jake leaned on the pillar and said 'I'm not going to apologize. But anyway, what is this place and who's that guy?' He was pointing at the sculpture of Mr. Lincoln sitting on his marble base. He had his hair combed and a short beard. His coat was long that it hanged down in one side. His eyes were lustrous, gleaming golden because of the lighting. I said 'This is the memorial of Abraham Lincoln, the sixteenth president of US. The building was finished in 1922 to honor the president. The architect was Henry Bacon and the sculptor; he's um . . . Daniel Chester French.' He grinned at me. 'You are a big nerd. So this is old man Abraham Lincoln. Hey dude! I've read about you. So what's up?' Maybe talking to a sculpture was weird but Jake was a weird guy so it was fine. I walked around the memorial; I was amused in a way. I've always wanted to visit here.

Suddenly I heard a huge noise. I turned to see the sculpture of Lincoln rise from his seat. Jake was awe-struck but he slowly pulled out his sword. What was going on? His big voice yelled 'Who are you?' Jake frowned and said 'I didn't know statues could move.'

- 'Who are you calling a statue? And why are you so tiny? You know I do not like trespassers in my area. And why are you pointing a toothpick at me boy?' Before Jake could say something stupid I said 'Mr. Abraham Lincoln. Please forgive us for trespassing. It's just that, you've inspired me a lot.'

The expression in his face changed. He smiled softly and said 'Oh really young lady, I bet you are a wise girl.'

- 'I've read a lot about you and many of your speeches.' I had no idea what I was telling but I just said it.
- 'You have? Then I think I should tell you something. A secret of mine.' He motioned me to come closer. I gulped and approached him. To my surprise Lincoln picked me up and made me sit on his lap. He said 'And please shoo this young man away, his presence is very annoying.' Jake looked at me for a reply. I said 'We'll meet by the lake.' He gave one look at the talking statue and climbed down the steps.

He said 'Young lady, do you know this man named Lucifer Cyrus?' I was shocked when he'd asked me. I said 'Yes . . . . sir.' His face twisted. 'He's very dangerous. I went through a lot of painful days. He killed my cousin. You see I found out something.'

- 'What is it Mr. President?'
- 'He's immortal but he can die only when his heart is stricken by a particular metal.'
- 'What metal is it?'
- 'It's very rare and very precious. It's hard to find.'
- 'Okay sir, but what is it?' I asked anxious to know the answer.
- 'Oh young lady, that is what I have forgotten. But will you do me a favor?' I was so disappointed.

- 'I will sir.'
- 'Can you kill him for me?'

I managed a smile. 'I will try, Mr. Lincoln.' He smiled and said 'I know you will. Good luck, dear.'

Chapter 19

My cousin makes a call

Jake was tossing pebbles into the lake. I sat away from him reflecting on the conversation I had with Lincoln. After a long moment of silence he asked 'What'd he say? You can tell if you want to.'

- 'Well . . . . he told me something about Cyrus . . . something that can destroy the immortal. He didn't exactly tell me what kind of metal can kill him he has forgotten that. He just wanted me to kill Cyrus for him.' I said. Jake just stared at the ripples. Katy and Luke came running. They sat down and said 'We didn't get any place to settle for the night within the budget.' I sat in silence for a while and said 'I guess I can talk someone in to lending us a hotel room for the night. I don't like doing that but we got no choice.' I stood up and the others followed.

I walked them into the Salvatore suits. When the manager saw me, he ran to me. He said 'Ma'am, what a pleasant surprise! What can we do for you?' Yeah, I guess I don't have to talk them into lending me a room. 'Give us a suit for tonight. We'll leave in the morning.' I said. The manager led us into the elevator and gave me a pass to the finest suit in the hotel. My body felt like lead, I really needed rest. I fell on the bed and told my friends 'If you guys want to eat something, you can order. And . . . um . . . don't use any technology in this room except the phone to order room service.' The minute my head hit the pillow I fell asleep.

My vision was very blurry; I could see a shadow of a man and nothing else. When it came on focus I realized it was my dad. 'How are you?' He asked. I rubbed my eyes and said 'I'm fine. We're in DC, and um . . . dad, we're staying in SS for a night, is it alright?'

- 'But you shouldn't go really high on the room service, or I'll never lend you any money.'
- 'Yeah dad. And um . . . do you have a hotel in Nashville, TN too?'
- 'Actually I never thought about that. I'll get working on one as soon as possible. But why do you ask?'
- 'Because we're going to Nashville tomorrow. And dad . . . . I kind of talked to the president.' I told my dad about Abraham Lincoln's memorial and what had happened there. 'Interesting' was

the only word my dad said. Then the connection got blurry and the scene shifted.

Everyone around was covered with grease and soot. The whole place smelt like gasoline and burning firewood. The noise of banging tools and metal scratching metal was heard. Sparks of fire blew everywhere. Then I noticed someone familiar. 'Hey sis,' He said. At first I didn't recognize him because of all the soot on his face then I realized it was Aaron, my cousin.

I said 'I'm sorry about the accusing. I never got to apologize for that. And what is this place?' He held his arm up and said 'This place is the basement of WPS. We volunteered to make weapons. It's my thing, making stuff.'

- 'You really make stuff, like weapons and all?'
- 'Yeah, why do you doubt that?'
- 'No, then you should know a lot about metals and what they're used for, right?'
- 'Yeah, of course I do.' He said.
- 'Can I trust you?' I asked. I still had a bitter feeling about my cousins.
- 'C'mon, I swear on my mom I don't work for Cyrus. If I work for him why would I be here helping them make weapons?'
- 'Alright then, can you tell me what metal possess the power to kill an immortal if it cuts through his heart?'

- 'Well . . .' Aaron was thinking hard. 'Not one kind of metal but . . . .'
- 'Could a mixture of different metals and minerals bring a weapon to kill immortals?' I asked curiously. His eyes widened.
- 'That's it. The mixture of celestial bronze with black diamond and gold could be it!'
- 'Really?!' I asked.
- 'I guess . . . . if I was right.'
- 'Then can you make me a weapon.'
- 'I'll get working on it right away.'
- 'And hey, how are you talking to me?'
- 'Oh well you see my sister Annabel, she can talk to the dead. So when you're asleep it's like dying for a while so she's helping me talk to you, you know the four of us sometimes talk to our mom.' That explained my dream. They were talking to their mom and she said that their dad will return.
- 'Oh right. Goodbye brother, and um . . . Good luck with the weapon.'
- 'Thanks sis, go kick some monster asses for me will you?'
- 'I will.' I woke up when Luke was shaking me. 'We got to teleport to Tennessee in half an hour.' He said. 'What?' I sat up and rubbed my eyes. 'Tomorrow's the eighth of November, it's a new moon tomorrow. Our powers won't work.' I shook of the sleep from my eyes and stood up.

The whole table in front of me was littered with food. 'Seriously? You guys ate so much food! My dad's gonna stop my allowance forever.' I moaned. 'On second thoughts we probably are never gonna taste food often and maybe you won't live long enough to get your allowance.' Luke said.

My stomach growled. I hadn't eaten at all. 'We got to get moving before it becomes twelve. And we got you some pizza.' Luke handed me a big plate with pizza slices.

I hogged on the pizza fast, partly because we had just a few more minutes and partly because I was dead hungry. Jake had cleaned up the table and left cash. I said 'I'll pay it. And that cash will be useful later on. We'll need it.' I dropped a note saying my dad will pay the bills and shouldered my pack. But anyway, the money will be returning to my dad. Katy shrunk her spear into a small hair clip. I felt my sword on my belt. It was so cold and it had a smell of the sea on it. 'Hey how come your weapons get to shrink?' I asked. Katy giggled and said 'Most weapon shrink.'

- 'Even mine?' I asked.
- 'Nah, your weapons are supposed to be a threat to people. They were used a lot in war. They don't shrink. Only your shield does.'

'Guys we got to get moving.' Jake said. Again we made our circle; I held Katy's hand and Luke's in the other.

Luke and Katy caught Jake's hands finishing the circle. I shut my eyes and thought of Nashville. I had never teleported before, but I just knew I could do this. The world around me spun and I no longer stood on the ground. I felt my instincts tingling and that cold feeling running down with that hard and painful tug in my gut. It was like something was pulling all my energy away, drinking my powers gradually. When I opened my eyes, the four of us stood in a highway which was dark and quite. I felt like something had sucked my organs out of my body and my body felt like lead. I could stand on my feet, and then I slowly lost balance and fell. Right before I hit the ground Luke caught me. He helped me stand up straight but I couldn't balance myself. Jake slipped his hands around me and took me off my feet.

He said 'We got to stay till the night gets over. Can you guys set a tent?' Luke's eyes widened when he mentioned tent. 'My pleasure!' He said with delight. I felt really cold but I could feel the warmth radiating from Jake. My eye lids began to feel heavy. I asked 'You don't love me, then why do you act like you care for me so much? And why are you actually helping me?' Jake froze in his tracks. He was still looking forward. His features relaxed in the moon light. Then he turned to me and said 'I was mad at you, that didn't mean I don't love you. And it's my duty; my purpose is to protect you. It just comes from within.'

'Do you really still love me and still care about me?' I asked, looking deep into his black eyes. He took a long while to think and said 'If you don't love me, why are you still wearing that necklace?'

I touched the locket, it was cold. I looked at him for a long while and he didn't shift his gaze either. 'I just think I need an apology. That's it. It has nothing to do with what I feel about you.' I answered. I clutched his coat and my eyes began shutting without my will. I fell into a light sleep, I could still hear voices of the three of them talk, but couldn't make out the words. When I woke up I realized I was still in Jake's arms, my fingers still grabbing his jacket. He had a stick in his hand, poking the fire. I was shivering, it was so cold. Rain poured outside and lightning stroke followed by booming thunder. Luke and Katy were wrapped in a blanket closed to each other to keep warmth. Jake said 'You guys can sleep, I'll keep first watch.' The others didn't have any objection. As soon as their heads hit the ground they fell asleep, tucked in that cozy blanket, hugging for warmth, they looked so beautiful together like they were meant to be that way.

I took my head off Jake's lap, he un-looped his arm which was around me. His breath came out like steam. He said 'You should get more sleep.' I tried to sit up straight but my body wouldn't move. 'You should sleep too, I've slept enough.' I said. My voice came out small, my throat felt dry. He nodded and said 'Go to sleep, you need it more than me.'

I finally balanced myself to sit; we were in a tent with fire inside. That was kind of weird but I guess only mortal fire can you know burn stuff used by regular mortals. I took a deep breath, I was shivering so much and eventually my teeth started chattering. Jake brought out a blanket from his backpack and said 'Put it around yourself, you'll be warm.' Why was he being so good to me all of a sudden? He was shivering too. I said 'I think you . . . could . . . . use that, it's . . . . yours . . . anyway.' To my surprise he took my hand. He said 'Come closer to the fire, it'll make you warm.' I drew closer to the hot, blazing camp fire. The fire didn't warm me up too much. I was still shivering. That's when tough guy did something so surprising; he pulled me into his arms and tucked the blanket over both of us. The warmth radiating from him made me feel better. Both of us stopped shivering.

'Jake . . .' I said. I could hear his heart beating. 'Huh?' He asked. 'I asked you something and I never got a reply. Do you still love me?' He kept his gaze fixed on the fire. I could see the flames dancing in his dark eyes. 'I . . .' He began but something held him back from saying anything. 'You still protect me like you care about me.'

- 'That's my job; I'm destined to do it. Its fate, like my scar's back on my arm. Everything is fate, whatever happens. I just know when you need protection and I know when you're in danger. It's all fate.' He said.
- 'So fate is only the reason you loved me, right?'

He hesitated. Then he said 'No, to be honest. I still love you. Look. . . . I know I was such a jerk with you but . . . .' Something unbelievable happened. He was tearing up. 'Deep inside I . . . . I still love you, SJ. I'm . . . . sorry. I'll regret breaking your heart, I regret it right now. And Lisa . . . she wasn't even close to how wonderful you are.' I wiped his tears. He took my hand and placed in on his chest. I felt his heart beating really hard. 'I swear on my own life, I will . . . never hurt you ever again my life. I love you; it's up to you now.' He looked away. I was so awe struck I couldn't react. Did he just apologize to me? Nah, I'm still dreaming. I leaned back on him; he ran his fingers through my hair. I said 'Jake, you love me so much. I'm so gifted to have a guy like you by my side. Its okay, even I did some mistakes. I'm really sorry about that. I never meant to do it. It was just for fun . . . until you got mad at me. And . . .' Jake drew closer to me and said 'and . . . . ? C'mon spit the words out.' I took a deep breath and closed my eyes. I said the words for the first time, and I was never sure about anything this much ever before. I meant it with all my heart 'I love you, Jake.'

Suddenly I heard a familiar voice say 'Guys, you mind letting me in, I got a surprise for you.' I realized who it was, 'Cody?' I said. 'Yeah, it's me, sorry to disturb but someone was pestering me to come visit you.' I zipped open the tent to see Cody with an umbrella. He said 'Surprise, surprise!' He moved to reveal a little girl with dark black hair just like Jake's and grey eyes. 'Oh, I totally forgot. I kept my burger in the microwave, I'll be right back.' Cody said. Within a few seconds he vanished. I brought the girl inside, sheltering her from the rain. We already had enough problems, now we were gifted with a kid to take care of, how wonderful!

I asked 'Who are you?' The kid smiled and said 'You don't know me do you?'

- 'Sadly yes. Who are you?'
- 'I'm Alice, don't you recognize me?' I nodded a no.
- 'I don't know any Alice.'
- 'Well, I am Alice'

Jake stared at her in awe. 'Who exactly are you? Why do you resemble SJ?'

'I'm from the future. I am Alice Martin. Eight years of age, the daughter of Mr. Jacob Martin and Mrs. Sara Jane Martin.' Wow, was I dreaming, or was I really looking at my own kid? 'Huh?' Jake looked at me for an answer. I was as surprised as him. 'You're so young.' The girl, I mean Alice, my girl said. 'I just wanted to wish you luck. Mom and dad, I mean you guys always tell us tales of this quest. You guys don't have regrets.' I asked 'So we achieve this quest?' She shook her head 'Maybe, maybe not. I'm not here to deliver news; I'm just here to wish you luck. I know you can do it, my mom and dad rock.' Jake was still awe struck. Then he cleared his throat and asked 'Can you tell me one thing, does Alex marry

Su?' I looked at him in a weird way. Alice smiled and said 'Oh, Uncle Alex just had his wedding with Aunt Su a few months ago.' Her eyes had a familiar twinkle which I realized as mine.

- 'How lucky, my brother and cute little angel.' He muttered. I stared at him. 'It's not like your less pretty or anything. Your sister is a kid; she's cute in the kiddy way alright.' He reasoned. I smiled. 'Oh I got to go. We've got the anniversary party in a few hours. Mom and dad are gonna love the surprise.' She said. Then she realized what she said and muttered 'And I just ruined the surprise.'

I patted her and said 'It'll be our little secret, don't worry, your brothers won't know.' 'You know Ryan and Noah; I thought they don't time travel?' Then a flickering image of Cody appeared. 'You've got to go child.' He lifted her into his arms. 'Good luck!' He said and winked at Jake. Then Alice's eyes widened as she peered at something behind I and Jake. She said 'Leo and Lizzy were right; Mrs. McQueen did have long hair even when she was young.' Then they're image flickered to a faint glow and vanished. 'Who are Leo and Lizzy? And why was she talking about Luke's mom?' I rolled my eyes and said 'She means Mrs. Katarina McQueen, and her children Leo and Lizzy McQueen.'

- 'Oh yeah.' Jake said. The rain had slowed down to drizzle. He hugged me and said 'Well, our kid's beautiful.' 'Looks like someone's made up!'I heard Katy's voice say. We turned to see Katy sit up straight and Luke was still snoring. 'Aw, I missed it!' She exclaimed.

Chapter 20

I run into the undead

'We were in a cafe, in Oklahoma City.' Luke said. It was five in the morning and Luke woke all of us up by murmuring something from his dreams. All four of us have begun getting dreams. Our destiny was getting closer. He was sweating, he seemed terrified. 'Cyrus' army doesn't only have humans; it also has some monsters; deadly ones, ten feet tall, filthy, ugly, beefy and freaky.' 'How many monsters did you see?' Jake asked. He was the only one who hadn't freaked out by the whole monster thing. 'A few dozens of ugly looking beasts, I reckon.' Luke said. Katy gulped. 'Okay, pack up; we've got to start moving to Oklahoma City. Luke, unfold the tent. Katy, a few kilometres away, there is a convenience store, get us some food and supplies, will you? I and SJ got some business to clear off.' Jake said that like we'd already planned.

I looked at him for answers, but he took my hand and pulled me out of the tent. 'You don't mind running a few miles, do you?' He asked. 'I love running, I'm ready. But where exactly are we going?' I asked. 'I'll explain later.' He began running and I reluctantly followed. We ran past the convenience store. A few metres away a man in camouflage pants and a hard leather coat stopped his motor bike and walked into the convenience store. Jake said 'I hate stealing, but I'm getting tired.' 'Jake are you out of your senses? You can't steal that man's bike!' I said. He pulled me towards the bike. He wouldn't listen. We boarded into our new vehicle and flew in high speed. 'You know how to drive motorcycle, a car, what else?' I asked. 'Well, I know how to drive almost anything. Except a plane, I should try driving my dad's private jet.' He joked. He was only fourteen and he drives. That still surprises me. 'Can I drive?' I asked. Was I out of my senses? Oh no, being with him made me lose my mind too. He chuckled at my request and said 'No way in hell.'

We got into the city after two hours or so. He kept driving till we reached a tiny street which wasn't big enough for the bike to go through. So I and Jake walked into the street. There was this big metal door; above it hung a board which read 'RSS recording studio' in big bold letters. 'Was it a dream?' I guessed. He nodded. 'What's in there?' 'I don't know! All I know is that there is something in there which awaits us.' He said.

He flung open the door. It was dark inside. I asked 'Can you find the lights please; I think I pushed something down.' I said. Jake switched on his flash light. There was a big circuit board and Jake was rattling with it. 'You can fix that thing?' I asked. He pulled out something and the whole building lit up. 'Alex has some influence on me.' Jake said. Then I looked under my feet to see a big head of a deer. I pushed back, 'That's not real.' I told myself. Jake laughed. The whole place was empty; dirt covered it, grease and soot everywhere. A soft voice whispered 'Walls, carvings, right.' The voice was so familiar. I know who it is . . . . my mind told me the answer but I couldn't grab the memory. I turned to my right and wiped the dust of the wall. 'Latin' Jake said. 'It's Latin.' He came closer and touched the carvings on the wall. It was too faded to read. But Jake translated 'Beneath the golden flower.' 'Upstairs, Jane.' The same voice whispered. Then it hit, the only person who called me JANE, 'Nancy!' I called. 'What?' Jake asked. I looked around, she was dead, how did she . . . ? There were so many questions in my mind. A faint image of a girl with blonde hair and golden eyes appeared in front of me. She was pale, it was so surreal. 'Hello Jane.' She said. 'How did you . . . I thought you were . . .' She didn't let me finish. 'Dead . . . Yes I am. Who's he?' She asked. 'Jake, my . . .' I began 'Boyfriend.' Jake finished. 'You are?'

- 'Nancy Quinton.'
- 'Are you real?' I asked.
- 'Yes, I just wanted to help. I found you, so confused; thoughts are having a traffic jam in your mind. You know too much, too much for

your mind to take. You have answers to your questions, but your mind is not organized. I have to leave, good luck.'

'Nancy, you can't go, I've got millions of questions to ask you.' But her image faltered and vanished into thin air. I climbed up the stairs as Jake followed. We climbed a million fleets of stairs. When we reached the first floor, there was a strong smell of sulphur. The place was broken down and had huge craters in the middle. There was a broken chandelier hanging from above, flickering. It was the only source of light to the whole floor. Jake pointed towards the south and said 'I think I saw this place in my dream. We got to cross the passage.' There was a very thin passage which looked old and fragile. But the sharp tipped spikes on either side of the walls were still deadly. I gulped. 'Do we have to do this?' I asked. Jake was as tensed as I was. He nodded. 'I guess we have no choice.' Jake counted till three and we ran through the passage like idiots crossing the road when the cars where driving at high speed. I shut my eyes, I didn't know what I was doing, all I did was catch Jake's hand and run for dear life. When we reached the other side, I opened my eyes to see both of us were unharmed. 'How did we do that?' Jake nodded his head and said 'I have no freaking idea.' We flung open the door. It was a dark room with absolutely no lights. Jake lifted his flash light. I kept my hand on one wall, panting. I felt something hard, like metal. I said 'Can you show the light my way?' I asked. Jake lit up the light and I saw something which would be the most useful thing. 'Armours, what is this place?' He showed the ray of silver light around the room and we found many armours lying here and there like someone had just thrown them here, just dumped them and walked away. 'I never knew a recording studio had armours.' Jake muttered. 'Okay, we'll grab four and leave the place.' I and Jake strapped ourselves in our armour and took two for Katy and Luke.

'But what does that have to relate to beneath the golden flower?' Jake asked. I shrugged, 'We'll figure it out later. Right now, we got another deadly run to make.' I looked back. I held out my hand and Jake caught it. 'Let's do this.' Jake said. We ran, just like the way we did before, but this time my eyes were wide open. Just a few steps before we reached the other side, a sharp spike injected itself right through my leg. My ankle twisted and I fell. But before I could digest the thought and start feeling the pain, Jake didn't only carry the armours, he also had me in his arms. When we reached the other side I felt the pain. It was burning, blood flowed in rivers. I couldn't look. It took me too much of my guts to look at my blood than fight monsters.

When I looked at the red liquid pouring out my heel I felt a different feeling, a feeling completely foreign to me, something that involved fright.

Suddenly a big chunk of rock fell just a few millimetres away from us. I looked at Jake. 'Oh holy crap!' he said. Jake was strong and fast even if he didn't have his powers. He swept me off my feet and he ran out the building and into the tiny street which smelt like drainage. The whole building came crumbling down, only if Jake wasn't fast enough both of us would've died. 'Thank you.' I said. I didn't really know what to say, he saved my life. I know it was kind of idiotic but I just couldn't think of anything else to say. Jake chuckled and said 'My pleasure, smarty pants. Now, we got to get you to a hospital.'

'It's just a sprain, you'll be fine if you take rest for a while and um . . . you kids still don't want to tell me how you got hurt.' The doctor said. 'Can we not talk about that, sir? Thank you very much for fixing my leg.' I said. He handed over some medicines and told me I'd have to apply it every day. I threw it away when we were getting back from the hospital. I'll heal tomorrow. I don't need the medicines. On the way back we dropped the bike back in the convenience store. I was moving with my crutches slowly and Jake was far ahead of me. Then he finally stopped for me to catch up with him. When we reached, Luke had already put down the tent. Katy had our bags packed.

'How are we getting to Oklahoma City?' Katy asked. 'We had food, I think you guys should have some. I'm taking that one.' She grabbed a breastplate from Luke's hand and put it on. After so many months, I was back in my armour and I know how to put on my stuff even better than anyone in the whole world. I helped Luke and Katy put on their armours. 'I guess we have to ride back into the city.' Jake said. 'I hate stealing.' I muttered. 'Me too, but do we look like we have another choice.' Jake agreed. But eventually we got a BMW and were racing into the city at twenty five miles an hour, but to our surprise the cops couldn't find us. The car could've gone faster. 'I got burger.' Katy handed me two plastic boxes. Jake wasn't interested in the food, but I was hungry . . . . and equally tired . . . . and pissed off with my broken leg. I held the burger so Jake could munch on it every few seconds. His hands were tight around the steering wheel, his black, olive eyes on the road, reflecting everything we saw ahead. His hair was uncombed and shabby. And my hair . . . . oh, it was a bird's nest.

It was twilight when we actually neared the city. Luke and Katy were asleep in the back seat. Jake strained his eyes to remain open. 'You really need sleep.' I said. He yawned and said 'We'll stop by at the inn, just a little while further. How much money do we have left?' I reached in my pocket to find only a fifty dollar bill. 'I've got fifty.' 'I've also got fifty bucks. Katy's got twenty, Luke's got thirty. We'll sort out something from that.' Jake said.

- 'How did you know about the inn and the convenience store back in Nashville?' I asked.
- 'The convenience store, I saw in my dream. The inn is right here.' He replied, pointing at a screen. It was a map. Yeah, I'm a total idiot.
- 'Right.' I said. 'I love you.' I heard Luke's voice. He was sleep talking; both of them did that a lot. 'Luke . . .' Katy murmured. Jake chuckled. 'Sometimes I used to feel lonely, alone when the three of us would hang out. We talked about it once or twice. I was never interested. Sometimes I envied Luke. He was happy; both of them were just so perfect together. Then you came, finishing the group.' I leaned on him and said 'I'll always be there for you.'
- 'You know you're really fragile, delicate, sensitive, and tender.'
- 'It all means the same.'
- 'Right. I don't think your right to fight the war. You are just so . . . . I don't know, I don't feel right.'
   'Oh c'mon. You think I can't fight. I'll show you when the time is right.'
- 'I didn't mean you can't fight, I dismissed that thought the day you turned me to ice at Sean's place.'
- 'You're scared aren't you? You're scared you'll lose me, after what happened at the studio.'
- 'Yes, how did you–'

- 'I guess I know you too well. Don't be afraid, be brave. If you lose confidence, I'll shatter.' We stopped when we reached a big gate leading us into a compound. 'I'll go drop the car in the parking lot, you guys can get down here.' He said looking at the rear-view mirror. I did something totally unexpected; I kissed him on his cheek and got down. When I flung open the door to the back seat, Jake turned back and stared at me. I shook my friends up so they'd wake up. 'Guys wake up, good morning!' Both of them were in a deep sleep and didn't even move. It was a very awkward situation with Jake staring and all. Finally Luke's eyes fluttered open. He woke Katy up and the three of us strutted into the gate. There were two buildings inside the huge compound wall. One was broken down and scary, it looked like the haunted ones you see in horror movies.

Luke stopped in his tracks. Katy asked 'What are you doing?'

'Do you hear that?' Luke asked. 'Hear what?' I asked. 'Just listen.' He commanded and all of us remained silent, listening hard. I heard a faint sound of a moan; it was a female voice, so melancholic. 'What is that?' Katy said in a soft voice and looped her hand around Luke's. 'I don't know, but it's coming from that house.' I said. Jake approached us. 'What are you guys doing here?' He asked. Then he froze when he heard what we heard. 'I think we should go in there.' I insisted. 'I'm not coming.' Katy said. I felt someone pinch my arm. 'Ouch!' I cried. 'Sorry,' Katy said 'Just checking whether this is real.' I rubbed my arm. Jake walked closer to the building. 'Let's go in. I think someone's in there, she needs help.' 'Or needs supper' Katy said. Jake rolled his eyes and rang the doorbell. The sound was so loud the four of drew closer to each other. 'Doesn't matter what the situation is,' Jake said and gulped 'we will not split.' The huge metal door was rusted and melted at one end. 'Why do I have a strong feeling that this place was burnt down?' Jake muttered looping his arm into mine. 'I guess it was burnt.' I said. No reply for so long we decided to open the door. I touched the rusted door knob, it was cold. I pushed the door open. The moaning grew louder. The place was lit up with shivering candles. It was dim lit. The floor board was made of wood, which was black and burnt. Two huge stairwells made of granite where full of soot. The wall paper was burnt down like rags. Jake took a deep breath and kept his foot in. A gust of warm wind blew around us. All of us stepped in. 'I think the moan's coming from upstairs.' Luke said. We crawled upstairs. Katy was shivering and sweating at the same time. Luke kept his hand on her forehead to check her temperature. 'You're sick.' He said.

We entered a dark floor lit with only five candles. There was a room straight ahead. Jake opened the door and the moan grew louder and more tempting to rescue.

I took out my sword; 'Eau' was engraved which meant 'water' in English. On the other side of the blade was written the words 'Blade of doom'. 'It's French, right?' I asked Jake looking at my glowing blade. He said 'Spark's sword was made in France and his wife was from France, he lived there for a couple of years.' We entered the room with the light from my sword and Jake's flash light. There was a door which looked like it leads into a closet. 'Who dares to open it?' Katy asked and all eyes turned to Jake. He rolled his eyes and said 'No way in hell.' 'I'll open it.' I said. What could we possibly find in there; there were nothing that can scare me. I already ran into a ghost this morning. I pressed my crutch on the floor. The floor board creaked. I walked forward and kept my hand on the big metal knob. I twisted it and looked around to see my friends step back. I raised my sword and flung open the door to find . . . . nothing! My heart beat slowed down. Oh gosh, what were we scared of? I limped back and said 'Nothing.' All the three of them widened their eyes. 'Holy . . .'Jake started but couldn't finish. Then the moan faded and the smell of a rotten corpse floated in the air. I turned to see a burnt, corpulent figure crawl on the wall. 'What is–huh?' I said. I raised my sword. It was a lady, with hair that was burnt and uneven, her teeth were black and three were missing in the front. Its eyes were blood shot; I couldn't exactly define a colour. It twisted on the wall and reached its hand out for me but I backed up. All of us stared in awe. A bat blew out of the window and past our heads.

Katy screamed and Luke tried to calm her down. It made a hissing noise like a snake and said 'Come to me.' The voice was so hypnotizing. My curiosity pushed away my fright. 'Who are you?' I asked. It sighed so loudly that I felt like an elephant exhaled. Jake pulled out his sword. It said 'One of you girls will have to give away yourselves today.' I gulped. Luke pulled out his dagger and Katy's clip turned into her spear. 'Who are you?' I repeated. 'I'm going to possess your body and take revenge on my husband.'

- 'Why?' I asked. It sighed again.
- 'Because, my husband left me for that bar tender. He burnt me in this mansion, he left me all alone. He killed me and ran away with that girl.'
- 'I'm sorry, but why do you want to possess one of us anyway?' I had to keep talking.
- 'I will possess one of you and take revenge on my husband and that girl. He told me I wasn't pretty enough. I will get married with another handsome guy, you girls are pretty and I can't make up my mind to choose one.'
- 'But she's just fourteen and I'm almost fourteen, you can't get married.'
- 'Oh then I'll pick one of these boys, they're hot.'
- 'Excuse me?' How could she even think about having my boyfriend! Katy's eyes widened and she yelled 'Don't even think about it you ugly

beast!' Luke and Jake stared at each other and began laughing. I gave an annoying look at Jake. Both of them controlled their laughing. 'I think I'll pick . . . . you!' It said pointing its ugly finger at me. 'Wow, this is not a beauty contest and there is no way I'm letting you touch my girl.' Jake said. But the corpse wasn't in the mood to talk anymore. It leaped from the wall over to me, I sidestepped and it went flying across the room and banged itself on the wall. I exhaled. It walked towards me in a weird way. I limped towards it and slashed my sword towards its neck but I missed. It pulled me and threw me across the room. My leg had hit the wall first and the wall cracked because of the impact. My leg began bleeding and my crutch was very far from me so I was unable to stand up. I felt like the blood was reaching out for me.

My head was spinning and my stomach wasn't feeling so good. But my leg hurt so much all the other pain in my body dissolved. Jake slashed through the women, she burned but then she said 'I'm already dead, you can't kill me! Oh that girl's broken her leg, then I'll—' 'don't even think about it.' Luke said. My eyes felt heavier and I couldn't concentrate on what was happening, I remember Katy's spear went straight into the corpse's head. It tumbled and fell down. But then again I remember it recovering quickly and, when it turned towards me I took my dagger out and threw at it, my dagger went straight through its neck. That bought the others time and distraction. Jake slashed his sword through it and yelled 'Nobody messes with us!' The corpse disintegrated but the words it spoke echoed through the manse, 'I will come again.' It had said. Katy chuckled and said 'Then we'll kill her again.' Jake ran towards me and hugged me. He said 'Oh God, I thought I'd lose you again.' He stroked my hair, the warmth he radiated spread through my whole body. Then my vision grew clear and my stomach felt right. I took a deep breath and looked at my bleeding leg. 'Let's go to the inn. We got to fix her leg.' Luke said.

With the cash we got we could afford only one room with two beds and the rest went for the food. Jake fixed my leg and we had food in silence. Nobody wanted to talk. Jake was so sleepy the second his body rested on the bed he fell asleep. Katy sat in one corner polishing all our weapons. Luke had a shower and got into new fresh clothes. I occupied the shower after him and drew out my new pair of clothes. A pair of camouflage pants with a purple T-shirt and army boots. It was my uniform we wore at WPS, it was the last pair of clothes I had.

At mid-night, the three of them were fast asleep. I sat on the couch by the window and looked at the winter moon. It was so bright above. I missed my family. I missed Sam and Cody even more than anyone. But being with Jake, Katy and Luke just made everything better. I'm the luckiest person in the world to have such friends. The clock in the lobby made a huge "ding dong" sound the old building actually shook a bit. My leg began burning. It was the worst form of pain ever. The burning spread through my whole body and the pain grew intolerable. I screamed my lungs out. It hurt so much that I felt I'd die. The three of them woke up, startled. Katy sensed what was going on. She said 'its okay, you're healing. I know how it feels.' Luke patted me on the shoulder and said 'its okay sis, everything's gonna be alright, okay?' Jake sat across me; he reached out for my hand. I grabbed it, the more the pain grew the tighter my grip was around his hand. He drew closer to me. The moment I fell into his arms, the pain stopped. My leg was fine. I sat back and observed his hand. It was scarred. I realized that there were many more scars on him. A big scar rested on his forehead. I touched it and it vanished. 'That didn't hurt so much.' He said. A shimmering image of Nancy appeared in front of us. 'Hey, I'm free now, we can talk.'

- 'Where are you coming from?' I asked.
- 'Heaven, of course. Good souls end up in heaven, and we get a choice, whether we'd want to stay in heaven and enjoy the beauties. Or become an angel and when you become an angel with power comes responsibilities. We angels have to make sure all souls end up in the right place, that's our job. We got to make sure

the right souls leave the earth at the right time and reach the right destination.'

- 'You're an angel?'
- 'Yeah, but you don't want to see my real from. I prefer showing you this.' She said holding her hands in front of her.
- 'Okay,' I said digesting that my best friend was an angel. Luke and Katy stared in awe. I said 'Yeah guys, she was my mortal friend back in NYC, when she was alive. Nancy Quinton. Nancy . . . Luke and Katy.' She waved at both of them and smiled. Her golden eyes twinkled in the moon light. Luke and Katy tried hard to smile.
- 'Oh no, I got to leave, some soul's creating a scene to get into hell.' She said. 'Goodbye Jane, Love you.' She vanished. The three of them stared at me like I was the one who came out of hell. 'You have an angel friend?' Katy asked. 'She's Nancy Quinton. She was the only best friend I had in New York. Everyone says she died because she had cancer, but I believe that she was murdered by a stupid cheerleader, that's student politics, that's crap stuff I don't want to talk about. I don't exactly know how she killed her without a trace, but I know Nancy was murdered, and later on she became angel, so I sort of have an angel friend.' I said.

Jake Martin

Chapter 21

We go to suicide cafe

My eyes fluttered open. It was four in the morning. SJ was still asleep. She lay in my arms and her hair smelt like jasmine. She radiated warmth when I felt cold. The spot she kissed me still felt warm. But the thought made me shiver. We had to go to this cafe Luke told us about. I didn't want SJ to go through this. I can't see her near death ever again. We have a long and tough journey ahead. SJ is strong but at the same time she just seems so delicate to me. She's amazing with that sword of hers, she's a born fighter. Every move she makes just seems to be so complicated and hard to read. The way she fights in combat is unpredictable. But yet, why do I feel like she feels insecure? Why do I feel that she's unsafe? The way she slept in my arms was so cute I was disappointed when she woke up. Her grey eyes reflected my image in the dim yellow sunlight. She smiled and said 'Morning, tough guy.' Her smile made all my worries fade, it made me happy. 'Sleep well, smarty pants?' I asked. SJ nodded.

We strapped our bronze armours and armed our weapons. Katy's done a good job polishing them. We drove into town with my new BMW. The cops spotted us and frowned at us but didn't say anything. While we ran into streets up and down the city for Luke to recognize one cafe . . . . but it was of no use. Finally after one hour of roaming Luke pointed to our north and said 'That one.' We parked our car outside and walked into the cafe. It seemed so tiny outside but inside it was huge.

There were dozens of tables arranged in intersecting circles. Only a few mortals wore bright red aprons and walked around. The smell of donuts filled the air. There was a huge stairwell at the back of the cafe which would've been enough for two giant monsters. A skinny boy with gold armour walked down the stairs and yelled 'Have you guys got enough food to feed him? He'll get mad if he's out of food and he'll eat one of you instead!' He had the sign of the eagle on his wrist. Instantly we knew we were standing in Lucifer's kingdom. The boy went yelling at each red apron.

Suddenly we heard a huge noise, a huge giant walked down the stairs and his yawning was like there was a tornado in the cafe. He was ten feet tall and two meters wide. He wore armour and his breastplate had an image of a duck with eagle wings carved on it, it was very odd. He said 'Donuts, needs donuts.' His voice echoed through the building. All the guys in red aprons picked a dozen trays and stacked then on one table. A million soda cans were tossed on the table. He sat on the ground and hogged his food. Katy whispered 'Can we just run back?' SJ took out her sword and started moving. The rest of us followed. The skinny boy noticed us and ran towards us. He removed his helmet to reveal his blonde hair and freckled face. 'Who are you?' He asked. SJ's sword glowed. She said 'Who are you?' He gulped. Luke stared at him and said 'Michael? You're Michael Alonski, aren't you?' The guy stared with no reply. Instead he drew his sword and slashed at SJ. She side stepped and hit his blade with the flat end of hers and Michael's sword went flying in the air and hit the giant on his head.

The giant stopped eating. He banged his donut on the table and turned towards Michael. The kid bowed in front of him. The giant got up and stared at the rest of us. Katy whispered 'Maybe we should bow too.' Katy began kneeling but SJ pulled her up. 'Never show your fear.' She said. He had a huge head which was pretty much human, but the rest of his body was terrifying. He had the legs of an elephant and the tongue of a snake; his hands were reptilian, scaly. The worst was his hair, he didn't have hair he had worms instead and he had two horns sticking out of it. 'Salvatore!' He yelled. All of us backed up and hid behind the pillars. But SJ stood there. She raised her sword, it glittered. The giant stretched and took out his spear which was ten meters longer than SJ's. He slashed but she jumped. It passed just a few millimetres away from her. She ran behind the giant and began climbing. When she got to its head she yelled

'Guys, you gonna help me or not?' The giant went crazy, running around trying to get SJ off its head. I shot at it, but the giant recovered fast. I charged it and slashed my sword through its big ugly foot. Luke shot an arrow on the other foot. The giant lost control and fell. Katy spear whooshed over my head and straight through the giant's eye. SJ got her balance and slashed his throat. The giant vaporized into thin air.

We turned to see that all the guys in red apron had run away including Michael Alonski. He was just a kid and he worked for Cyrus. I actually felt sorry for him. 'Let's go upstairs.' SJ commanded. 'Finally, the leader of the quest is actually leading the team.' I said. She turned and smiled at me. 'Let's get moving.'

The first floor was nothing like we'd expected. It was a garden full of yellow flowers. Big French windows lined the walls. They were open and let in the cool breeze and sunlight. SJ was startled. She was standing at the last line of flowers. I approached her and asked 'What's wrong?' She looked at me and said 'Beneath the golden flower, all the flowers here are yellow, except this one.' She pointed at her feet. There was a golden daffodil smaller than the rest of the flowers. 'Then let's dig' I said. I and SJ began digging. Luke and Katy were standing guard. We found a vial covered with mud. There was a small label which read "Love potion, creates love at first sight!" which was handwritten. SJ looked up at me, 'What are we going to do with this?' I shrugged. 'Maybe we'll find a way to use it later.' Only after months did I realise its use.

Chapter 22

SJ blows the house of monsters

That afternoon we teleported to Phoenix, Arizona. SJ wasn't as tired and drained of energy as she was the last time. 'I've learned how to control it a bit,' she said 'I just need a little more practise.' With our final scrapings we bought cheese burgers and ate at a picnic table. The food was the best of what we'd had since the quest began. Katy had her head buried in her hands and was snoring. Suddenly we heard a big "Boom!" from a building a yard away. We approached the building. It seemed like there was a party going on. A huge sign hung on the door which said 'All invited to Chessy's party!' 'Who's Chessy? What kind of person invites strangers to their parties?' Katy asked. 'If trespassers are allowed, let's have a sneak peak.' Luke said. We turned to SJ, she nodded. 'If they got nachos, I'm in.' I said. The four of us flung open the door. The music was so loud we couldn't hear each other. Everything seemed normal till we saw someone unwanted. The Alonski kid wore his armour and was dancing like crazy. His armour pieces were like huge metal pieces that hung on a skinny kid and were dancing with him. I pulled him by the shirt and the four of us cornered him. 'You guys again!' He said. Katy knelt down and put her hand on his shoulder. 'Who are you kid? And what are you doing here?' The kid kicked her and Katy held her leg in pain choking back a scream.

SJ pulled out her weapon and kept the tip at the kid's throat. 'Who are you and what are you doing here? You work for Cyrus don't you?' That was something that SJ would never do to a kid but I felt her nervousness. She hated harassing people, but the situation was like that. The boy took notice of her sword and said 'Blade of doom? You are Sara Jane Salvatore!' The boy stared at the sword and was more frightened now. He knew something about the sword and was not telling us. 'What are you not telling us?' I asked. SJ held her hand and said 'He's Michael Alonski, age nine, born in San Francisco, serves our enemy but he does not know many things. He's got only information that we already know nothing new. He's in charge of feeding his monsters, in all a slave of Lucifer Cyrus.' 'How do you . . . ?' The boy stammered. 'I can read minds, scanned your filthy brain, it's filled with garbage but not knowledge.' She retrieved her sword and sheathed it. Then SJ's eyes widened like she'd heard something she didn't know, and mostly she knew everything. 'Water, huh?' She asked. The boy gulped. 'Thinking of not thinking is also thinking kid.' SJ said. The boy melted into some kind of green liquid. Luke poured milk on the goo; none of us knew what he was experimenting. 'Nice one Luke, the kid's allergic to milk.' SJ said. Luke smiled 'Yeah I knew that, Leom's told me 'bout him.'

We turned to see a huge bunch of ugly beasts staring at us. Their armour pieces hardly fit them. They had big hairy bellies popping out from their armours. We readied our weapons and turned to SJ for command. But she had other plans. She said 'The three of you, please go somewhere far. I'll meet you a few yards away, I got this trust me' with a wink at me. 'SJ, you can't defeat the whole . . . .' I protested but she said 'I told I got this.' She snapped her finger and flames sprung out of her finger. I lit myself up and flew out the house with Luke and Katy.

'I'll just go check on her. You guys stay here.' I said. 'No way, if you're going we're coming with you.' Luke said. 'I got this buddy, I'm not going to do anything, and I'm just going to watch.' I continued. 'Take us with you.' Katy said. 'No, I'm going to have to go alone.' I flew away before they continued the dispute. I landed near the window and watched. SJ was standing in the middle surrounded by monsters. For a second I thought I'd have to help too but then she rose into the air and water flushed the whole house. I was drenched, myself. The water level kept rising and all the ugly monsters were confused and were not sure of what to do. They locked their shields expecting another huge wave of water to splash. But slowly my breath began to steam.

Frost covered the walls and then the whole building was covered with ice. SJ walked out from the crowd. I stared at her, star-struck. I never knew she could do something like that. When she came out she noticed me. 'I told you to keep-'She began 'they're not here, just me.' I said. She kicked a pebble of ice out of her boots. 'How did you do that?' I asked. 'The boy, when he saw the sword, he guessed its name right and he knew the power it possesses. I get to control water! Can you believe that? I feel so powerful.' She exclaimed. I was so glad to see her happy on this travel which leads us to death. For some reason I felt it was unfair. 'You get water and ice, but what do I get? Doesn't it seem unfair?' I asked. Her smile faded. She began thinking 'Maybe it is.' She said finally. 'Maybe you got something we haven't discovered yet.'

We walked in silence to Katy and Luke. SJ told them what had happened and they were shocked to hear it. Suddenly Nancy appeared in front of us, this time with a big box in her hand. She said 'You guys got a present from Sillvius Spark, Jake please sign here.' She gave me a pen and a book. I signed on it. 'Mr Spark sent this to me?' I asked. 'Well, he said the four of you. But he wanted me to deliver it to you, I don't know why but he seems very fond of you.' She said. 'You guys want a ride to LA?' Luke and Katy nodded before we could think. 'First I'll distribute your gifts.' Nancy said. She pulled out silver arrows in a quiver made of fresh teak wood and a bow and handed it to Luke. Those arrows belonged to Hillary. They gleamed in the sunlight. SJ sighed; she didn't seem interested for some reason. 'What's wrong?' I asked. She nodded and said 'I was expecting something from Aaron.' Nancy gave Katy Helen's golden spear; the tip was so sharp I shuddered when I saw it.

Then Nancy pulled something that caught my fancy, the knife, the knife I've always wanted, Hermine's knife. The hilt was strapped with leather and the blade was gleaming bronze. Nancy sheathed it and said 'It's yours, Martin.' When she took out the dagger SJ waved her hand and said 'It's okay, someone else could use it. I have my sword.' Nancy looked at me for an answer but I shrugged.

Nancy slipped the dagger into my hand. She whistled and a big chariot pulled by a flying horse descended from the sky. 'Hop on.' She said. All of us climbed the chariot and SJ was the last one. Nancy slowly changed from normal girl in jeans to a girl in a white dress. A faint silver light glowed around her. Then she spread her milk white wings and climbed onto the horse. She spoke in some different language that only the horse and she understood. All the weapons had an owl on it. That's our sign and the deadly eagle is Cyrus'.

Then we were up in the air flying to Los Angeles, California.

Chapter 23

Sweet Dreams: Jake

After flying for about an hour I fell asleep. In my dream I saw myself flying in the air, all by myself. It was so strangely quiet. That's when I remembered what Trish had told us. Under any circumstances we should avoid flying by air. And right now I was flying in the air.

I heard cries of pain and war after a while. I followed the noise and saw many strange creatures fighting flying monsters. These creatures were shaped like humans from the waist up and were swirling storms from the waist below. Then I felt something grab me on my shoulder. I turned to see a face form in the sky. It had multi-coloured eyes, I felt like I was looking into a kaleidoscope. His hair was till his shoulders, assuming he had them. They were long strands of shabby chocolate brown hair. His skin was pale. He smiled weakly. 'Jacob Martin.' He said with a French accent. 'Jake Martin.' I corrected. 'Son, as you can see the storms are still defending our worst enemies from descending to the land. I don't think I can stand it any longer.'

- 'What do you mean, who are you and what are those?' I asked.

- 'I mean that I'm growing weaker as well as my army. I guess I've grown old now. I'm Charles Spark. My younger brother, Sillvius has laid in his death bed already. He'll die soon. So will I and my two brothers. I may not be the oldest of the four but I also want to give up my life and rest in peace. My power has kept me alive and I want to give it away. It's a great responsibility to control the components which make up our world. Surely the young girl has understood it. And I believe you will too. Everything that rests in the sky is mine. My kingdom has weakened. You shall inherit what I inherited from Helen, my son. I'll give you the sky and everything that lies in it. And as for your last question, Cyrus possesses the ability to transform his emotions, anger into deadly creatures. Those are his furiousness fighting to get to earth and destroy our kind. These are only the beginning. The worst of all is their leader, who is yet to come.'

- 'Who is their leader?'

- 'The Black Fury.'

- 'Are you serious? The one that-'

- 'Began all this chaos aeons ago. Yes, it is.'

- 'Are you sure I'll be able to control all of these? I mean the whole atmosphere, five layers of the atmosphere, that's a difficult task.'

- 'I know my son, but you are fit for the job. I believe in you. You can learn how to make storms from Orageux. And then all the rest of the creatures that dwell here. He was the first storm spirit I'd created. He will guide you and help you through your difficult tasks.'
- 'Orageux? That's stormy in English right. I'm sorry but I'm not so good at French.'
- 'Yes, Orageux means stormy in English. You see I named him when I was twelve.'
- 'Oh right. So which one of them is Stormy the storm spirit.' I asked pointing at the war in the sky.
- 'Stormy is in my castle, training the new born storm spirits so that they can fight in battle too.'
- 'Okay, do I have to live in that castle or am I allowed to go back to earth?'
- 'You can go to earth, my child. But you'd just have to come up once in a while. Now let me take you to the castle.' His image floated to the south and I followed it.

As we continued our journey I saw clouds building weapons and armours. They were sweating and covered with grease. The floating head of Charles Spark stopped. He said 'You can send a drizzle and have some lunch then get back to work.' I felt water droplets hit my face. I said 'Why do I feel rain drops on me?' Charles smiled and said 'Because in reality you are still asleep on the chariot.'

A huge door made of clouds and storms appeared. The gate flung open when Spark walked in. 'Blanc, please come to the conference hall, also you Orageux and . . . Where's Tornado? Tell him to come too.' He led me up the stairwell of clouds. We walked into a huge room with a table in the centre and chairs surrounding it. 'Please sit Jacob.' He said. 'Jake.' I corrected again.

The door opened to reveal three things which were human from waist up and storm, tornado and cloud from the waist below. The three of them sat down.

All the three had kaleidoscopic eyes. The cloud had blonde hair; Stormy had black hair like mine. And the tornado had honey coloured hair and was pleasant looking. That was so different from the rest of his body. Spark said 'As you can see, this is Orageux,' then he pointed at the cloud guy and said 'Blanc, which means white in English and Tornado.'

Charles Spark's whole body shimmered to life. He was just like any other human, nothing unusual and powerful about him. He sat down next to me and told the three of them he had to leave. He told them I'd be the next ruler of his kingdom which gave me the creeps. I don't think I could take care of the whole sky; I can't keep everything organized and all.

I began to feel drowsy by the time we finished our conversation. The three of them told me they'd teach me to build things later and now I had to leave and get back on my suicidal quest.

Charles Spark brought me to a room which I guessed was something like a throne room. There was a huge throne in the centre and three others by its sides. There was a tall statue that stood on one end, it was Helen. Spark began chanting and suddenly a ray of white light surrounded me. I was lifted up in the air and circled above. When I set my foot back on the ground, I felt so powerful and unbeatable. It was like all the bad stuff out there was just a piece of cake. I took a deep breath. Spark began aging, his hair withered to a shade of grey, his face wrinkled and he coughed. He grew unstable and before he fell I caught him and helped him back to his feet. 'I shall go now and you can complete your journey to San Francisco and come back up to rebuild the kingdom as yours. Today you have been claimed the king of the sky, my son. It is a great responsibility and you are the only one who can carry the burden.' With the last words he passed out and I caught him. The three of them took their ex-emperor into a room and laid him on the bed.

I woke up to find a miniature of the sky in my hand. The battle was still continuing but the enemies were few in number. More troops joined in and fought. I guess my side was winning battle for now. The worst is yet to come. I slipped it into my pocket. The sun had begun setting.

𝔖weet 𝔡reams -2: 𝔖𝔍

𝔐y father's image shimmered to life. 'Hello!' He said. 'Glad to know you're still alive.'

- 'How are you, dad? How's everyone, Sam, mom, Su? I miss you guys.'
- 'We also miss you, SJ. All of them are fine. Sam's really worried about you, more than anyone else. I hope you're doing fine.'
- 'I'm great dad.' I said. I told him about what had happened at Phoenix, how I'd frozen all the beasts and how I could control water. Dad smiled, but the smile had worries. 'You inherited it from Sillvius Spark, SJ. Have you read the stories, how Hera could rule the seas and Helen was queen of sky and Hillary owned the flames and Hermine was mother earth? The Spark brothers inherited it from the four sisters and Sillvius has trusted you with his burden. With great power comes great responsibility SJ. The world is depending on you.' With the last words my father's image turned to mist.

The dream changed. I was underwater and Mr Spark's image floated. He said 'I will die in a few days; my brothers are also giving up. The four of you need to inherit our powers. We can't stay any longer, our time is over and now it is yours.'

- 'You mean, I'm going to-'
- 'Yes, you are responsible of every single drop in the oceans and seas.' A blue light shimmered in my hand. He said 'You are queen now. After you finish your journey to destroy the army, come here. Soak yourself into the pure liquid and my creatures will help you when you are in trouble. As an exchange you will be empress, you will civilize my kingdom. Water is a natural element which keeps every living thing alive. So maybe you can't really control it all but a part of this,' He said waving his hands around 'Is yours. Make me proud, young lady. Now I shall say farewell and lay back on my death bed. I will die leaving you with all the great power I have. And remember with great power-'
- 'Comes great responsibility, yeah, I know.'
- 'No, no child. With great power comes great weakness. Your biggest enemy will be someone close to you. Your biggest threat, the only one who can destroy your kingdom will be valued so much by you. And you also happen to be his biggest threat because you are the only one who can destroy his kingdom.'
- 'You mean Jake is my biggest threat?'
- 'No, Jake is your guardian, he can't be killed by your hands and neither can he kill you. He's someone you love, someone you haven't realized the importance of, someone who is a

caring brother and loyal friend.' The words sunk into me like needles. What if it was Sammy? That question troubled me. No, I told myself, it can't be. Then he gestured his hands to one way and said 'I will show you my castle as well as the creatures that dwell in my kingdom.' I have no idea how long I slept because we kept swimming like forever. When we finally swam over, probably five countries a big building appeared. It was so tall an aeroplane could've fit into it. It shimmered blue. It had huge gates of metal. The doors swung open by themselves and I stepped into my empire.

A shimmering sliver carpet lead till as far as my eyes could reach. Beautiful aquatic creatures swam around, they looked very busy. All of them went around like they knew they had something to do and they seemed engaged. There were so many beautiful fishes and eels and many other creatures I couldn't name around me. When they saw Mr Spark, they bowed awkwardly, at least I guess that gesture was bowing, but it was weird that fishes could bow and all.

He showed me around the place. It was beautiful. The throne room was made of sea weed, which was odd but it all just blended together. Sillvius Spark said 'My kingdom is in your hands now. All the creatures know their job and they will organize themselves. You just have to visit once in a while and consult. Now I shall say farewell and rest, the throne is yours.' He snapped his fingers and a crown appeared on my head. All the living creatures gathered in the throne room and bowed. 'You are the new queen of the seas.' I said to myself. With the last words I woke up with a start. I realized I was sweating. I took a deep breath and began digesting my dream and the fact that I ruled the seas.

Sweet dreams-3: Katy

A ray of light flashed before my eyes. It was so bright that it blinded my vision. When my eyes adjusted I realized I was buried in soil. Was I dead? Even if I were dead I would've been in a coffin. To my surprise I didn't feel suffocating. Then a big hole appeared in front of me. I stood up. Wet earth surrounded me. A middle-aged man appeared from the hole. He had dark tattered hair and a goatee. His eyes were as brown as the soil around. 'Hello' he said like he'd already met me million times before. But something told me he looked familiar. He resembled someone . . . . someone not so close to me, someone old. He chuckled like he knew what I was thinking. 'How are you doing, Miss Katarina Robinson?' His voice was soft and mystifying. Who was he? I had a strong feeling I was going to die. The only thing I could think of was Luke. 'Who are . . . you?' I stammered. 'Where . . . . . am I?'

'I' he said 'am Henry.' I was blank. Nothing gave his answer a ring in my head. Henry? I knew no Henry. 'Henry Spark.' When he said his second name I stared at him with astonishment! He was Henry SPARK, the Henry Spark! The emperor of earth, himself. I bet I was going crazy right now. 'As for where you are' he continued 'well, physically you are asleep on a chariot rode by flying horses tamed by an angel. This is your dream, dear. I'm connecting our minds so I can send you a message.' I was confused but yet I asked 'What do you want to tell me? I'm no hero, I'm a "nobody", how would you, Henry Spark, want to deliver a message to me?' The man just smiled and said 'You are my favourite among the four. You're not just a 'nobody' you are more than that. You have specialities, young lady. That is why I have picked you.'

- 'Picked me for what?' I asked.
- 'I picked you to give everything I have. To be the next ruler of the earth.' The words sunk into me like blades.
- 'How could you trust me so much? How could you believe that I could possess such a great post? I have done nothing incredible. I think you should have SJ instead.' He rolled his eyes.
- 'SJ already carries a heavy burden on her shoulders. I'm not going to let my kingdom crumble, she can't rule here. This is your territory. And anyways, she carries the seas in her

hands. That's very hard; almost three-fourth of the earth is covered with water.'

- 'Then why not Jake, he's perfect for this.'
- 'Oh Katy dear. Jacob is king of air, the sky. He has the most complicated, heavy, and biggest element to care about. His kingdom is the farthest from mine.'
- 'You mean the two of them inherited the kingdoms form your brothers. Charles and Sillvius Spark?'
- 'Yes, that is why I have decided to inherit the empire I was given by Hermine to you.'
- 'This can't be. I'm not right for this Mr Spark.'
- 'Call me Henry.' He took out a glowing object from his pocket and tucked it into my hand. 'It belongs to you.' When I looked up at him he seemed to age. He said 'Good luck dear, come by after you finish your quest, I will take you to my palace.' With the last word my dream vanished. I woke up to see a smudgy black thing like wet soil in my hand. But the thing glowed and dissolved into me.

Sweet dreams -4: Luke

As soon as I sat on the comfy chariot, I passed out. I had many images floating in my head, it felt like I was looking out the window of a moving train, but only the images were fading, I remembered them vaguely. Then I saw a bright image of fire, it looked more like peeping into hell, a huge abyss full of flames. The more my mind focused on the picture, the more it felt real.

A split second later I was falling into the big pit. I kept falling for . . . . forever. Then suddenly the flames below my leg turned to hands and caught me. The fire spread like a sheet below my feet and I was standing on a sheet of fire. I hadn't realized it but I had changed form, I had the form of a dragon. The fire seemed very calm for some reason, it seemed to be friendly, and it didn't hurt me. I had the odd feeling that I could feel what the fire felt. A man shimmered to life. He wore a black leather jacket above a black T-shirt that had a skull printed on it. He wore a hood over his head and thick black shades which covered most of his face. When he removed his hood I swear I got a heart attack. He had flames on his head instead of hair. And when he removed his shades, I got even more terrified. His eye sockets didn't contain eye balls, but had balls of flames instead. I guess I now, know the literal meaning of sparkling eyes. 'Oh my God, you're Ghost rider!' I exclaimed and I immediately felt embarrassed for saying that. The weird dude chuckled and said 'No, no son. I'm no rider.'

Suddenly he began to change form. He began aging and he turned into a very familiar adult. 'You're Alin Spark; Hillary gave her power to you.' I said. 'Yes, you are right. I knew you were smart, kid. That is why I chose you.' He said. 'Lucas, I'm old. My brothers have rested. The oldest, Henry, has laid down in peace. Next will be Charles. Sillvius has already rested in his death bed, awaiting his turn. And so should I.' I didn't understand a word he said.

- 'Can you be clearer, sir?' I asked.
- 'I mean that I am going to give you the throne.' He let that sink. I was beginning to understand and I didn't like it.
- 'Why me?' I asked.
- 'Because, you are just right for this. Hillary would be proud of me if I give you my power. My kingdom, Hillary's kingdom has to be left to the right person. And you are fit for this young man. And can you please turn human; it's very distracting, that form.' I turned back to normal.
- 'So, I get the throne of fire. Don't you think Jake needs it more? SJ's got the seas, and Jake needs something too. And Jake is fighting war, not me.'
- 'I know my son. And you have mistaken by saying you are not fighting war. Katarina and you are supporting Jane and Jacob. Without the two of you both of them will grow unstable. You are destined to fight war with them. The four of you side-by-side, defining the true meaning of friendship .... love .... care. All

the things that Lucifer Cyrus doesn't possess.'
That hit my like sharp needles.

- 'Okay.' It was the only thing I said.
- 'And, the four of you will discover your biggest fear. Whatever the four sisters feared will also be inherited to the four of you. Now I have to say farewell, and rest.'
- 'Wait, you said each one of us will begin fearing something. What did Hillary fear?'
- 'Darkness. I haven't slept with the lights out since I ruled this kingdom.'
- 'What about the others?'
- 'Well, Katarina will fear heights. Jacob will fear water. And Jane will fear blood.'
- 'Wow, Jake can't fear water. SJ is queen of seas, he can't. Is it like phobia? Don't tell Jake's going to have hydrophobia, I guess that's what you call it.'
- 'Don't worry. It's not as severe as phobia. And you seem to worry about Jacob more than yourself.' Why wouldn't I worry about Jake? He's my best friend. He's more like my brother. And to be true, I always worried about him. He was . . . . always a kid. And lately, he just seemed to grow up, and he grew up too fast. He changed since SJ was around; she made him grow up into a fourteen year old. He was always so dependent on me and suddenly he became another individual. It's not like SJ's fault or anything. It's actually a good thing. But I just couldn't seem

to digest it. I mean, he probably feels what I feel for Katy, but.... a guy who hated every girl around suddenly fell in love?

- 'He's like my little brother. I can't bear to lose him.'

- 'Loyalty to friendship, I like that. Does Robinson know this? Doesn't she feel jealous?' The question was so stupid I actually laughed.

- 'Of course not. I love Katy too. If I told you I loved anyone, even Jake more than Katy, I'd be lying. And Katy cares for Jake too. We've been friends since I remember. Jealousy can never come between us.'

- 'I see.' He said. 'When you wake up, check your pockets.' He vanished within a second and I woke up. Katy's head was rested on my lap. Jake was awake, he kept rattling something in his pocket. SJ was staring down. Katy kept opening her palm and closing it like she expected something to appear. Then she sat up. The minute she looked down she held my hand tight and drew closer to me. 'I've never been afraid of heights.' She said.

'Guys, I want to tell you something.' The four of us said in unison.

Chapter 24

Luke blows up

I was shocked when I heard their tales, and they were no less surprised. The four of us are as strong as the four sisters now that thought scared me a bit.

Luke searched for something in his pockets. Then he took out a bright glowing mist that was in the colour of fire. It surrounded him and dissolved into him.

We rode in silence when I felt a stone knock me on the head. I looked up to see the dark figures of the Furies roaming around. I took out my miniature and saw that our chariot was surrounded with Furies. Nancy said 'I have to leave. My horse will take you to your destination. This is your fight, I cannot intrude. Goodbye and good luck!' With the last words she vanished. SJ grabbed the air at the spot Nancy was standing and yelled 'Nancy!' but she was gone. A rain of rocks kept falling on us. In no time, we'll be surrounded. I summoned the air and knocked down a few. Luke shot fire balls at them. Katy kept the chariot running and dashing sideways to make sure our ride didn't get hurt.

SJ had made an invisible shield around the four of us. 'Can you expand it and cover the whole chariot?' I asked. She gulped like she was holding the whole earth together and said 'I'm trying; I can't seem to expand it any longer.' I fell on my knees; I was losing all my energy. I had already begun to feel drowsy. But I still kept knocking down the Furies. They just seemed to recover very soon. Looking at SJ, I knew she couldn't hold it any longer. She was struggling. She fell on her knees; she was sweating and breathing hard. Luke was not any better either. Luke's feet began to wobble.

The wind around me was doing fine, but my tornadoes and little storms seemed to slow down. My whole body felt like lead. And the great, Ms. Katy did the one thing we had told her not to do—she looked down and began to panic! Then she passed out and I caught her just in time before she fell. Immediately after wards Luke passed out too.

I and SJ were the only ones who were still progressing. When I and SJ were hopeless, Luke's eyes fluttered open. He stretched and sat up straight like nothing ever happened. 'Mind giving us a hand?' I asked. Instead of starting to shoot fire balls again like I predicted, he asked me to do something so stupid which would've got him killed. 'Hey, help me fly. I have to get to the centre of the Furies.' He said. SJ gulped and panted and said 'Are you serious? That's suicide!' 'She's right.' I agreed. Luke sighed and said 'Guess I'm on my own. Guys, please don't tell Katy what I am going to do after she wakes up. It'll be our lil' secret.' Before we could do something to stop him, he turned into a vulture and flew into enemy lines. 'Oh, Lucas!' SJ muttered. She sat down, the shield was broken, and she was breaking. She panted for a while and stood up and drew her sword. 'I got to get into battle.' Instead of charging, she jumped down. Ignoring all the pebbles and stones falling on me I raced to the edge and yelled 'SJ!' Oh my God, what's going on? My best friend just flew into a suicidal trap and now my girlfriend fell of the chariot. Was I going nuts, or was it everyone else? I fell down and covered Katy from getting any hurt. SJ was gone. Luke was gone. My life's over. I failed in the only job I was given, protecting SJ.

That's when the crazy thought struck me, if SJ was dead; I'm supposed to be dead and probably should end up in hell because I haven't done my duty right. If SJ dies there is no need for my presence in the world. I felt someone pat my shoulder. I turned to see SJ, floating in the air, with a fresh smile. She looked so much better than she was a second ago. 'Missed me?' She asked. I hugged her and said 'I thought I lost you.' She ruffled my hair and said 'You're stuck with me for now.' Before either of us could get into combat, there was a huge explosion above us, which knocked off most of the Furies but some of them had flown away. 'Luke!' SJ said in disbelief. Luke had released all the energy he'd had inside him just to save us. When the smoke cleared I saw Luke's body falling from the sky. At that moment I was just glad to know that my best friend was in one piece. I grabbed him as he fell into my arms and laid him down next to Katy. SJ decided to ride and I passed out immediately.

My dreams were a blur, just like the dim rainbow in the sky, pictures ruffled by. I saw bits of Charles Spark's funeral. The old man had died, having all faith on me. I woke up to hear SJ say 'Welcome to San Francisco, California, USA!' SJ and I put up a camp and put Katy and Luke in sleeping bags. I put up a fire and SJ said she'd get some food. I didn't know how she would get food without cash but I just plopped down and slept. When I woke up I saw SJ with McDonald's happy meals in her hand. It'd been so long since I had those. It'd been so long since I had good food. Luke and Katy had just fluttered open their eyes and the four of us hogged on our food. SJ told us to pack up and went to polishing our weapons and armours. 'How do we know where they are?' Luke asked.SJ sat down and closed her eyes concentrating. Then her eyelids shot open. 'Were close, I can't name the exact location, but I know where they are, but it's only a guess.'

'How did you find out?' Katy asked. 'Alonski, the kids mind is very bright. He's just a kid, how could Cyrus be so heartless, so many innocent kids like us get brain washed.' 'How did you get the food?' I asked. 'Nick, the charm speaker. I just talked them into giving me some food.' I rolled my eyes and said 'Do not speak of such names when we are this close to the army of doom.' My mind was rewinding my life, I was flipping to that one page of my journal which I didn't dare to see again, even now I don't want to recall the past: the ugly part of my past, just when I was beginning to have my perfect little life again. Things were going so well at school, at gym, at home, Luke was back from France. The year I became ruler of Mid-Springs Academy, everything broke down because of one stupid fight.

Like every other school, there was an opposing party for the school's hot shot in the soccer team, and that role was played by Nick. The freak's granddad had spent almost all the savings he had on a car for Reed which wasn't even out yet in the U.S. That's when Nick got his ego raised up, before that he was nice guy, a person I actually respected because of what he went through in his life. He envied me and I couldn't do anything about it. His brother's foes had broken the car into thrash and he assumed it was I who made the disaster. The car was the biggest luxury and property he owned, the last thing his parents had left him with, why would I destroy it anyway? We had a little fist fight in school. He told his brother he wanted revenge, he charm spoke his brother. And his stupid, drug-addict brother and his friends decided to set my room on fire. I don't know why he wanted to kill me just for a stupid car, he could've just asked for it I could've got another one. At that time my grandparents were staying for a while and it was my turn to share my room with them. I, Alley and Alex always fought because we wanted to spend the night with granny and grandpa.

When they were in my room, Reed set the fire and Grandparents died. And everybody blamed me. I spent the whole night out in the rain, ashamed to confront my family. Only Luke and Katy were there with me. I was sitting in middle of the road in the cold rain. Not crying, but . . . hurt and dying inside . . . but not crying. The next morning at the funeral, Nick was there. All he said to me was 'I'm sorry Jake, my brother didn't know what he was doing.' Reed did go to jail and my name was clear, but that wouldn't bring my grandparents back, would it?

'How come I can't read your mind?' SJ's questioned snapped me out of my flash back. 'The more strong our bond gets the more normal we become to each other. You can't use your powers over me and I can't use my powers over you.' I replied. She smiled and deep dimples fell in her cheeks. Her smile, her presence just makes me forget all the bitter happenings and it was like I was reborn each time. 'Okay guys,' she said 'let's charge.'

Chapter 25

War with the Army of Doom

I had to confess that Cyrus had pretty good taste of architecture. I was impressed when I saw the ten storey glass building soaring into the night sky, reflecting the usual traffic. That's when I remembered something important. 'SJ,' she turned towards me. Her eyes were confident and stiff, revealing no signs of fear. They were stormy and at the same time fierce. 'What is it Jake?' She asked. 'Happy birthday, you have turned fourteen.' I said. She looked at me and actually laughed. 'What's the date today?' She asked. 'November 11.' I said. Her laugh turned into a smile and she looked at me with a pleased expression. 'Aww, how sweet, you remembered.' 'How can I forget?' I asked. She hugged me hard and flashes of the day I'd asked her flew past. 'I love you.' I whispered. 'I love you too.' She replied. 'Aww how cute it is to see you guys together.' I heard Katy say. That's when we realized Luke was missing. 'Hey, where's Lucas?' SJ asked. Right before we began to panic Luke showed up. He held out a small muffin with a candle poking out. 'Make a wish, birthday girl.' Luke said. SJ closed her eyes and blew the candle. We split the cake into four and ate. SJ thanked Luke for being so sweet. I actually envied him at that moment and then I pushed that thought away. How could I be jealous of Luke? SJ suddenly changed from happy to suspicious. 'Oh my Gosh,' she said like she'd just solved a mystery and the result was surprising. 'You are the one. You are my greatest weakness. A caring brother and loyal friend, I should've know, your fire, I'm water, Mr Spark was right.' She said. None of us understood. Then she reminded us of what Sillvius Spark had said about her kingdom is a threat to Luke's and Luke's is a threat to her and all that.

'Okay, let's not get distracted. You guys remember the plan right?' SJ asked. We nodded.

We went to the security booth and it wasn't hard to knock out two guards. We disabled all the cameras and switched off all the alarms. Then we stabbed the two ugly monsters that stood guard at the entrance. SJ turned us invisible but I just turned into a gust of wind so when I pass by people would just think it's a cold day out. But in wind form my stomach wasn't doing so well, neither was my head, both were churning like crazy.

The ground floor was full of weapons and machines for moulding weapons and food and all that. So we decided to go to the first floor. When we stepped on the carpet, chains flew from the sides and strapped themselves around our wrists and ankles. A huge floor filled with kids our age and older stood there lead by a very familiar person, Lisa Brown. 'I didn't expect you guys to just walk into the trap.' She said. I pulled the chains of me, you see there is no use strapping me to anything, I'm pretty strong and that is a clear fact. SJ probably got through the chains because she turned around without thinking and began unchaining Luke and Katy.

'I didn't expect to see you here too.' I said. Her red lipstick curved into a smile. 'You broke my heart by joining with her again.' She said pointing at SJ. SJ stood between both of us and said 'Please stay away from him.' I would've sat down with popcorn to see two girls fighting for me but the situation was not like that. 'Oh Sara Jane, you didn't only ruin my life, you also ruined theirs.' She said. Two blonde girls walked out of the crowd. One I recognized, Candice, the other I didn't want to. 'Sara Rachels and why did I ruin your lives?' SJ asked. 'You stole the spot light. I killed that dork, what was her name . . . . Nancy so that you'd be all depressed and then you show up all confident and happy two months later. I had the crown just for two months. All because of that brother of yours, he was the one who made you smile after two months, so we decided to eliminate him first. You are the chosen one; you always get all the glory, so we sought the same glory from someone who would be the ruler of the universe and not just a silly little neighbourhood.' The girl named Sara Rachels said. 'What?!' SJ looked astonished. A flat screen TV popped out of the wall and there he was.

Sam was tied up in chains, blood flowing everywhere, his face was covered with blood I didn't recognize him at first. 'Oh, Sammy.' SJ muttered. 'You just got me angrier; I don't think that's good for you guys.' She said. The whole swarm of people were lifted in the air and clutching their throat like they were choking. SJ stared with anger. 'Can we get to the fighting part?' She asked. When SJ dropped them down, I summoned a huge wind and knocked them down. I tore some chunks off the floor and threw it at them. Katy and Luke had charged into battle slaying anything that got on their way. SJ had the three girls cornered. She was in a hard battle.

I summoned a big tornado and knocked down everything on my way. But suddenly I felt a something sharp pass through me. I fell on the floor. A couple of guys dragged me to the corner and in front of me was a barrel with water. At the sight of seeing it so close I started to pant. The guy dipped my head into the water and I understood that they had found my biggest fear. I blacked out.

Sara Jane Salvatore

The two girls were NOT good at combat. They were slashing their swords at me. They had no aim, they couldn't even hold the sword properly. But Lisa, Lisa was not bad. I raised them into the air and slammed them on the wall. I looked around for Jake, but he was missing. Sam, how could they have captured him? The three of them were knocked out. I focused on their friends. I stabbed and slashed and ripped. The anger surging through me made my cuts and bruises numb. I, Katy, and Luke had sent all their troops flying around or passed out on the floor. When the crowd was cleared, we found Jake in the other end of the room. He was breathing hard, his shirt was wet. His arm was bleeding. I looked at the blood, it seemed to tell me something, and it forced me into being frightened. I knelt next to him. I looked at the blood. 'Jake . . .' I said. His eyes fluttered open. 'Jake, are you alright?' 'Water, no water . . . . water . . .' He said. The more blood that flowed the more fear climbed up my body. I had no time to pass out. I looked away. 'Please fix him.' I said looking at Katy and Luke. They nodded.

I stood in the balcony, crying, crying out of frustration. I had no particular reason. They had Sammy, they almost killed Jake. How could people be so cruel? 'SJ,' I heard Jake's voice tell my name. I wiped my tears and put on a brave smile and turned. 'How are you feeling?' I asked. 'I'm fine, but you're not.' He replied.

- 'Why, I haven't even got a scar.' I said. I covered a big burning wound on my shoulder.
- 'I know how much Sam means to you. We'll get him.' I broke into tears again. I couldn't hold it back.

- 'I can't bear to lose you.' I said hugging him hard like someone else would take him away if I let go.
- 'I know hon, we'll figure it out. We got more fighting to do. Be brave, don't give up already. Stop crying like a girl, man up SJ.' He said as he stroked my hair which was a bird's nest. I looked at him. His shirt was torn and tattered, mine was no better; it was the last pair of fresh clothes we'd had. We hadn't bathed, we hadn't rested well. For some odd reason I felt like I am the one who put them through this situation. 'C'mon, sweetie, let's go.' He said. I looked up at him and asked 'What did you call me?' He smirked and said 'You heard it.'

When we got to the second floor, I got a heart attack. The big huge giants that we were spying on were the nastiest of all the nasty creatures in the world. 'Oh gosh!' Katy said in a low voice and gulped. 'I'm going first, I and Katy will get on all the small ones and distract the bigger ones, and you guys go get the biggest.' Luke said. 'Are you sure you wanna go first bro?' Jake asked. He nodded. He crawled to the door and closed his eyes. Then slowly he began transforming into a . . . . wow . . . . the biggest two headed dragon that I'd ever seen. 'Where did you see those?' I asked. 'Myths' I heard Luke's voice say but the dragon hadn't even moved his mouth. Luke broke open the door and bared his fangs. He charged into the building, breathing fire and the ugly beasts just stared in amusement and fear. Katy looked down at the city and held her hand out. To our surprise the earth below rumbled and shook. The beasts began to panic and try to fight the dragon but that's when I realized, it was time for us to get into battle.

At first things were going really well, we had vaporized most of the small, ugly, four armed beasts. But the tallest and the biggest of all had just woken up after a nap. I pulled my sword out from the last beast and stared at the big opponent. That's when things went incredibly wrong. Jake had sent spinning tornadoes but for the giant it was like toys floating around. Jake even tried reducing the room temperature and increasing it but it only made us to sweat and shiver but had no effect on the beast. The huge thing slammed Jake on the wall. I froze him, I concentrated on trying to push him out the balcony, make him tip over and then Katy could just make the earth swallow him. I worked so hard on it my nose began bleeding. Oh no, the blood got me tensed up. A wave of fire radiated form Luke which didn't help much. I silently talked in my mind with Luke to not disturb me. After trying hard I froze him but couldn't push him out. That's when Jake yelled from the other corner of the room and ran with all effort. He slammed into the beast and the ice statue broke into life and sent Jake flying again. I guess he hit his head really bad because he had passed out. I would've run to his aid but before this guy hurts any more people, I had to kill him.

I pulled out my sword and deep inside, I concentrated on summoning a power I had no knowledge that I had possessed it. All the frustration and anger I held back from everyone had been released today. All those days came rushing by, when I'd found out that Nancy had not died of cancer but Sara had killed her but yet I didn't have proof to put the truth in front, the time when Cyrus had tried to kill Jake's dad, when he'd possessed Micah and made him fear the outside world, killing the life that the guy would've had. Each time Candice flirts with Jake, each time Lisa would try to take Jake away, all those times when people would make rumours about me behind my back. I kept my anger down so I didn't hurt anyone. Anger was the feeling I never showed to anyone before I came here, it had been buried inside, so deep I didn't know it existed within me. The day we'd fought, Jake had brought it out. The fight we had was meant to happen to bring us both closer. The time when I saw Lisa happy when she'd known how worried I was inside when I saw Sam on that plasma TV screen.

The water roared into the building. Thanks to the Pacific Ocean. The water tightened around the monster and pulled him down to the ground. 'I can't hold it.' I said. Katy immediately darted out the door into the balcony. I fell on my knees, I was dehydrated. Yet I fought my body's weakness because my mind and soul were still fresh. I turned to look at Jake but he was gone. 'Where's Jake?' I asked to Luke. He turned back to human form and looked around. Both our eyes were searching for him. Katy stumbled inside the room; she was so drained of energy. 'That ugly, huge, filthy thing probably tasted horrible. It took so much effort to make the earth swallow him entirely.' Luke walked to the spot where Jake had passed out. 'Oh dude, where are you?' He said. Suddenly something from the top sucked him. 'Luke!' I and Katy yelled but he was gone. I looked up but I couldn't see through the ceiling. 'What's up there?' Katy asked. 'I can't see through the god damn thing.' I said. I felt thousands of tiny needles piercing my shoulder; I was so tired I couldn't feel the pain. Both of us gulped and stared at the ceiling.

Chapter 26

The Black Fury

We had to climb a million fleets of stairs which took up more energy than it should have. The odd thing about this place was there were no rest rooms. No source of water within the building. There isn't even drinking water. When we opened the door and stepped out, a whole bunch of bigger Furies stood awaiting our arrival lead by a kid, Michael Alonski. I silently looked at Katy and we both understood the message we conveyed through our eyes, she'll go get Luke and I'll go get Jake and Sammy.

The kid smiled and said 'You can't use your powers here ladies. Let's see how your fighting skills are.' I didn't believe him but the confidence he radiated made me check. I tried to summon a wave of water, but I couldn't. My sword has almost lost the immortal power so it didn't have that glowing aura around it. I remembered the dagger Jake had silently slipped into my belt. I pulled out the dagger and said 'Immortal power can never be blocked.' The Furies weren't going to wait. The first one came encircling my head shooting lightning at me, I pulled it from the air only after three attempts and slammed it on the floor, passed my dagger over its neck and it was finished. One Fury kept pecking me on my head, I had ignored it and I kicked on a Fury which was getting to Katy behind her back and it went flying across the room. The one on my head kept disturbing me, I pushed it away but it came back. Katy had disappeared into the crowd searching for Lucas. I stabbed one Fury which had cut my wrist. The blood, how did they know about it? I began feeling dizzy and felt like puking. And I surely did puke on one Fury. While I was puking my guts out I felt someone hold my hair back for me. I turned in hopes to see Jake but when I did I saw Michael standing and he smiled. 'What's up?' I asked. 'Nothing, I'm just helping.' He replied.

- 'Why are you helping me?' I asked.
- 'Because . . . . I don't know.' He said. He swatted the Fury that pecked my head and it disintegrated at my feet. 'Lucas is in the store room. Kate . . . . whatever her name is found him. Jacob and Samuel are on the Black hill. Get there before dark, the Black Fury's waiting, darkness is his strength. Good luck!' I saw the mark of the eagle on his wrist burn away. 'I guess Cyrus will get me first after he's down here.'
- 'I'll make sure he doesn't.' I said and slowly walked towards the store room. Luke had

passed out on Katy's lap. Katy was so tired she couldn't move a bone. I said 'You guys are safe here. Alonski will keep guard. Trust him.' I said. Luke's eyes fluttered open. I knelt next to the couple and said 'Take rest, I will get Jake and Sam back. Thank you so much guys, you're the reason we even came this far. Thank you so much for everything. If we don't make it back, just remember that I love you guys, and um . . . tell my family that I love them. I hope you . . . . will . . . be proud of us.' Katy took my hand and said 'We already are proud of you.' She kissed me on my forehead. 'Jake . . .' Luke muttered. 'Luke, whatever it takes I promise you I'll get Jake back for you . . . . I promise.' I said. With the last word I walked out of the room. 'I'll get them home safe.' Michael said. I patted the kid and walked to the Black hill.

My heart raced when I saw the hill. The hill actually had a shade of black. I climbed the hill with the little energy left within me. For some reason I knew I wasn't going to make it back, but I also knew I would save Sam and Jake but I doubted saving myself. At this very moment, I really don't care whether I'd make it back, but I doubted if Jake and Sam could be alright if they lost me. My body was beginning to give up. The cut on my shoulder burned like someone had rubbed salt on it, I couldn't move that arm very well.

When I almost reached the top unharmed, I spotted the creature I feared meeting. It was the oddest monster I'd ever met. I hid myself behind a rock. It had a face of any normal human. It's skin a shade of green, like bile. It's nose pointed and sharp. Its eyes were bloodshot, sunken into its sockets, red in colour. His head had poisonous vipers instead of hair. He would've at least been ten foot tall and three foot wide. He was beefy and wore the world's biggest armour pieces I'd ever seen. He wore a robe over his black armour that flowed on the ground like a carpet. In his breastplate were written the words we all feared **"THE BLACK FURY"**

'I can sense you, my dear foe!' A voice boomed. 'Sara Jane Salvatore. I didn't expect you to be alive; I thought you'd die before you made it here.' I breathed in, maybe the last deep breath of my life. I shut my eyes and saw Sam, I saw Jake, I saw mom, dad, Su, Cody, Katy, Luke, I had to save Sam and Jake doesn't matter what happens. I'd give anything right now for them, anything, even my life. I looked at the sun which was about to set in about half an hour. I don't have much time. I'd have to destroy the Fury before twilight, or we're all doomed.

I unsheathed my sword and stood, revealing myself. The Fury roared with laughter and the sky changed to a shade of grey, but sunlight was still lit up. I saw Jake and Sam chained behind him. Both of them hung their heads, I doubted whether they had life. 'Hello!' said the Fury. 'Hi.' I said. I walked forward till both of us were face to face. Without any warning the Fury attacked. I flew past him and landed near Jake's feet. 'SJ' he muttered as his eyes slowly opened. 'Help . . . . Sammy . . . . I . . . can save . . . myself.' He muttered. But I knew he couldn't make it and I had promised Luke. Jake was my heart and Sam was my soul, how could I pick, if I lose either of them, I'd die. 'Don't worry; I can save both of you.' I promised. He gulped and said 'I love you.' I almost cried when he said that but I put on a bold smile and said 'me too, Jake.' I looked at Sam. That second I knew I had to save both of them; I loved them both too much to let either die.

Jake Martin

I slowly lifted my head to see how SJ was doing and that took so much of my energy. After I was knocked out the Furies sucked me up and spat me up on the black hill. I had slid through the hill top; my whole left side was bruised. On the other hand, chunks of the hill had broken.

I saw Sam and tried to help him out the chains but that's when the Black Fury spotted me. A battle with such a monster was the hardest task I've ever done. And I guess I lost. I felt my heart beat slowing down when I knew SJ was here. For an odd reason I knew if there would be a situation where she'd have to pick me or Sam, she'd pick her brother. After all we only knew each other for two months, we were together just for a week. But to be honest, if I'd have to pick her or Alley, I'd pick her. Of course that doesn't mean Alley is not important to me, she is. But yet SJ just means so much more to me. But deep inside I hope I don't ever get into a situation like that.

SJ slashed her sword and black goo flowed out the Fury's unprotected left arm. 'You maniac!' The Fury screamed and charged. SJ made a shield around her and shot balls of fire at him. But they bounced off him harmlessly. They're swords clanked for a long time, flames roared; fire was shot at one another. SJ made sure the Fury didn't come close, he could just whack her. Black goo had been released from his wound; the goo was thick and disgusting to even take a glance at it. It smelled as sick as coal tar. SJ's shield began flickering, all her energy was taken. At that moment I hated myself so much I wished I'd die. I'm supposed to be the one saving her life. But I was helpless, I couldn't even breathe. My energy was drained and my vision was blurry. The Fury shot a ball of flame at SJ and her shield betrayed her. The flames burned her and pushed her away. She flew over to the steep end of the hill. She managed to crawl her way towards a tree and leaned against the tree. She panted.

The Black Fury wasn't doing well either. The black goo which was his blood I think had made him weak because of the overflow. SJ opened her eyes and slowly stood. Water climbed the hill steadily and surrounded itself around the Fury, choking it, crushing everything

ZEETA SHERIN

within it. Sam's eyes fluttered open. With the last bit of
energy the Fury sent a huge explosive ball of flame from
the other side of the hill, the flames coming towards me
and Sam. I wanted to tell Sam he could go through his
chains and move away but my voice was buried deep
inside. I looked at SJ who raced to us from the other
side. She removed Sam's chain and right before, just
seconds before the flames exploded, the last few seconds
I was supposed to live, she dove and pushed me out of
the way, leaving her brother unchained but to die.

I stared at her in shock, what had she done? Had she
really picked me over her brother? Was I that important?
Did I even deserve it? I heard a familiar voice yell 'They're
up here!' Alley's voice, it was my sister's voice. Her voice
made my heart come back to reality and tears flowed
out. SJ fell on her knees. 'You . . . . Sam' was all I could
say. 'Sam . . .' she said and her eyes widened with guilt.
She crawled towards where Sam had died; his body had
been perfectly alright. I also accompanied SJ.

Nancy's image flickered to life. 'A good soul' she
said. 'A good soul's body is always as pure as the soul
itself.' Alley fell on her knees and cried. She took Sam's
hand, SJ took the other. Tears poured out. 'Please don't
cry . . . . it's my entire fault.' I said. SJ looked at me with
her sad eyes. That second I knew I had to fix this mess,
doesn't matter if it takes me my own life. SJ passed out
and I followed immediately.

Sara Jane Salvatore

Chapter 27

Trade of souls

'Please don't burry him, the funeral can be tomorrow.' I said. I looked at Sam. I remembered what Alice had told me 'You guys don't have regrets.' How could I not be regretting this when I was old? I'd regret it throughout my life. My brother, my sweet brother was gone. I would raise my hands in prayer all day long, crying, standing, not drinking nor eating if I did have a chance to save my brother. It was my fault I could've saved them both. 'Okay hon.' Dad said. Mom was in tears. I walked to the balcony and sat on the swing. My mom sat next to me. Even with her tears she was trying to console me. Her language grew foreign; I didn't understand what she told. The atmosphere tightened around me, mom's gestures were trying to convey something but I couldn't understand. I heard footsteps, footsteps which brightened my soul, which gave some hope out of the hopeless world.

I could sense his presence behind me as well as his guilt. I could smell the pain in his wounds on his body as well as his heart. My mom left the balcony closing the door behind her. He sat next to me and said 'I'm sorry.' I looked at Jake. 'Why are you sorry? It's not your fault, it's mine.' I rested my head on his shoulder and began crying. 'It's okay . . . . I promise I'll get him back for you. I know how to get him back, please don't cry SJ. Please smile, smile for me.' I wiped my tears and asked 'How will you get him back for me?' When I asked the question Jake looked like he was holding back tears. 'I talked to Nancy and figured a way out. Don't worry I'll get him back. Now, you just have to focus on regaining your strength, you still have to fight Cyrus.' His eyes were puffy and tired. They didn't have that mesmerising feel.

- 'What do you mean me? We still have Cyrus to fight.'
- 'Right. SJ, if I ever hurt you in any way I'm sorry. Please forgive me, I didn't mean to.'
- 'I know you would never hurt me.'
- 'Why did you pick me over Sam?' His question startled me.
- 'Because . . . . maybe you mean a lot to me.' I said. He looked at me one last time. His eyes were sad and filled with shame and guilt. 'It's not your fault.' I said.
- 'But I can fix it.' Suzie dashed open the door and said 'Nancy's here.' Jake patted my sister and said 'I have to leave.'

- 'Jake, please stay. I can't go through this without you.'

He looked at me with an expression that told me he had something sad inside, which he didn't share with me. Why was he baring something painful all by himself? What was so bad he wouldn't even tell me? I grew suspicious. 'You'll be back right?' I asked. Jake left the balcony without a reply. But he glanced back, once.

After Jake had left I asked Nancy what she'd told Jake. She said the heart breaking words short and sweet. 'To bring a good soul back another soul must be sacrificed, a trade of souls must take place.'

Jake Martin

I drove to the woods all by myself. I stared at the sharp blade on the passenger seat next to me, the seat where SJ usually sat. Now, there sat the blade which would end my life. I can't see SJ depressed anymore. She needs Sam more than she needs me. She'd made a mistake.

I walked deep into the woods searching for the perfect spot for death, my last wish I suppose. I raised the blade but my fear got the upper hand. I put the blade down and sat on the ground. I closed my eyes, my whole life was flashing before me. I heard a voice say 'Daddy . . .' I opened my eyes to see three kids with black hair, just like my own. Among the three, I recognised one as my own daughter, Alice. The other two were boys about the age of ten and five each. The ten-year-old's face was so familiar, with a sharp jaw and deep black eyes. A face so similar to mine. The five-year-old too, looked familiar but he had sparkling grey eyes . . . eyes that reminded me of my beloved. 'There are other ways.' said the oldest one. 'I'm Ryan, if you're wondering. Ryan.A.Martin. And that's Noah, your youngest son.' 'Hey.' I said not knowing what else to say. 'I'm sorry to say this but you guys are not going to even be born. You understand me, don't you?' I asked. The three of them burst out with laughter. 'What's so funny?' I asked. 'Not every kid gets to watch their dad like this.' Ryan said. Noah walked forward and reached out for my hand. His skin was soft and his touch was powerful. I wish I could live long enough to have these kids, but I can't. I won't be happy; I'll feel guilty for the rest of my life. 'Daddy's not going to go. Gramps is on his way, searching for you. Mom's probably upset. She keeps telling us over and over again how you freaked her out.' I smiled at the kid. He reminded me of the time when my mother had brought out all the old stuff from the attic and that was the first time Alex had known that not all TV's were flat screens. He even asked whether he could open the "box" behind the TV.

'What do you mean?' I asked. 'Mom thinks you're going to sacrifice yourself for Uncle Sammy's soul, the whole family is going mad searching for you, dad.' Alice said.

'That is what's going to happen. Please leave. I'm sorry I'm doing this, I'm sorry about the fact that I'm not going to be your dad. Now leave.' I said. 'Crap! Dad's searching for us. Let's leave before he knows we're time travelling again!' Ryan said. 'Ryan, you just told dad that we time travel!' Alice said pointing at me. 'Leave.' I said looking at Alice. 'Dad, don't do this.' She said. 'I'm sorry kids. You know how much I don't want to do this, but SJ's . . . your mom's happiness means more to me than my own life.' I said. 'If you die, what happiness will mom have? You are her happiness, you are her world and if you die she'd never smile her whole life. She'd never feel happy ever.' Alice said. She pulled Noah away from me and said 'We are leaving! I know I would never get another opportunity to say this to you, you're going to become the world's best dad, you understand that, because I want my daddy, who is the best dad in the world. If mom is really important, wait and think about it once more.' With the last words they vanished.

I raised the blade; I felt the cold blade touch my skin. I was going to die. The thought made me shiver. Each time I brought the knife close, SJ's face flashed in front and I put it down. Finally, I breathed in, closed my eyes and put the knife at my throat; I said 'I sacrifice my soul in exchange of Samuel Salvatore's soul.' My hands trembled as the cold steel slowly pierced my skin but I heard a voice 'Wait, Sillvius Spark awaits you in his death bed. Perhaps a two minute visit wouldn't delay your suicide.'

I sighed and followed Nancy.

𝔖𝔞𝔯𝔞 𝔍𝔞𝔫𝔢 𝔖𝔞𝔩𝔳𝔞𝔱𝔬𝔯𝔢

'Did you find him?' I asked desperately when Alley came in. I sat next to the dead Sam who was laid on his bed. 'No, Uncle Jay, the sheriff, he's sent cops to search for Jake.' She sat down next to me and looked at Sam. 'I'm very sorry.' I told her. She chuckled sadly. 'Either way it would've been a loss, a brother or boyfriend. Don't be sorry it's not your fault.' She took my hand. 'I know how hard it is for you. But . . . why did you pick Jake?' She asked. 'I . . . at that moment, I didn't know what to do. I had unchained Sam and told him to move, he just nodded. I expected him to run away but I was an idiot, I didn't realize that he was tired; he didn't have enough energy to even move a bone. But I knew I had to pick Jake. Because I love him, for everything he had done for me. He told me to leave him and save Sam. But I knew that I could save them both. Loosing Sam is like I lost half of myself, and if Jake is gone too, I'd kill myself. Jake means the world to me, I can't let him die.' Alley smiled. 'I guess I can't ever have as much love both of you have for each other, ever.'

'If Sam was there, you could have. I could've saved them both. What kind of sister am I?' I sunk my head and began crying. Alley hugged me and said 'You tried, you tried your best.'

'Sam was the one who gave me life after Nancy died. I knew she didn't die because of cancer, she was murdered. Sam was the one who consoled me through the two darkest months of my life. He made me smile, he taught me that there was something called happiness and hope still out there. He told me there would always be enough love for me when he was around and he told me I'd never need anybody else. I feel like a betrayer.' I said. I hugged her hard and both of us cried. I felt an attachment with her, something I'd never felt before. 'Sam will be proud of you SJ. Sam will be proud.' Alley said. 'In case Jake dies . . . . if Sam comes back, you can keep him, you don't have to share him with me.' I said. 'Don't worry, whatever happens he is no less your brother.' She replied. 'I can't see him wake up in the morning every day, reminding me of Jake.' I said. She hugged me harder and said 'We'll get both Sam and Jake; we'll get them both somehow.'

Jake Martin

'Jared . . .' Mr Spark said. I corrected. He coughed. I sat next to him. He said 'Heard you were . . . going to sacrifice yourself. Don't do it.'

- 'I don't have any other option sir. It's my decision.'
- 'Remember when I told you to . . . . do me a favour in exchange . . . of the sword.'
- 'Yes sir.'
- 'I was conveying . . . . a message through you . . . . to my . . . brothers . . . . saying I found . . . a smart . . . one. You are the smart one, son. I never expected you to make . . . . such a decision.'
- 'Sir . . . it's my situation-'
- 'You could've asked me for help. How many more minutes . . . do I have?' Nancy glanced back and said 'One.'
- 'I'm going to die, son. In one minute. I trusted Jane with my world and I trusted you . . . with her.' He coughed.
- 'How can you help me sir, you have just a minute-'
- 'I sacrifice my soul in exchange of Samuel Salvatore's soul.' When he said that I was so shocked. I didn't have to die.
- 'Thank you so much.'

- 'You have a long life to live. Destroy evil for me . . . . Jake.' He finally said my name right. But he closed his eyes and Nancy looked at the half open door. She nodded at someone there. A blue mist erupted form Mr Spark and dissolved into thin air. 'Samuel Salvatore has been granted life.' Nancy said. 'You shall be gifted Jake, for the goodness of your heart. Goodbye, keep SJ close.' With the last words she vanished. 'Thanks.' I said just before she faded. I'm going to miss that angel. I looked at Mr Spark. 'Thank you very much sir. I respect you a lot sir.'

Sara Jane Salvatore

Sam's eyes fluttered open. He sat up. Alley hugged him and said 'Sammy!' He stroked her hair, they both seemed so happy. My heart crawled up my throat. Jake was gone, the only person who could make me feel safe even when I was in enemy lines was gone. 'I'm alive!' Sam said with a smile. 'You're alive.' Alley said. Then she looked at me. 'Oh no.' She said. I began crying again. Jake was gone, why did I have to live? I hugged Sam. 'What's wrong?' Sam asked. 'Nothing.' I said. Alley tumbled on the couch. 'Oh, my brother.' She said. I walked towards the balcony. 'It's cold outside.' Alley said. I looked at her and Sam. 'I love you guys.' I said.

I opened the door and stood outside. I climbed over to the other side of the railing. There was no SJ without Jake. There was no saving the world without Jake. Why die as a loser in the hands of an enemy when you can die as a loser in your own hands? Jake was gone. Sam and Alley will be happy. I don't have to worry. Mom, Dad, Su, Katy and Luke will learn how to get over it. I didn't have to give false hopes to people and pretend to save the world. I stood at the edge and closed my eyes. I felt the air blow through my hair. The times when Jake stroked it . . . . The time we met, when we fought like kids. The day of the party, in his back yard, the lights, the candles, the time we were in Nashville when Alice showed up. I stood over the chilled railing, the scream of Sam's voice behind me fading. If Jake is gone, I'll go stay with him. I have no life without Jake. He was my every breath. He was my world. He was everything to me. I need a protector, I need him to shoulder this burden with me, I need him to guide me, I need him to hold me, I need him to live! I squeezed my eyes harder and slowly released my hands from the railing. That moment felt like forever, falling into an abyss, everything was blurred, my mind wasn't clear; all I knew was that it felt like looking into Jake's warm, melting coal-like eyes, it felt like I was falling into his arms, and that's all I cared about: to reach him somehow. But that's when I felt a warm, strong, muscular hand go round my waist and pull me up. 'It's cold outside. Let's go in.' I smiled when I heard the voice. All the sadness I ever had in my life washed away. I didn't know what sad even meant anymore. I turned to see Jake with a smile on his face. 'It's very cold; we better get you inside, love.' He said.

- 'What did you call me, tough guy?' I asked.
- 'You heard it smarty pants.' I hugged him hard.

The whole night was a blast. There were the Martins, the McQueen's, the Robinsons, Uncle Jay, Cody, Aunt Jess, Aunt Leah, and so many others. We narrated our stories and cut off the violent parts which would get our moms concerned. 'It's really cool that you let your son have a TV in the washroom.' I said. Mr Martin looked at me with surprise. 'I'll go get some coke.' Jake said and got up. 'Jake, you have a TV in the washroom?' Mr Martin asked. Jake turned with an apologetic look. 'I'm sorry, dad. I thought you knew.'

- 'You're grounded for a month.'
- 'Dad, I'm sorry.'
- 'I am not going to change my statement son.' Jake sunk on the chair next to me. 'I'm sorry.' I whispered. 'its okay.' He said grumpily.

That late night I and Jake sat on my bed the whole night talking about the quest, recalling memories. That's when our kids showed up. 'I told you, you guys don't have any regrets.' Alice said. 'Cyrus is coming, but for now everything's fine.'

We talked with the kids too and every time they called me mom I felt so awkward. After they left, Jake looked at me with a smile. 'We are going to make beautiful kids.' I smiled. 'And you're blushing again. God, do you know how beautiful you are?' He asked. My house was jam packed because all the ninety something family members were staying over. It was fun.

Our adventure isn't over; there was a long way to go. But right now that doesn't matter. Thinking of all our inside jokes, the time we shared thoughts and said remember when we did this or that are the precious moments we shared.

I took out the paper Ms. Green had given us for our assignment and wrote down the day of the party when I and Jake were officially together.

Even today when I look at Jake I remember that day.

I have a hard task at hand; we were going to do this together. Even with all the bad stuff, I can say my life is beautiful. I had succeeded a big task but I had a bigger one coming up. I felt proud of myself. But I'll always remember 'one victory never makes history'.

To be continued on . . . "Slaying the immortal"

Acknowledgements

Everyone at Partridge Publishing.

My parents for helping me through this wonderful journey of becoming a published author at such a young age. For discovering my talent and nurturing it.

My big sis, Afreen, for giving me the idea of becoming a story-teller. To my little bro, Murshid; he unintentionally choreographed my action sequences.

My friends whose silly jokes and warm moments and sayings created prolonged chapters of this book.

And a special thanks to S.T Jabeen ma'am, for doing the hard job of editing. For being my teacher, most importantly a critic, a guide and of course a true friend. Will always be grateful for all your help!